He had seen some~~~~~~~~~~~~~~~~~~~~~~~~~~~~~
space.

A vast mass, for~~~~~~~~~~~~~~~~~~~ing away
into the Deep, blotting out the stars from Rigel to Ursa
Major. He guessed it must be 1,000 kilometres long and
maybe fifty kilometres from where the scoot ship lay
becalmed. The nebulous object was closing rapidly as
though driven by some titanic cosmic wind.

Within seconds, greenish, fibrous-looking matter was
billowing past the scooter ship in long luminous
strands.

Morgan rushed down the steps to the recreation deck.

'Guys,' he said to all of them. 'Forget the engines. We
don't have to go to the Gas Cloud. It just came to us!'

# CHRIS BEEBEE
# THE HUB

Futura

An Orbit Book

Copyright © Chris Beebee 1987

First published in Great Britain in 1987
by Macdonald & Co (Publishers) Ltd
London & Sydney

This Futura edition published in 1988

ISBN 0 7088 8214 5

Printed in Great Britain by
Collins, Glasgow

Futura Publications
A Division of
Macdonald & Co (Publishers) Ltd
Greater London House
Hampstead Road
London NW1 7QX

A member of Pergamon MCC Publishing Corporation plc

## Acknowledgements

Excerpt from *Yellow Back Radio Broke Down* by Ishmael Reed. Copyright © 1969 by Ishmael Reed. Reprinted by permission of Doubleday & Company.

W.S. Burroughs

Louis Aragon

Sonny Boy Williamson II, *Sonny Boy Williamson Volume Two SLP 170*, Storyville Publishing

*Route 66*
Composer & Author: Bobby Troup
© 1946 Burke & Van Heusen Inc.
British Publisher: Chappell-Morris Limited

Professor David Bohm

Gwyn and Mair Jones, *The Mabinogion*, published by J.M. Dent & Sons 1974

New New Riders of the Purple Sage

Herbert Marcuse

Iceberg Slim (Robert Beck), *The Pimp — The Story of My Life*, published by Holloway House Publishing Company, Los Angeles, California, 1969 edition

Lester Willis Young

Bruce Feirstein, *Real Men Don't Eat Quiche*, published by New English Library (UK) and Pocket Books (USA)

F.T. Marinetti, *The Futurist Manifesto*

James Drever, *A Dictionary of Psychology*

Mircea Eliade, *Myths, Dreams and Mysteries*

"... and sure enough, there in the distance could be seen rising a really garish smaltzy super technological anarcho-paradise. The people began to trot in slow motion towards the blue kidney-shaped swimming pools, the White Castle restaurants, the drive in bonanza markets, the computerised buses and free airplanes, the free anything one desired."

Ishmael Reed, *Yellow Back Radio Broke Down*

## CHAPTER 1

DATE: 8.30 MARCH 27 2031 TCT
LOCATION: DODMAN'S LEY
DEVELOPMENT SUSSEX UK
WESTWORLD CENTERCOM
REGION 1010

*"... all monopolistic and hierarchical
systems are based on anxiety."*
W.S.BURROUGHS

'Some people say it's the system – not the people.
Others hold that it's the people not the system. Well I
don't believe that because I believe in people. So it has
to be the system. That's why I believe in the New
System.'

The face on the television screen smiled warmly.
Reassuringly. The face was round, clean-shaven beneath a crew-cut head. Ball-like, fleshy. Maybe fifty
years old. It was hard to believe the head was nearly
twice that.

Turner snarled angrily at it.

'Salcoo!'

Goodrich was salcoo. Amalrik was salcoo. Madame
Feng was salcoo. They were tying the whole thing up.
No more room for the little guy. To hell with the whole
bunch of them.

'Already CENTERCOM has established peace, stabi-
lity and prosperity the world has never known before.'

A split screen showed freighter helicopters dropping
aluminium cylinders into an African village. The other
half of the screen showed villagers erecting geodesic
domes. The round face of Goodrich returned.

'Precession not Recession is the key tenet for CENTERCOM.'

'Oh yeah? Go tell 'em that in the Stack – asshole!' Turner was still snarling as he buttoned his shirt.

'You see we aren't satisfied with what is possible. Our goal is the conquest of the impossible.'

AW NUTS!

Groping for his tie with one hand Turner reached out and punched the channel changer on the remote control viciously.

President Goodrich flickered and vanished. Turner sank to his knees. The crippling burst of pain in his right side had brought tears to his eyes. It had gripped him from chest to groin. Iron fingers. Looking up through the mist – a girl – pouting at him – sitting on a king-sized bed – thighs wide open, knees bent – her skirt up around her hips, her hands moving slowly and sensously towards the crotch of her black lace panties.

'Damn,' Turner growled. 'This must be the fiftieth rerun of *"Crotch Crazy"*. He stretched again and got the off button (reflex). The pain was gone. Silence almost. Somewhere a tiny mains hum and muffled drone of house service equipment.

Turner got the tie fixed around his neck. He went into the toilet. It was a modular unit including shower and bath that all snapped together in about half an hour. It had first been designed in America in 1937, rediscovered in Italy as high tech in 1981. Now it was being marketed again. This time from Japan. Most of the apartments in the block had dry toilet systems. Hygenic, water saving etc. – the latest thing. Turner's wife, Tracy, couldn't stand it. Hence the 'Modular Bathroom'. The hell they'd had with the plumbing. The whole block was designed for Dripac Toilets. But that was Trace.

Turner's bowels moved slowly. His digestive system acidic and hot. Liver thick and sluggish. 'Have to change my beer' he thought. He groaned loudly. It was over. Part of being human. Physically a robot. A machine of flesh and blood, that had to void its waste

2

matter as surely as a diesel or a nuclear plant. Somewhere in that machine a ghost maybe. Nobody knew for sure. Hot water sprayed him intimately. The toilet had a mini jacussi built into the rim. The Japanese thought Westerners barbarian. Didn't wash themselves after defecation. Now Turner could enjoy the height of civilisation. Salcoo or *sale cou* as it really was when not warped into the polyglot argot of WestWorld English. He laughed. Jeez. Poverty, radiation, unemployment, Pranksters loose in the streets and they come up with this!

His side still ached from the sudden baffling attack. They'd been going on for about a month.

Turner switched on his work station screens. He was almost at the stage where he was too afraid to call a doctor. Too many heavy rumours going around. If Tracy had still been there she would have made him. Tracy's face suffused with orgasm, moist with sweat. Her mouth around his penis head. Gratuitous glimpse in mirror of them on bed – doing it. Funny when they're gone you only remember the good times. Think about it. The moods, the tantrums, the stupid wallet-busting ideas. Bitch!

'Turner we have a live one for you.' Quiet, American voice on speaker – quiet face with horn-rimmed eyes on screen. Turner's manager, UK spearhead of Reclaim Inc., USA.

'Don – any chance of putting the gist of it on tape? I just had another attack.'

'Frank – you should see a doctor.'

'Well I intend to.'

'Okay I'll put this on tape. When you're through with the doc run it through and come back to me 'kay?'

Screen blank.

I'll have to go out there. It was starting. The fear all urban people felt. He called the Health Centre. 10.30 am or five o'clock. He took 10.30 am. Dr Sheer. He had just enough time. He was out all the time Reclaiming – but it didn't make any difference in the long run. To the fear habit. He flipped on the security scanner screen.

Blank roving pictures of empty concrete. Access conduits and empty parking lot. No cars in there he didn't recognise. But so many places to hide. His car stood in the corner by a heating duct. Just where he'd left it. Alone.

Turner was lucky he didn't actually have to live in the Stack. This was Dodman's Ley, Sussex. A new out of town luxury development.

A 'berm' was what they called the condominium – a complex of apartments set into the earth of an ancient hillside, half buried underground. Solar heating from eight huge high tech collectors on top of the hill. Insulation from the earthen berms. Tracey liked it because 'it looked all old fashionedy and like something from space'. The estate agents preferred 'Fabulously modern architecture with primordial values'. The architect who designed it claimed he had 're-invented architecture. The Dodman's Ley venture takes the mind back to building's state of nature.' It took Turner's mind back to atavistic panic when he thought about the price. But Tracy had liked it until that morning she caught the monorail to Paris and had never come back. Salcoo. Slut. Better off without her, Turner thought.

Yes, it was certainly safer out here in the New Developments. Total security. But it didn't console Turner. Everyone was full of fear. If Don went back to the States I could have his job. Admin job. Stay at home all day, work screen to screen. Porno breaks on vid. Yes sir? You want to hire the services of Reclaim Inc? Excuse we while I switch my vid off and er, pull my trousers up.

Had to go out there. Be at the doctor 10.30. Worst is yet to come he thought. Is disease worse than getting wasted by Pranksters? Or being torn apart by rioting Leisure People? He shook his head.

He kept the number for getting out of the apartment in a little book. There was only so much you could memorise. 15 32 34 37 47 32. That would open the front door into the hallway.

34158916865947323793946793

The door swung open into the parking lot, gliding on its silent bearings of lirium. Lirium the wonder metal. Researched, synthesised and manufactured entirely in space. Impervious to the strongest explosive. Yes, you'll be safe behind a lirium hinge. Turner stepped into the parking lot tunnel.

This part was worst of all. If they got in here – nowhere to run to. Why bother with ten security doors on the apartment?!

Okay but he had to get to his car to get into town. Pull yourself together. Let your mind flood.

She was naked but for black nylons and high heeled shoes. Turner held her at arms length, his eyes devouring her.

The car! Get in the car! This sex fantasy is only permissable as an opiate – to overcome the anxiety you feel. Securilok module. That will open the car.

She's saying, 'Come to bed, come to bed.'

No! Think of the number!

13432343?

43223223?

No! 1343243 2325432

The door opened with a soft deadly click.

Moving up the exit ramp. Radio ... town today ... bzzzzzzzt! ... (under ramp doors) ... rioting Leisure People ... click! Off.

For godsake Goodrich you'd better be good if you get elected. Because if Goodrich fails, WestWorld fails. Couldn't make his mind up. Thought he'd vote for Calvin Gold. Gold would do more for the NMS Faction.

Turner accelerated. Up feeder ramps, around cloverleafs, along motorways. In the distance the sun shimmered grey and forbidding on the dense tonnage of the Stack.

Thirty years ago they'd still talked about tearing down high rises and building for high density at low level with modular :welling units staged on piers. Out in the flatlands, central America say, they still could. But here no space. And so many people. The Stack rose half a mile into the sky. A dwelling – a complex – a

5

city. Bridged out across the Channel, it linked up with Beltburg – La Ville periphique – ran from Tashkent to Madrid. Every big country had a Stack. Tokyo Stack, Mexico Stack, New York Stack. A Stack was just a stack.

The motorway zipped past the Stack, forty storeys high. Levels above that you didn't dare look at for fear of highway vertigo.

Radio. Shock troops have entered the lower levels to pursue the ringleaders to their hideouts. Fierce fighting ... Click. Off. It was out there – just beyond his car window. All that trouble. The car glided him along. Big warm comfortable expensive. All the time an urgent current. What will the doctor say?

His eyes wandered from the backs of speeding cars. She was a hundred feet high, naked holo enhanced woman on ad screen, her clothes at her feet, bending towards the highway, beckoning. Her hair blew in the breeze. Invitingly she ran her hands over herself and beckoned towards the nearest exit. Naked holo woman standing over four mile complex of Adult Leisure Inc. She was suddenly dressed again. She started stripping. Height of goddess 100 ft (30.48 m.) Size of bust 66 ft (20.15 m.) Length of thighs 20 ft (6.20 m.) Duration of strip 2 min 13 sec. Time naked 40 sec. Total length of cycle 2 min 53 sec. Danger to traffic. Voted down. Cast steel projectors in lirium shells set in concrete 300 ft up after sabotage by women. Bigger one outside Las Vegas. Indicates underground entrances to Pleasure City, world headquarters of Adult Leisure Inc.

Turner couldn't resist her. He was up there with her. A sex giant above the freeway. The riots in the Stack were gone.

Disentangled himself from giant sex act. Nearly missing exit. He moved fast at surface level through narrow crowded streets towards white glittering hospital.

The appointment card read – Dr Sheer. Level 8 Room 901. No security screen by the elevator. Just one big one by the door. Maybe that's enough. Maybe no one can get past that. Nope. Noway am I going in an elevator I can't screen.

Turner took the stairs. His heart was racing when he reached level 8 ...

SCAN SCAN SCAN. Turner buttoned his shirt. Printouts clicked, spewing from the banks of analysis equipment built into the long sunlit wall of Room 901. Doctor murmurs quietly.

'These are the ones I want, isn't it?'

Assistant leaves discreetly on crepe soles.

'Level with me Doc,' Turner said. 'Is it cancer?'

The light brown skin of Sheer's face suffused darkly. He pursed his lips together. Recomposed himself, leaning back in his green leather chair.

'I am sorry Turner,' he said. 'I know we medics are not supposed to show emotion. But emotions are natural I think. This one always gets me on raw nerve you know. No. It is not cancer, and if it were there would be nothing' – he paused, projecting energy – 'absolutely nothing to fear. Cancer was an old Piscean nightmare. It makes me so angry because I remember how my family feared it. When I was child you know – how is so and so? Cancer. Oh my God!

'Now – no longer. Today we know. Cancer is virus!'

He said the word 'virus' powerfully, so that it became plastic with a long rolled 'r' and heavily accented 's'.

'Over the years when epidemic started in 1950s – since that time – the human body has built up resistance.'

He said 'resistance' the way he said 'virus'. Powerfully, like a guerrilla politician.

'We have drugs to do that also. What remains we can eliminate. Rebuild with fresh new cells – immune cells. The only ones who die of it now are those who want to.'

The anger hovered in his voice. Fiery vibration.

'Is that why the Exit Ashrams are so full?' Turner asked, bitterly. His brother Tony was in one. Comfortable – genetic pain killers were very good. He had old movies and magazines, plants and flowers, soft lights and gentle touch of kindness to help him while he listened. Listened for the last fatal whisper from his flesh.

Life was changing so rapidly here in the twenty-first century. Life span lengthening. Rumours circulated of a government immortality programme. In the orbital locations and satellite settlements there had been no reported deaths from natural causes at all. It seemed like some people couldn't live up to it. Hence the Exit Ashrams. Death as a psychological problem.

'You ask me this?' Sheer said. 'I am not man of religion or psychiatrist. What I am saying is true! Of course it is when man now can live ninety, a hundred, hundred and thirty years!'

Fury.

His tone changed.

'No I am sorry,' he said suddenly. Very calm. 'What you have is the new thing.'

Turner said nothing. He felt his whole body convulse slowly.

'Organ Implosion,' he said.

'Yes.'

The evolutionary codes were set for optimum population level. Optimum life span. Mankind was overcoming the controls. One by one. His brother Tony was subliminally suicidal – he knew that. That's why he got mad. Tony didn't have to die. But the codes were finding more and more violent ways to wipe a proportion of the race out. Including those who wanted to live. Biots programmed to self destruct in response to a genetic trigger – the terminal fault. Turner's body was now such a biot. The terminal fault had activated.

Turner sat down and lit a cigarette. A recent T.V. show had told him that the smoking scare had been a kind of Montezuma's revenge by Mother Nature on modern atomic civilisation. Her agent had been a Yakut Indian shaman – an initiated confidante of the tobacco spirit. His name in the Yakut tongue meant 'The Plants

Fight Back'. He had cooked up the spell on his sad reservation. Once you knew this it was safe to smoke.

Sheer casually pushed an ashtray in Turner's direction, across the green plastic desk top.

'At the moment,' he said, 'this illness is attacking lymph glands in right side of your body. The pain you experience is caused by sudden contraction of the internal organs. This is first stage of Organ Implosion – an organ contracts suddenly – like this ...!' Turner shuddered at the graphic movement of Sheer's hands '... and expands again.

'At first, these attacks will be momentary and infrequent, but, as you already know, excruciatingly painful. This stage may last one year, or two years.' He shrugged. 'Sometimes five years. Gradually, however, it will spread – to another part of body. The organs continue to contract – but eventually they do not expand again.'

The words floated round Turner's ears. Cold, clear, terrifying.

'You see, the conquest of cancer and other major diseases has brought its own problem. We stand on the threshold of immortality but – some theorists believe – nature has other plans for us. Nevertheless, as always, situation is not hopeless. There is treatment.'

Turner watched the astonishing clarity of light reflecting from the doctor's coat. Essentially, how odd he should be from India. But now everyone lived everywhere. You never saw a passport. The linear cities had taken care of that. Every detail is clear. His bone structure. The waves of his hair. The desk, designed exactly for human height – so inevitable. Why is it in a crisis everything is so clear? So beautiful? And essentially, so meaningless?

He realised the Doctor was talking to him.

'... and at this time I was actually studying with Kesh you know in Calcutta before he relocated on DEV. So I have no hesitation in prescribing Stellachlorazine A. This one is to strengthen organ walls against collapse. And of course Enketholin to counteract ...'

Sheer voiced the next two words carefully. '... the pain.'

'Enketholin?' Turner's mind sidetracked. Strident letters on a garish screen. Rise in murder rate blamed on teenage keth addicts. 'I thought ...'

'Please! Forget what you read on Olfax. This is mostly sensationalism. More Enketholin is distributed through licenced medical outlets than dealers on the streets. As you know probably, Enketholin is most powerful painkiller known to man. Synthesised from brain's own natural analgesic. Third factor here is time.'

'You mean there is a chance Doctor?'

'Oh yes. Most definitely. You are still relatively young. A forty-two-year-old man. Fit, active. All this plays its part you know. Naturally, the most important thing is Stellachlorazine. Next most important thing is you.'

His eyes were clear, liquid, sincere. But Turner felt no trust for him.

'Is that it?' Turner asked. 'Drugs are the total treatment?'

'No – you see if we can catch in time – and restrict to one or two organs, there is always chance of transplant. You are lucky so far – lymph glands may heal. First we must strengthen them though and arrest the implosion. Next one to go almost certainly is liver. You see?'

'Alternative therapy,' Turner said.

Dangerous drugs. The cult of surgery. Turner felt the fear everyone felt. Fear of the Doctor in his White Coat. Alternative therapy ashrams were big business now. Even UniMed had a division for it. Tracy had come out of anorexia with herbs, hypnotism and orange light. But she had believed. Turner was only afraid. The devil and the deep blue sea.

'Yes, you can if you want to.' Sheer's voice was calm. 'This is free world. But they won't give you Enketholin.'

'That's why people go to alternative therapy.'

'Listen Mr Turner. Controlling blood pressure is one

10

thing. There is not one Yogic adept outside of India who could handle the pain of advanced Organ Implosion through mind control alone. And without treatment we know works, this stage will surely come. But yes. Herbs, relaxation, environment and so forth. Very good. But look, when you go there – take the herbs and other thing that you want – enjoy the atmosphere. But at same time – please – take this one also, eh?'

Sheer tapped the prescription he had written with an urgent forefinger.

'Side effects.'

'One and only one. People using keth for purely medical purposes rarely become addicted. No one knows why this is so. But it is so. Stellachlorazine, however is something else.'

Turner said nothing. He waited.

'Total loss of sex drive.'

Turner grinned. Baffled.

'You know I don't mean like with a hormone type of drug. There is no change in sexual characteristics. Nor is it like the loss one may occasionally experience through tiredness, depression or bad diet. No, I mean you will cease to exist as a sexual being. Sex will become totally meaningless. A concept you no longer understand.'

'Permanent?'

'No. Only so long as medication period lasts.'

Turner shrugged. He was past understanding the places the forces of his life were leading him to. He understood suddenly the inherent helplessness in the Doctor/Patient relationship.

'Okay,' he said quietly. Then, 'how about my job?'

Sheer smiled earnestly, his head on one side. Hands spread.

'You will be able to work normally for as long as you feel able. If treatment is success – you may never have to stop at all. Certainly, for a long while these attacks will become less intense because of drugs you will be taking. Come back in three weeks time. We will be able to assess how you are progressing'.

The Doctor smiled.

'You realise this treatment is very expensive? Now because of New System people all over the world get this treatments free! Something to be thankful for. You don't pay a penny of it!'

Turner said nothing. He had no reason to thank anyone for anything yet. The door opened. He left.

In the corridor – great white dazzling electric corridor – smell of lysol and surgical rubber. Turner stopped fifty feet from the pharmacy. Looked in the paper carryall he was holding. Strangely exciting. Like a kit. Service equipment for the repair of the robot. Clean plastic. Very usable. Green spherical capsules of Enketholin. Like a soft paste visible through the capsule surface. 500 micrograms.

Translucent plastic Stellachlorazine gun – for thigh injections – in a sealed polyweld container. Pink ampules of Stellachlorazine A. Pearly white ampules of Stellachlorazine B. Tightly packed in brown plastic tubes with snapfix lids.

He shut the bag and kept on walking. This groove was a defence mechanism.

Were nurses good as naked under their overalls? Like did they just slip the overall on over their bra and briefies? This thought kept his mind protected. Weird in hospitals. Fussed over by young women. Really nice some of them. No wonder patients fell in love with them. Criptphunktweeeeeerreeeeeep! Criptphunktweee-eeeeereeeeeeeep! of crepe soles on bright linoleum. Woman coming with hands ready for medical intimacy. There – in the sound – knowledge of ptisk! ptisk! – her body touching buttons and material inside her uniform – the seeds of a fetish.

In the parking lot fear returns. There, out there somewhere. Bright sunlight on concrete. Clear daylight. That didn't mean you were safe anymore. They could be behind those cars. Machine gun, mills bomb, machete.

'Bomb toting banditos blast hospital Implosion victim.'

He took from his pocket the securilok module.

*You know I can't help it. Everytime you examine me. Your hands are so lovely.*

The codes were getting longer and longer.

Harder to remember.

What was the longest serial number of digits the human mind could hold?

He thought carefully. Desperately.

*She was unbuttoning her uniform.*

Soon society would find out.

*Just as I thought. No bra. Just panties.*

He tapped the number out. Slipped the securilok module into the space above the doorlock.

*Nurses don't generally do this but – heck! I'm gonna derby you, you big hunk! After all you poor klutz! – you are suffering from organ implosion!*

The catch released with a satisfying click.

Okay, what have they put in my ignition? Movies always fade then don't they? with the dame going down. I mean straight movies not hard core. But bullets you always see them penetrate. Why is that?

Turner ran the safety sensor over the instrument panel (E.Z. Coder-Security model – 'the Bomb Squad in your Pocket'). No trace. Okay no bomb. Cool. IT'S COOL FRANK! He almost screamed aloud.

He reset for 'Drive'. The securilok module pushed into the ignition slot. The car started. Wound up the feeder ramp. Onto the street. Almost silent purr of electric motor.

Two mecs in Levi's 'Space Drifter' jackets lounging by an 'Electron Glider' car. Electron Glider covered in probes and antennae. Custom 'Shuttle' nose cone. Yeah, funny how space is really the thing. The new fashion. Space suit jackets. Usta be plain old denim. Space Drifter! Christ! These brand names! The closest these fools have ever been to space is the top of the Stack! Ha ha. Some laugh!

Across the windscreen – gray flashing sheets of information gray flashing sheets of information gray flashing sheets of information gray flashing sheets of information gray flashing sheets of information gray flashing sheets of information gray flashing sheets of information gray flashing sheets of information gray flashing sheets of information of information of information of informa

From satellites, from cables, from screens, from rays, leaking from conduits, escaping through the universe – gray flashing sheets of information. Blind across the streets, flickering between IITS (Instantaneous Information Transfer Systems) user booths on street corners. Turner driving on the city streets between bright slots of daylight – gray flashing sheets of information.

DATE: LOCM 727 – 5335 J = 8.30
MARCH 27 2031 TCT
LOCATION: SPACE

*'Who's there? Ah splendid, show in the
infinite.'*

LOUIS ARAGON

'Engine trouble? What do you mean engine trouble?'

Morgan turned angrily from the holo set. The work
that the crew's minds had been through in the last few
days had left its own karmic weight.

'I mean engine trouble – like has bugged human race
for the last 300 years. No kind of reaction taking place
in the transit stage motors.'

Platinov grinned annoyingly.

Morgan cancelled the final act of the holo drama.
The figures blurred into vague colour and vanished.

'Yeah. Knock it off Platinov.' Angela accentuated the
similar sounding phonemes intentionally as she looked
up from the Moog key board built into the scoot ship's
wall. Dissonant chords jangled – faintly piercing, from
the private play headphones hooked back loosely
around her neck.

'Engine trouble?' Datsun smiled and shook his head
in calm denial.

'It's what I'm telling you. We aren't getting any
further.'

Platinov's broad impassive face registered only
exhaustion now. Bags under the eyes grey.

Morgan flared angrily. 'I'm gonna get on that transmitter right NOW!'

He remained motionless in the middle of the deck.

Why them? Expatriates even on the wacky world of Cipola, the European Orbital Location 120,000 miles from Earth – at a point called L5 – where the gravitational pulls of Earth and Moon would hold a third object in position (technically) forever. Could have picked from millions of French, Germans, Dutch, Spanish, Brits, Yugoslavs, Albanians and Poles.

'Four days to pick us up.' Platinov shrugged. Morgan glanced around at the crew fighting off negative feelings. The Scooter was a plain hull in the shape of an inverted saucer, fifty feet in diameter and three decks high with a simple nuclear motor installed in the base. But it seemed plagued by gremlins just now. The mission was not being a success. The crew had left the Seven Cities of Cipola to investigate the 'object' scanners had detected in deep space. An object whose path drew rapidly closer to the Seven Cities' orbital track.

They didn't have to go. Cipola was equipped with all kinds of sophisticated robot probes capable of carrying out the investigation. They went because 'the Council' wanted them to. To find out if they could 'communicate' with the object. Because Dralon, Most High Magic Man of the Seven Cities of Cipola had dreamed that the object was alive.

Dralon, a person of English origin. Charles Fishbourne – Smythe D.R.A.L.O.N., spiritual adviser to The Council and Director of Religious and Analogous Lines of Necessity for the mysterious 'OCTAVE' group which carried out consciousness research for scientists and enquirers on Earth.

The crew had volunteered. No one was coerced on Cipola. It followed the New System, the same as that which prevailed on Earth. The only difference was that on Cipola ideal conditions existed where the New System could actually be made to work. On Cipola, the New System had almost flowered to the designed end point of its evolution. A co-operative anarchist society of free people.

The cloud was still a long way off and the Scooter had stalled for the third and, according to Platinov, last time. No reaction taking place in the transit stage motors.

They had worked hard. They had used all kinds of meditation techniques to open their minds – to project the content of their consciousness. Archetype matrices – symbolism mantras – universal abstractions – pure math – music patterns. The consciousness of the object could be alien to anything they could conceive.

Morgan's irritation was all the greater. He had been appointed 'ORGANISER'. Non authoritarian co-ordinator of the group.

After three days of the advanced 'MED' techniques he had felt his mind really expanding. Quiescence. Receptivity. Tao. Now he would have to shut all that down. Energy. Focus. Control. Return his centre of consciousness to an operational area where he could concentrate, organise and work. It angered him.

His dark bearded afroskinned face with the high oriental forehead, hedgerowed into a frown. During his leisure period he had been watching holo drama. His favourite – the twentieth-century Terran classic *Lotr*. The perfect thing for sustaining his mood of aware relaxation. The interplay of psychic archetypes soothed him. He really could dig it. He had queried for the fiftieth time if it implied the racism and classism which had run riot in the twentieth century or whether it transcended them. He wondered again at the casual acceptance of mass violence in the midst of such tender spiritual beauty and marvelled at the brilliant analysis of addiction patterns conceived and presented by a man who had apparently never messed with anything stronger than the mild neural stimulant, tobacco.

Now these trains of thought were gone. As 'ORGANISER' he was faced with a hangup. Damn! On Cipola – that technological anarchist paradise with its smaltzy high tech minarets and beautiful gooey plastic tube elevators – Dizo twinkling lights – where the synthetic rain was always soft and warm, – nothing ever went wrong.

INTERJECT - ARCHIVE - ENTRY - REF:

CIPOLA - Centre Industrielle Pendu L'Orbite
Lagrange d'Autour.
Structure: 7
Form: Six cylindrical units around a central hub.
Conceived: (Spacek: Limoges, France)
Components Launched: 2002
Assembled: 2004

Cipola 1
    Industrial plant assembling solar panels for
    Geosynchronous Ad Terram Energy Transfer
    stations. Owned and operated by Global Energy
    Foundation. (GEF)

Cipola 2
    Engineering and Chemical works operated by
    GALCOM (Terran socialised manufacturing
    combine)

Cipola 3
    Ultima. Prime residential zone for
    scientist/workers and visitors to Cipola.
    Includes 'Astrohedron' concert hall. Site of
    first Eulipion Congress, 2031

Cipola 4
    Farm Zone. Output equivalents 1/3 combined
    European yearly produce (Terran Calendar
    Time). Includes 'Space Park' freedom area with
    famous synthetic forest, mini mountains, lake
    shore and waterfalls. Includes Lunadome' sport
    center. site of quinqueannual Weightless
    Olympics.

Cipola 5
    Part Residential. Main area of island occupied
    and operated by SCICOM (Socialised Terran
    scientific and research combine). Includes
    pure research labs, astronomical telescopes,
    data processing. Extra Terrestrial
    Communications Probe (ETCP) situated here.
    Headquarters of 'Octave' a consciousness
    research group jointly funded by Global Govt.
    and private trust funds on Earth.
    (Controversial)

## Cipola 6

Lab and factory complex leased by SPACE
INDUSTRIAL SERVICES (SIS). Privately owned
company. This unit instantly recogniseable by
rings of orbiting junk. Known colloquially as
'The Space Ghetto' Cipola 6 is also the home
of the 'Immigrants' – humanoid beings from a
supposed parallel universe who appear to have
materialised on Cip6 through a quirk or quark
of nature. This is an hitherto unpredicted
property of Lagrange Point satellites.
The Immigrants' – primitive and uncouth –
most closely resemble Barbaric tribal peoples
of bygone Terran eras. Many have been hired as
'casual labour' (sic) by SIS. (Controversial).

## Cipola 7

Central Hub. Incompleted. ⅓ mile peripheral
belt occupied by small robot operated SCICOM
installation. Remainder and central core
empty. Unit leased by SIS. Purpose unknown.
Laser shields enclose large areas. Access
restricted. This policy believed to be in
direct conflict with drive and directive of
New System Constitution Preamble para 4
(Controversial).

'Well okay,' Morgan thought. 'The sweet life is for
the closet buddhist. If expanded consciousness can't
handle hangups, then you're nowhere. You're building
skyscrapers on paperbags or toothpicks. But I'd better
go easy – or they'll think I'm like some kind of orc.'

'Datsun', he said suddenly. 'Man this whole trip is a
fiasco.'

'Not necessarily' Datsun said. 'The complete pattern
is not yet unfolded.'

An energy vibration passed between them. It said 'I/
You wanted to be Organiser.'

Morgan turned to Angela thinking, 'It's just crises
you got to go through. To become perfected – supra
planetwise. We'll get there.'

'Don't get uptight Morgan,' she said. Doll circles of
pink lit up her cheeks. 'Just don't get emotional.'

'Okay. Plat –'

19

The broad impassive face had masked up again, the corners of the mouth curved in a fixed smile.

'Come and see for yourself.'

The crew trooped to the engine room. Morgan took the E.Z. Analyser Platinov had been using and ran it over the transit stage reactor.

The E.Z. Analyzer was simultaneously aware of all the nuclear reactions, electronic circuits and chemical processes powering the ship and all the cybernetic link ups that ordered them. A wand-like cylinder less than a foot long, the E.Z. Analyzer could organise repair, tuning, modification or improvement while in flight. It was a failsafe for the design engineers and their computers.

NOW IT WAS SILENT. Everything intact. But nothing was working.

'We are becalmed huh?' Platinov said. 'I can't fix it, if that is what you are hoping I can do.'

'No Plat – I accept that" Morgan's voice was quiet and tense. 'But what I can't accept from you ...'

Platinov' eyebrows raised slightly. The broad tired face grinned. 'Yes?'

'The fact that you seem to think it's funny.'

'Oh boy,' Angela said. 'Morgan, you aren't going to be one of THOSE Organisers are you? Because if you are – barf!'

'Don't let's get dingy with each other,' Morgan said. 'Remember what The New System is about. Think of Cipola. I'm going to the observation deck.'

```
INTERJECT - ARCHIVE - ENTRY - REF:
NEW SYSTEM - the
Inaugurated: TERRA 2001

History/Structure:
     The New System. A Global political system
     resulting from the Superpower rapprochement
     brought about by Arnold Effects. (Discoveries
     in the field of mathematics that made secrecy
     impossible). A system strongly influenced by
     the political theories of La Comtesse Simone
     de Lautrec. A synthesis of centrist
```

democratic and syndicalist ideas, championed
by Edwin O. Goodrich (US) and Andrei
Tsarchovsky (USSR). A world government system
based on the shape of an egg. A supra
national system allowing for a national
identity.

## PROPONENTS:

Proponents believe that the New System is
designed to evolve to a point where it no
longer exists.

## OPPONENTS:

Opponents believe that the New System is the
old tyranny, statically enslaving the world
under the mortmain of bureaucracy and
committee management forever.

## EXAMPLE OF THOUGHT:

N.S. Constitution Preamble Para 4. We also
hold this truth to be self evident that it is
the inalienable right of every Wo/Man and
Child on Earth or any Planetary Colony or
Orbital Location to demand and be granted
free and unrestricted access to all human,
cybernetic or printed sources and repositories
of information, all artificial or natural
resources and means of nourishment, all
commonly owned or public property, existing
anywhere on Earth or in Space.

The environmental computer had programmed a
beautiful synthetic dusk for them. Soft blue light crept
into the blazing purity of day which faded pinkly to
purple then it was all soft blue and then dark blue.

Morgan thrust his hands into the pockets of his
jacket and stared out through the transparent dome
that roofed the Scooter's combined observation and
flight deck, the top layer of the saucer-shaped hull. He
stared out at 'the Deep' as Cipolans termed the visual
experience of the vastness of space.

'I shouldn't have spoken to Plat that way,' he

thought. 'That was sick. I failed the New System when I said that.' Minimum age 65 years and details of four previous incarnations on the application. But that was Dralon. Now, all that heavy Med. Really he knew. His consciousness was OVER sensitized.

'Light,' Morgan murmured to the Scoot Ship's audio sensitive electronic switch system, simultaneously aware of light as energy, light as equation, light as the last of the last words of the Nineteenth Century Terran artist Turner. The light faded up quickly, but before it peaked he barked 'Cancel!' He had seen something out there in the darkness of space.

A vast mass, formless and dense, stretching away into the Deep, blotting out the stars from Rigel to Ursa Major. He guessed it must be 1,000 kilometres long and maybe fifty kilometres from where the scoot ship lay becalmed. The nebulous object was closing rapidly as though driven by some titanic cosmic wind.

Within seconds, greenish, fibrous-looking matter was billowing past the scooter ship in long luminous strands.

Morgan rushed down the steps to the recreation deck.

'Guys,' he said to all of them. 'Forget the engines. We don't have to go to the Gas Cloud. It just came to us!'

Now, there was frantic activity on the observation deck. Before any attempt was made to fulfill the main purpose of the mission as defined by Dralon – telepathic communication with the gas cloud – there were the obvious scientific tests to do. Facts, as far they could be determined. All members of the crew were perfectly aware that the validity of these facts existed only in proportion to their ability to measure the data that produced them. But all residents of Cipola were convinced of the need to follow the disciplines of the mystical cult known as scientific method – of the key importance of the sword of reason in the armory of any voyager. Anyhow you had to start somewhere – you didn't just ease on up to a weird alien gas cloud and start right in to communicating with it. First of all you could measure a whole lot of stuff like – density – volume – length – composition and so forth like that. After that basis – well then you could get heavier into it, on a supra subatomic consciousness/information level.

Sensor – computer – screen – right? The computers were processing the information as fast as the sensors could collect it.

Naturally, as Morgan had suspected all along, nothing made sense. As though the 'cosmic wind' effect had suddenly stopped blowing, the cloud was slowing down. Like the atmosphere of an alien planet it hung under the belly of the Scoot Ship whorling and twisting inward upon itself, spreading and flattening out beneath them.

The test results were crazy. In places the cloud appeared to have a very dense molecular structure, concordant with the fibrous appearance – yet quite equally – it appeared to be very loose. Molecules placed so wide apart that it seemed impossible that the thing could hold together in visible form. The crew collected and collated data – faces full of puzzled frowns.

Angela voiced their confusion first.

'It's very long,' she said 'but the sample I just tested says it can't be.'

'How long?' Morgan asked.

'About 3,000 kilometres' she replied.

'That's not so long – in space terms. Not if you consider the Magellanic clouds or something like that,' Datsun murmured.

'Yeah, it's just a cute, little gas cloud,' Angela said in a tired voice, 'drifting happily through space.'

Morgan glanced at her through half-lidded eyes. Does she have to be so negative?

'A *weird*, cute, little gas cloud. Because – you see what I mean ...' Platinov was pointing to the wide, curved windows of the deck, 'it's solidifying!'

One quick biovisual check – out the window – all that's needed. PLATINOV IS RIGHT. The Scooter appeared to be standing on a long, roughly rectangular island 2 km by 1 km surrounded by a vast mass of gas. The island was growing rapidly in size. Pretty soon it looked like it could be the size of a small state.

There was a definite appearance of a landscape. Vague, shadowy, greenish, in soft relief against 'the Deep', with the land falling gently concave between the horizons.

'Range finder's report: situation consolidated,' Datsun read from the VDU. 'The island has stopped growing. Length – 2,300 kilometres. Width – 2,300 kilometres. Beyond – gas. Fluctuating. Wave motion irregular – density variable. Kind of like an ocean'.

Complete silence.

Angela moved slowly to the Moog keyboard and pushed down a strange dissonant chord, as though demons from the Terran mountains of Tibet beat with bronze hammers on the edges of a vast frozen bell.

Morgan's eyes turned towards her. They smouldered with a deep inexpressible anger.

'Gravity field?' Morgan stared at the white plastic ceiling his voice scarcely above a whisper.

Datsun answered. 'Yes'. He muttered figures to himself. 'Just a little bit heavy, but it will do.'

'We didn't need sensors for that,' Platinov said, grinning again. 'We got no transit motors – so why else are we in position here if not for some gravity?'

'Right!' Morgan said, vectoring a long finger on Platinov's face.

'Atmosphere?'

Datson smiled. A wide, peaceful contented smile. 'Breathable,' he said.

'Oh boy,' Angela murmured quietly. 'That old thing.'

'Did you ever watch that holo –' Platinov's broad face had lit up with interest.

'No need to remind me.' Morgan grinned wryly. 'They're all the same'.

'It's obvious,' Platinov said, his face now radiating heavy Slavonic joy. 'We got to go outside and explore this thing!'

24

Morgan hunched. Hands deep in the pockets of his sharp, off white Space Drifter.

'Okay. But we'll take suits. It could be sneaky out there.'

DATE: MARCH 28 2031 TCT
LOCATION: UK WESTWORLD
CCR 1010

*'I look at my television, see pictures of all
kinds but I never did see no pictures of that
darling girl of mine.'*
SONNY BOY WILLIAMSON II

The vid screen flickered dimly. Bad prints. The voice
over crackled. Static. There were bad connections to
Turner's antennae. But they were all he had to work
with.

Turner thought – this is crazy. A potential death
sentence – but I carry right on working. It's the best
way. Organ Implosion doesn't make you immune from
bills. If only. Damn! Why did I let it go by so fast? If
only I'd taken the time and trouble. Sorted out a decent
bio mechanic – or a bio analyst. Hundreds of 'em in the
directory. Used to laugh at Tracy. Hypochondriac.
Could have though. Gone to an Ashram every month.
Public Sector too busy for all that. Private Sector. They
want your money. Alternative therapy can cost. Thing
is they do believe in it. Prevention – is better. I coulda
got a prognosis. Well keep on it's better. Or I'll be a
medication junkie drooling by a cold vid. No – die with
boots on. Maybe I'll live. Three weeks. I'll know better.
Let's check this new assignment.

'Turner this is the girl.'

Tall, leggy, slim, brown-haired girl. Seventeen years
old maybe. Looks sophisticated. Sitting on a rail fence

– big farm somewhere. Mountains in background, brand new, and huge ancient forest with that just planted look. Ride fit for an Earlking. West Germany maybe.

Tall slim girl. Smiling. Chewing a hay stalk. Bridle in her left hand. There, on Turner's work station screen.

Turner at work sipping drink. Notes taken on a clip board.

'Subject is Ellene Novotny. Age eighteen years. Born November 28th, 2013. Sign of Sagittarius. Father is head of Quinline Metal Pressings. Mother hysterical.'

Quinline Metal Pressings. Multinat. Subsiduary of SIS. Whoops! This could be very heavy.

'Believed to have joined INK. Initiated Neophytes of Knowledge. Turner they're raising wigs on the green. She has got to be reclaimed and deprogrammed.'

Turner thought, 'She's a lovely girl Don. It'll be a pleasure. Well just a joke. I'll be going for my "usual" soon.'

'She's West German, Turner. Second generation. Russian extraction. Grandparents defected from the Bolshoi Ballet 1969. Her father is UK based by choice. Anglophile – 'kay? Naturally he's just thrilled his darling daughter disappeared over here.'

What difference did it make, Turner thought, in Westworld? In France, haricot vert. UK, fish/chips. Germany Vienerschnitzel. And if you went to Head Office, hamburger and apple pie. And you could get all of it everywhere. Maybe France had the best art galleries, if anyone cared. Ask Tracy. That's where she'd fucked off to.

'Last seen outside the Fun House Auditorium. Concert featuring "Heavy Period". Three months ago. She leafleted fans on the way out. Here's a piece of Site Security's film of the subject.'

The image shifted. Milling groups of teens and twenties leaving a gaudy 'effect architecture' building. Getting into cars. Cars jamming an exit by a wire fence. Arc lights.

Standing by slow-moving cars and crowds on foot,

the girl Ellene – jeans, anorak – wool hat low over ears. Intense facial expression of smiling – appeal – entreaty. Handing out leaflets, Xeroxed sheets. Turner put the machine on 'pause'.

The cults. Oh boy. What he didn't know about the cults, dem. It was his job.

Children of God. Scientology. Moonies. Catholics. Sons of Ahmitsu. Fellowship of St Jack. Hare Krishna. Teeny Masons. IBM. The Police. The Pranksters. The Riverbrook Foundation. Process. Entropy. Dissolution. Thesis. Antithesis. Synthesis. Sexus. Nexus. Plexus. The Brotherhood of Breath. The Sisterhood of Spit. Daughters of Kali. CofE. The Great White Way. The Holy Overmind Church. The various Death Cults. Mah Religion and INK.

One of the weirdest. Believed in the possibility of absolute knowledge and hence, absolute achievement for every human.

Stage One. You were contacted. By someone like Ellene. Soft sell. Nice, normal-looking kids. Xerox. No gloss.

Stage Two. Four days of intelligence tests and investigations. If you tested out high enough, you were in on the ground floor. You began taking courses equivalent to majoring in Economics, Politics, Architecture, Astronomy, Maths, Navigation, Medicine, Metallurgy – then Physics – genetics ... So it went on. At various times there were secret rituals of initiation in which great secrets were imparted. Like, so rumour had it what brekekekex koax koax really meant, and how it had nothing to do with frogs.

Periods of seven years, fourteen years ... even twenty-one years, depending. On your stamina. And beyond that – the final secret. Il Segreto. The secret of secrets.

A high pressure-achievement method with a quasi religious overlay. Nothing wrong with the basic idea. But full of conceptual flaws in the basic application. Turner knew. To be good at his job you had to know a lot about education.

Incredibly competitive. Most Neophytes took jobs in industry and business, where they tended to advance. But, very high rate of mental and physical breakdown. Last case he'd reclaimed – but couldn't deprogram. Pathetic drug addict. Using vast quantities of 'Drive' in a hopeless attempt to keep up with the incredible demands of the system – and keth to calm down. Turner had no intention of deprogramming the know-ledge. Only the controls, cunningly and ruthlessly installed, that kept the poor guy struggling on and on to achieve past what flesh and blood could endure. NFG though, too far gone. Gibber gibber gibber. Organic smoke from burned out circuits pours from ear cavity. Eyes glazed with dead figures stare at scratchy mind screen. Fingers twitch at broken buttons. Private nursing home job. Parents with lots of money. Soon a nurse will come. Bring Keth in big needle.

Origins. Basically it was business mysticism. A legend circulated. Movement started by Henry Ford and J.P. Morgan in secret. After they had deciphered the mysteries of the Great Pyramid. This faboid borne out by events. INK world headquarters was a pyramid shaped sixty storey block in Indianapolis.

Fact. Movement started by Clyde 'Fuck da Japs' Finster, a Detroit auto worker who, having lost his job bolting bumpers onto Toronados in the Recession of 1973, attempted several astounding business ventures of his own. Including a chain of disco laundromats. All these failed, but he decided to sell the secret of his success anyway, as an education plan. (Pyramid selling – mythical linkup No. 2)

This took off. Then one day, his top salesman, Artie 'Blue Sunshine' Grunewald – previously unemployed ex-hippie gone straight, had a vision while staring fixedly at the tail lights of his '82 Seville Cadillac. It was not big, that Cadillac. Downsizing of automobiles had begun in 1978. Cars were getting progressively smaller in four yearly increments. By the end of the century people would be riding around in 1/32nd scale AMT construction kits. The end of civilisation was approaching. He saw the logic of it with unusual clarity. A vision. 1999 would be the last model year of the Western World.

Lost in a reverie, picking up on creepy paranoid vibrations, gazing vividly with his inner eye upon scary vistas of cracked and empty freeways, crumbling buildings, deserted lawns, tattered flags fluttering abandoned above the brown hulks of rusted out cars (even this must pass away) – a panel truck drifted by. The sides of the truck were lettered 'Iverson and Quail ltd I.Q. Products. Intelligent products for intelligent people!'

Wow! That was IT! The cosmic forces has spoken. The answer was to found a new religion – but not one based on hocus pocus. Salvation lay in Intelligence! Clyde 'Fuck da Japs' Finster's idea extrapolated to the mind expandin' limit.

It was the dream of a poor man, who had finally struggled to succeed. To liberate, for everyone who would listen, all the knowledge and ability that lay in the intellectual storehouses of the privileged and rich. This was the dawn of the Age of Information. This was Freeland, despite the unspeakable conditions obtaining. Everything was available to everyone everywhere. All you had to do was get the books and learn what they put in 'em.

There would be a vigorous programme to raise intelligence at all levels. Knowledge would be increased. The magic ingredient would be hard work.

Basic flaws in the application. Artie equated knowledge with learning. He equated intelligence with a quantifiable ability to manipulate given problems. He equated motivation with desperation. But he did have a secret. Definitely. But that was for later.

He quit selling and started preaching. He was supported only by the Neophyte's donations.

INK did not appeal to the troubled masses Artie had originally intended to liberate. It appealed to kids from the lower echelons of the superstructure who faced a life of dependent boredom with all the privileges and no real achievements of their own. It appealed to middle-class kids who were fed up with the stagnant world situation and their washed out parents – and really wanted to get somewhere. The fabulous fat bellied future their grandparents of the high rolling nineteen fifties had envisioned for them. The Neophytes, of course made all their available money over to the Neophyte Holding Co. (Pres: AG) Lawyers made personal fortunes trying to get it back.

Artie Grunewald traded in his Cadillac for a Mercedes. He dropped the 'Blue Sunshine' tag. He had a pyramid built in downtown Indianapolis.

Soon the cult had spread all over the world. It had been in existence now for decades. Artie Grunewald was a very old man. He wore long white flowing hair and a pink, shot silk business suit.

So what? Turner thought. The way things were going, GALCOM and everything like that, you'd need to join INK or be born into a Dynasty to get anywhere anyway. No room for the little guy. So why did he intend to Reclaim and Deprogram? 'It's a living' as the little bird Fred Flintstone employed as a motor horn was wont to say.

The facts. Head of UK operation? Graeme Fisher. INK's greatest personal success story. A great name for a young man who was really going somewhere. Turner imagined him as a school leaver on the first day of his first job, picking up the phone and saying 'Hello, this is Graeme Fisher. Can I help you? I've just started here today.' A voice reedy and thin. Thin as a golf club. Flat as a mock Georgian front door.

Achievement profile. At age 28 – youngest ever General Secretary of the TUC. At age 37 youngest ever Chairman of the CBI. Retired now at age 41 to run INK UK.

Turner released the pause button and the film ran on. Any closeups? he wondered.

'This is the closest we've got,' the voice-over rumbled by synchronicity. 'It's only a surveillance film.'

A boy stood beside Ellene. About the same age.

Same expression. Handing leaflets also.

Turner freeze framed them both alternately. Memorizing. He moved on.

There appeared to be no obvious supervision or control. They were merely in the parking lot leafleting the crowds. A few hands grabbed from car windows. Walkers took leaflets and smiled or scowled or shrugged and walked on by.

After a while the area cleared. Ellene and her companion walked off camera.

Turner replayed the sequence two or three times. Then he entered the authorisation code known only to himself and Reclaim Inc. He switched to the coded part of the transmission that had played through earlier, silent and invisible, safe behind a Diophantus Lock.

Personal and Confidential. These were items supplied by the subject's parents. Intimate details and touches that might be of use to the investigator.

'Daddy I love you. Mamma you're the greatest. Daddy I love you. Mamma you're the greatest. Daddy I love you. Mamma you're the greatest. I'm so happy.'

Westworld English. No German. Home movie sound track. Fourteenth birthday.

Turner played it over and over. Split the screen. Voice prints hovered and flickered across the cathode tube.

He watched them. Played them over and over till he could read them. By now, she might be heavily disguised.

'Daddy I love you. Mamma you're the greatest. I'm so happy.'

Good examples of her speech? The parents were claiming it was kidnap.

Just hope I get a good clean run at it. No fuckups. No OCTAVE snoopers creeping around. Goddam 'consciousness research'. Deprogramming and The Violation of the Mind. He'd read the report. 'Possibly the very act of joining a cult, a motivation spurred by a deep inner need, authentically expresses the "true will" of the personality concerned, as acting conscious mind.

Deprogramming, at best a panacea, at worst a nightmarish recourse reminiscent of the worst fears of the Laingians for both the family and society, driven by the basest aspects of surviving free enterprise capitalism that refuse to be subsumed ... like a long arm of unwritten law dragging the refugee back through the barbed wire kicking and screaming in to the claustrophobic psychic prison cells of monogamy's myriad microhavens of reproduction ... a gray zone of quasi psychiatry shrouded by a blank wall of faboids ...'

Yes. Fine words indeed. But I know better. Bleeding heart wimps I call them. I've seen what the cults can do to people. But now OCTAVE have initiated a research program at the behest of CENTERCOM. How in hell can they call it research when their recommendations are CENTERCOM mandated?

Turner cancelled the screen. It was time to go. Time to start an investigation. Turner flicked through numbers accessing doors, tunnels, his car. Out on the hard road again. Highway vertigo. Gray sunlight on the dense tonnage of the Stack. Feeder roads spiralling into it like galactic arms. Always he tried to judge the moment you were actually 'in', but he couldn't catch it. At one instant out in the gray sunlight. Next moment gusts from ventilator units rocking car body. Condensation drips from rooflayers overhead on windshield wipers. SOX lamps replace the pale sun.

Crowded crowded crowded. Magnetic grabs winch Turner's car up and away to a narrow slot in a parking structure. At the kerbside illegally parked cars are wrapped in sheets of 'SupaTuff' – the strongest plastic known to man – and dynamited. So crowded. A million feet on every street.

Shoulder to shoulder. Nose to nose. *Le Siècle vingt et unième est un paradis de frottage.* Downtown, Turner struggles through the crowds. Fifteen minute wait to cross the road. Flashing sheets of information gray flashing sheets of information ... *uberweisung gekommen* ... gray flas ... *o-ne-gai ga arimasu* ... sheets of informa ... *depositare in una banca* ... ay fla ... *que pasa* ... ing shee ... in the hub? ... of information gray flashing sheets of information – arcing across between IIT booths nearly blinding Turner.

Looking around. Girls sell cigarettes. Girls sell cars. Girls sell food. Girls sell everything on every holo – every billboard. He desires. The pantyhose girl. The lipstick girl. The car upholstery girl. Girls everywhere. Turner's mind is colonised till he reaches his destination. INK UK 429 E. Malthus Rd.

Girl at reception.

'Can I help you sir?'

'Yes. I'd like to talk to Mr Fisher.'

'He's busy at the moment. Do you have an appointment?'

'No.'

Flashes ID card from wallet.

She looks at him very displeased.

'Oh dear Mr Turner. I hope there isn't any trouble?'

'Not as yet. Let's keep it that way.'

'I'll tell him you're here.'

She shifted from behind the desk, her skirt to her buttocks softly moulded. Breasts like shells of sheerest aluminium. Machine turned legs tapering into high heels. Tack tack. Tack tack tack tack tack. Sweet and sour exhaust of bio warmth and stale perfume.

He glanced around the foyer area. He'd seen it all before.

Suspended from the ceiling a huge plastic metronome dominated the reception area. It must have been all of twenty feet tall. Symbolic of time and the discipline needed to control it. Also a pyramid. Mythical link up No 3. Huge three dimensional holo portraits of INK heroes shimmered in deep softly lit conical wall alcoves. Giants of super achievement through inner motivation. Nikola Tesla the mathematics whiz who made scientific discoveries through self induced trance states and dreams. Ransom Olds who invented automobile mass production because he hated the smell of horses. Theophile Gautier who said 'inspiration consists of sitting at my desk and picking up my pen', thus demythologising the idea of inspiration forever.

'Come all ye who hunger . . .'

'Life is short and the art long'

'No man is an island . . .'

'I am you and you are me and we are all together . . .'

The holos and slogans shimmered and flickered all around the walls. 'Apply the seat of the pants to the seat of the chair' flashed past Turner's head in a rainbow of brightly coloured laser beams. It was an effect architecture building. 'Genius is . . . (in simulated ticker tapes of focused light) . . . an infinite capacity for taking pains.' Turner glanced at his watch. A low table spread with INK pamphlets and elegant recliner chairs stood by the reception desk. But high fashion 'effect' decor lighting had flattened and synthesised their forms until they looked like a painting by Juan Gris, or Georges Braque. Turner decided to remain standing.

Tack tack tack tack tack tack tack TACK TACK.

The secretary emerged or appeared to emerge from the base of a ceiling-high VDU across which flashed a repeated series of dazzling calculations ending in the formula $E = MC^2$.

'In the long run,' Turner said, 'You can't beat the good old'uns,' gesturing towards the display.

'He'll see you.' The girl smiled angrily from a perfectly designed face with lips of candy.

'Third floor. Second office on the left as you go along the corridor.'

'Thank you,' Turner said. He didn't repeat the instructions in case the sound of his own voice made him forget them.

The elevator was screened. Screen blank. Good. A numb ache gripped the right side of his body. The medication began in very small doses at first. He wondered if he would be being crippled by an attack without it. He knew also soon – there would be – side effects. Were the elevator walls expanding? Could be the building. Effect architecture. No. Control fear.

The second office on the left as you went along the corridor was open plan in a large area. Stale smell of men and girls working. Soft chill of air conditioner. Fisher rose from behind a steel and copper executive special, which bore his name – Graeme Fisher – on a plastic plaque and a photo of his wife and children. He was grey suited. Forty-four. Dry. Nondescript. Efficient English accent.

'Hello. I'm Graeme Fisher. How can I help you?'

Turner smiled. Turner smirked.

'Turner. Frank Turner. Reclaim Inc.'

'I know who you are.'

Pained voice. Pained expression.

Turner didn't sit down or kid around. He tossed a photo of Ellene onto the heavy desk.

Fisher leaned back and compressed his fingers.

'Turner, you might benefit from several of our indoctrinations you know. Improve your manners. Get yourself a decent job. Ever consider emigrating? Space for example?'

Raw nerve. Hit him on. Bastard. Too old. Too stupid. Too ugly. They didn't want Frank Turners out there in the future. Oh yes, that's where the real jobs were – if you could study physics, or learn to be weightless – or be ten years younger. Real careers are in space now. Fat chance. Study electronics. Goddam this Organ Implosion. Could work in construction. Building solar panels and what have you. That's the glam industry. But it's an elite thing I reckon. Lucky to get a Space Drifter jacket or a little cheap energy for my home. Look at me. A dirty old deprogrammer.

Coulda had my own agency. But this System! Sewing it all up for the govmnt dem. Be damn lucky if they don't incorporate 'Reclaim' into the FTPA.

Soft beep of phones. Clickertik of keys. Grey flashing sheets of information. Sight of Fisher. Smell of women.

Sheets of light in a deep well. Below in the pool hundreds working. Rumour had it they were copying out the Bible. Just there to look good like in the old days when the world was young and offices were full.

'Thanks, I'll remember that and you, Fisher. I'm here to negotiate. Up to four hundred Euro units – if you want to. Or else we track her down and grab her.'

'Turner – this conservation is being recorded. As far as I know, Westworld is still a free state within the CENTERCOM structure. This girl is eighteen. Do you really have the right ...?'

'Fisher. Give me a break. Her old man is a director of Quinline.'

What the hell was the use? Four hundred units couldn't buy anything Graeme Fisher needed.

'All the more reason Turner –'

'No. Think about it. If it was your daughter and you were him. Would you want an insane over achieving robot in your home? Or even your business?'

'Of course, I don't accept your definition of our products.'

Turner laughed. The tape. He wanted that on. The laughter. Get up their fucking noses.

'Okay Fisher. Let's break it up.'

He tossed a card – F.B. Turner, Reclaim Inc. – onto the desk.

'You probably don't need this. You must be familier with us already.'

Fisher ignored the card.

'Turner, have you considered how fortunate this girl really is? Faced with a useless life of unending leisure, she came to us. Experts in the art of self advancement. What if a Death Cult had got her?'

'No job for me most likely. But they didn't. So why not hand her over?'

Fisher smiled. A wan despairing unfriendly smile. Button pressed on desk console. He began to read softly from a built in screen.

'Turner, Frank. Age 42 years. Married but separated from wife. Resident of Dodman's Ley Development, Sussex. Seven years Southern Regional Security. Left to found own company in North Wales, "Gelert Protection". Business failure ... Downwave of '23 ... yes, not surprised with a name like that ... returned to yes, yes, ah yes ... Reclaim. Six weeks suspension! Induced null program through intravenous "Real" shots to unconsious subject. A fifteen year old boy, David K. Horowitz, son of Denise Horowitz, leading European Evolutionary Survivalist Party candidate. Really Turner, this is a bit much . . .'

'You cunt!' Turner's mind was raging. 'That kid was with "The Stiffs" the worst death cult there is. Woulda done five or six god awful ghastly murders then topped himself. I saved his mind with that Real, and his mother's. Insult to fucking injury. You hypocritical bastard!'

'Turner, don't take it all so personally.' Fisher shook his head sadly. 'This is the *Age* of Information. Has been for decades, will be for the foreseeable future. Can't you see that? People live daily with the knowledge that there are hundreds, perhaps thousands, of others who know more about them at any given moment than they know about themselves. You of all people should be able to appreciate this. But you're still shocked I can tell. Why? Because you're so hopelessly old fashioned. You're in the wrong job, Turner. You care too much.'

'Mr Fisher, think it over' Turner said. 'Four hundred units or we come and get her anyway. Old fashioned see? And so simple.'

'Good day Mr Turner.'

'Yeah. Checkyer.'

Better get ready to bust her out. Fisher is going to clam. Four hundred units won't buy anything he needs. No way to put the chill on him. Clean sheet. Damn. Price of recovery? Price of mind. Price of body. Price of bio unit complete?

Prostitutes ask the same question. How many units can I raise on my body? How many units can I raise on my brain you can also ask. Different kinds of prostitute of course – but we're all inmates of the same culture.

Clinkadinkadinkadinka

Left here. Noisy indicator. Look out! Nice that – Fiat I think. It's a prostitute culture. Or else a leisure culture. I'm an old whore. So is Good King Thing and Graeme Fisher.

Shell vibration.

Third here. Funny how the old manual stays in business. Shades – yes, glove compartment. Coulda been a mechanic. Thought about forms and principles. Shift big hunks of metal – make adjustments. Precision and oil-based existence. Never get your hands clean. Girls don't like that. Oh, look, the thighs before your eyes trick. Mighty good advertising that. Put your product at the top of a girl's thighs. Magic vee will do it every time. Jesus. I would love to. And oh – girls too I guess. They come from there don't they? So – girls sell everything to everyone everywhere. Thought Madame Feng would have put a stop to that by now. I see the Women's Committee have started on poor old Edouard Manet. Explicit sexism implicit in 'Dejeuner sur l'herbe'. Men in tall hats represent the ruling sexist classes of the nineteenth century. She is their plaything. Degrading. Funny she doesn't look very degraded from what I remember. Wonder what old Trace thinks about it. She's over there. Jeo de Pome.

Rain wet trees dark. Sunsplash on sidewalk. Rain pools. Hiss of tyres on rain wet tarmac. Pearly banks of purple cloud.

These dark spots here. Oil on the windshield I suppose. That's polaroid for you. No glare and eyes like infra red. Not really infra red. But like that kind of idea. The tits on that! Seventeen maybe. Yes. But I'm too old for her. Imagine it. In white and gold bedroom maybe. Off with her bra. Rose bud lips.

You bastard. Where did you learn to drive? In a whorehouse? Soft – when you push it in. Straight into top gear. Brilliant engineering. Good feeling gear sticks made for men. But women use them too. Mish mash. Mish mash.

Kiss of tyres on wet tarmac.

RED LIGHT

Brake slowly – if they'll fucking let you. I hate the thought of skidding – into say a cyclist. We need grooved pavement. Arise and overthrow the people! Hm, like that one. No connection though. Is that the answer? Probably. Must get a spray can. Nearly as good as 'Good Morning Lemmings' on the eastbound Stack feeder.

Ellene. Funny little girl. Says mummy I love you, daddy I love you. Goes through changes. Runs away from home. Crams head with knowledge. The Sex Slave Eggheads of INK. That's what the papers say.

This seat is going. Car is going. Fat chance of a new one.

dinkadinkadink

Turn left only. Hm. That's new. With these VDU road signs they can make it up as they go along. Get back on the pavement! Nearly there now. Got to park somewhere.

Grey flashing sheets of information.

My 'usual'. Can't say I really feel like it. Stop you bastard! I'm reversing!

The business was franchised from Adult Leisure Inc. A chain of sex shops, sex cinemas and legalised brothels. No risk. Check by doc. It's cool.

Turner checked his reservation at reception. Third floor. Room 2. Jennine. He looked at the movie screen on the desk. Yes. Nice. Dark skin. Flashing eyes. Big tits.

'Your shower is in Room II sir. Same floor. If you want to get changed. Here is your cap of "Desire".'

He always ticked the box marked 'Stimulants?' yes. Hell, you paid enough for it. Or he had. Ever since his wife had left him.

His usual.

The stiletto heels were grotesquely high. They gave the long slim sinewy legs a look of ruthless fetishistic beauty.

The skirt was cunningly cut to end exactly level with her crotch. She wore nothing else. She extinguished her cigarette in the bedside ashtray, stooping with casually revealing elegance. She straightened up and folded her arms under her bosom. Her fingers drummed lightly on her forearms.

'Did the "Desire" start to work yet?'

'I think so', Turner said.

'You think so!' She laughed. A hard knowing callous professional laugh. Disbelieving.

Waves through Turner. For a second at a time his naked skin would tingle, reaching that deliciously agonizing electric peak in the palms of his hands and soles of his feet. But it wasn't right. No way. By now his whole body should have been a burning craving pillar of erotic energy.

The feeling tantalised. Then ebbed.

He looked at the girl. A nice jouba. No doubt about it.

The sample movie did not lie. She had pick picked her way on high heels to the edge of the bed. She clasped her hands over her naked breasts and sat down. She pushed her tongue from the edge of her mouth and spread her legs. She lay back against the wall. Mighty hot and porno.

Turner's knees felt weak. A good sign. That's how 'Desire' was supposed to feel. He fell slowly to his knees and slid his hands up the aquiescent thighs. He shook his head. No taste for fish today. Come back Friday. Part of his brain laughed a manic titter. Hihihihihihihiheeeeeeee!

He stood up, turned around and reached for his cigarettes. He stepped into his trousers and pulled them up with one hand, the other snapping the ignition button of his lighter. Smoke wreathed his head.

'What's with you!' the girl said sitting up, hands fallen limply to her sides. 'Jesus! "Desire" can make a dead man hard.' There was a rising note of anxiety in her voice. Turner was laughing through the smoke. Conscious voice less manic, but still quite eerie. He could see the mouth of a baby at her breast. The child grew two years old and stood clutching the girl's leg – staring upward, wide eyed. Peasant girls in black shawls, African woman birth drop squatting. Broad backs in rice fields. Slack breasts. Coil pottery.

He laughed again.

The girl's hand moved rapidly to the pillow – came

up clutching a TrankPak Personal Defense aerosol.

'You're wasting my time Mister,' she said. The voice angry and afraid. 'Are you some kind of pervert?'

'It's my medication,' he said. 'The Doctor told me it would be like this. I didn't realise it would be so soon.'

Turner buttoned his shirt and stepped into his shoes. He opened the door.

The girl's voice softened slightly.

'I mean you've paid for it. Why don't you have it?'

He pulled the door shut behind him. He couldn't tell her how nutty she looked in those weird clothes.

## CHAPTER 4

DATE: 8.10 JAN 10 2031 TCT
LOCATION: SSET FLAGSTAFF,
ARIZONA USA WESTWORLD
CENTERCOM REGION 436

*'If you ever plan to motor west, travel my
way, take the highway that's the best.
Get your kicks on Route 66.'*

BOB TROUP

The Lear Jet zoomed crazily into the sky. Below and
very far away now, faint smoke from the last of the
battle. Patch (not her real name) smiled. She was sailing clean. By now her cell would have self destructed.
No one to talk. The mission had failed. The SSET
station would soon be working properly again and the
city of Empyrean Park had not been destroyed. But the
guilt she felt about escaping when she should have
stayed and exit tripped with the others was evaporating
fast. Because now she had this! She looked down
triumphantly at the small plastic object on the seat
beside her.

All she had to do now was to pass it into the cells
and it could stay hidden and in circulation forever. The
Prankster cell system was massive and world wide.
Units of five in concentric circles. The concentric circles
of a circus ring. Inner circle – the arena. Area of Prankster organisation. Outer circles – the audience seats,
tier upon tier. Area of Prankster action. And in the
centre – emptiness! A circus without a ringmaster.
Some folk believed that the cells were organized by a
mad computer. They were wrong. It was something far

more dangerous. In the center of the empty arena lay a book. *I Am The Clown* by 'Herlechyn'. It contained the whole thing. You could buy it in any bookstore. You only had to pick it up and charge it. Millions had read it and never understood. Thousands of others had.

Herlechyn (not his real name) was the first Prankster. 'Herlechyn' was an old form of the word 'Harlequin'. But the name did not refer to the sad lover of Columbine. No. The old form of the name referred to a figure whose meaning was far more ambiguous, even sinister. In legend Herlechyn was leader of the 'Wilde Hunte' – a band of masked and eerie madcaps who haunted the fringes of society in Medieval times, causing mayhem and alarm. Some traditions suggested that the 'Wilde Hunte' were not of human origin.

*I Am The Clown* by someone calling themselves Herlechyn appeared in the last decade of the twentieth century, and became a frequently reprinted best seller. It was a simple, funny and slightly macabre tale about a circus clown who liked to play practical jokes (pranks).

The performing poodles whom he has taught to speak with human voices make their trainers do humiliating tricks.

The juggler, an unfortunate alchoholic, drops one of his clubs which Herlechyn has packed with laughing gas. The club bursts and the audience laugh themselves unconscious.

During the Big Parade, the Ringmaster's braces which Herlechyn has doctored suddenly snap and his trousers fall down. During his sleep Herlechyn has painted the Ringmaster's backside with luminous paint. While the clowns are laughing, all the animals escape to freedom. But of course the show must go on. Here follows Herlechyn's silliest trick. In the middle of a trapeze act without a safety net, all the lights go out. There are predictable and tragic results. As the lights go up again Herlechyn appears with his tearful painted eyes, and his laughing painted mouth. He tells the audience not to mourn just because the trapeze artists are all dead. 'The rictus is only another type of smile,' he says.

The end was very sad. Mawkish even. Herlechyn climbs to the apex of the Big Top and throws himself down on top of the fallen trapeze artists. Because, all of a sudden, no one finds him very funny any more.

Millions of readers had read this part through a mist of tears. But if you could see through the mist – and read between the lines ... Into the text of his book, Herlechyn had coded the perfect blueprint for revolutionary anarchist nihilism. Unfortunately, the type of people who saw this were so excited that they forgot also that Herlechyn was the first Prankster. *I am the Clown* was only a joke. No one, not even his agent or publisher knew Herlechyn's identity, race, eye colour or sex. Yet daringly, there was an indistinct photo on the back cover of the book. A slim figure in traditional parti-coloured clothes, wearing a heavy black mask and tricorn hat with foxtail pendant. Some people speculated that Herlechyn was an eccentric millionaire, a disgruntled politician, a famous movie star. A gangster on the run, an injured sportsperson, a disillusioned game show host. Each of these identities confirmed in the minds of the public by a thousand irrefutable proofs.

But there was only one fact. Herlechyn had vanished. And in that mysterious abscence the Prankster cells spawned – a great amorphous body without a head – fired with its own life as though by the imprint of some evolutionary code – mutating everything it touched like virus – floating around an imaginary circus ring like specks of sawdust kicked up by the hooves of performing horses. Tiny light, invisible almost – till they caught in your throat.

It had been tough getting out of there as the Government forces broke in, but Patch had clung to the side of one of the ponies grazing under the shadow of the huge SSET receptor banks and as the herd stampeded in the midst of the shouting and gunfire she had escaped.

At the edge of the site as Patch rolled clear of the thundering hooves, an operations truck was directing the stake-out and the final bust. Inside, two men. Patch shot the men and drove away in the truck. In the truck, an object. She knew what it had to be. There was no way they could have paralysed all the functions of the site without one. And the two studs she had shot had been Shadow Command, White Echelon. That proved it. Now the treasure was hers. And through her – the Pranksters'.

The jet had belonged to a nearby rancher. Now Patch had it. She was armed and extremely dangerous. Each member of any one cell knew one member and one member only of another related cell. Patch had a name and a location. She flew the jet low and fast in that direction, trying to stay under the radar. The object had to be passed on.

A thousand miles away in Washington DC, another mind was musing.

'Give me the luxuries and the necessities will take care of themselves' Frank Lloyd Wright had said in the dark heart of the 1930s Depression. USA president and CENTERCOM candidate Edwin O. Goodrich smiled when he thought about it. It sounded like the gambler's motto – upward mobile, positive and carefree. An ideal for an ideal world.

Like his forebear and mentor Franklin D. Roosevelt, Goodrich was a good panhandler – an expert conman en grand seigneur. With the New System he had perpetrated a massive but benign confidence trick. The massive Global Welfare State he had created and the world wide syndicalisation of the prime contractors precluded the power of political parties – yet they still existed at national level under the CENTERCOM blanket. There was a danger that they could increase their power in the future, distorting the shape of the CENTERCOM egg. It was vital he win the election and seize the reins of CENTERCOM again. Then he would press ahead with his Life Support Plan. That would restore the balance. His ideal was to make work and politics leisure activities, while the world system – smooth, efficient and bountiful, supplied both the necessities and the luxuries.

But for the time being, he was only President of the United States. Goodrich lay back on the massage table. Soft, firm fingers probed the sore spots on his back, where the tension was stored. Light brown oriental fingers. Edwin O. Goodrich relaxed. He began to dream.

His mind drifted back to the 1930s, the world of a hundred years ago – when he had been born. He saw it dimly lit like an old movie. Shadows of blue gray. Roosevelt presiding over the era, his cigarette at a weird angle. Men in felt hats. Crude rattling autos evolving into primitive streamlines, side by side with wagons and teams. A world rigged with telegraph poles, pylons and wire. Click click of ancient switchboards. Mr Wright's residence? Men in rags line by soup kitchens. Corseted women spoon gravy. Felt hats. Masked faces. Rochester's smile. Distant music. Another President, presiding over the era with his saxophone at a angle. Tiny lights begin to twinkle in the darkness. Patterns of coincidence.

The table side phone rang once. 'Pee whit!'

'Goodrich.'

'Pres – do you want the good news – or the bad news?'

'Both. But first, the good news.'

'Okay. The SSET stake out over. Site secured. All onsite hostiles terminated. Empyrean Park is safe.'

Goodrich breathed a sigh of relief. This much surely was good news. The SSET stake out had been a thorn in the flesh of American based security forces for over a long tense week. SSET was the main provider of the fuel that powered the world, CENTERCOM and the New System. Solar Satellite Energy Transfer. Huge solar panels assembled in ideal weightless conditions at L5, under GALCOM auspice and contracts held by SIS, were towed by nuclear tugs to Geosynchronous Orbit 22,300 miles from Earth. There the panels refocused the light of the sun into microwaves directed to various sites on Earth where they were picked up by banks of receptors and converted into Terra-usable energy.

Pranksters had seized one of the receptor sites near Flagstaff, Arizona. They were threatening to divert the massively powerful beams the SSET station collected across the Painted Desert until they affected the rain shadow of the San Juan Mountains, causing rain to fall at a mean temperature of 98 degrees on the futuristic new American city of Empyrean Park, Colorado unless ... unless the world leaders agreed to perform a joint suicide pact on GTV. Needless to say, the world leaders, ever worried about their popularity had received thousands of less than reassuring letters in their mail, especially from Colorado. Meanwhile the media fumed against the Pranksters with righteous indignation.

Now the security forces had managed successfully to break in and it was all over. Thank God.

'So what's the bad news?'

'Well Mr President, like I said – all on-site hostiles are terminated. But before *we* broke in, one of *them* broke out. And – uh – took a Mordell's Conjecture Probe with him.'

Goodrich blanched. His forehead broke out in fresh beads of sweat. A Mordell's Conjecture Probe. The Mordell'sConjecture Probe! Goodrich had personally authorised the use of it to enable the government agents to immobilise the receptors while the buildings were stormed. A Mordell's Conjecture Probe. The most powerful informational tool in the world! Why, in the wrong hands it could ...

'Find it!' the President said. 'By whatever means necessary!'

Groaning inwardly, he cradled the phone. He hated to authorise that kind of thing, but it had to be done. He turned over and lay back breathing deeply like a series of sighs. He knew it would be next to impossible. The Probe would be lost in the Prankster cell system.

'Anything wrong sir?' the attractive, swimsuit-clad

Japanese girl masseuse asked, smiling sweetly. 'I didn't finish your back yet.'

Goodrich stared at her as though suddenly seeing her for the first time. The swimsuit had a pattern of black and white diamonds almost like part of a harlequin outfit. As she moved, the diamonds moved. It was giving him a headache.

'No. Forget it' Goodrich said. 'I've got to go.'

'Better stay. Finish the massage.'

'No. Sorry. Pressing affairs of state.'

Grinning wanly he pulled a towelling bathrobe over himself and left the room, still groaning.

How long could he stall, he wondered glumly, before he had to phone Madame Feng?

The Japanese girl was still smiling. Thoughtfully she tapped a forefinger against her left temple. The tiny tape recorders installed in her left temple stopped rolling. By coughing lightly, she switched off the nose microphone.

It was time for her to catch the plane to Geneva.


'CENTERCOM Headquarters in Geneva (Mzrcski – Pierce Design Partnership) is an afternoon's ride from Washington DC by supersonic jet. It is a concrete steel and glass construction in the shape of a globe. Tasteful use of polished granite and copper sheath facings lends an air of grandeur to an essentially simple form. Subtly cantilevered on four flying buttresses (reinforced concrete – cast bronze decoration) which represent the four winds while being totally frank about their function, the plane of its axis inclines backward at a slight angle of tilt on the low but massive basalt plinth in which consists the building's foundation, conveying vividly and dramatically the impression of movement. Spaceship Earth in orbit – hurtling around the sun at 30,000 miles per hour.

Despite their natural penchant for a kind of expressionist neo-classicism, Mzrcski-Pierce have been unable to resist a few modish 'Effect Architecture' features, hence laser projectors bathe the entire building in a globular capsule of brilliant blue light – representing the atmosphere of Earth as seen from outer space ...' (*Geneva – An Architectural Guide for Tourists* by Ernesto Fallietti)

Behind that capsule of brilliant blue light, high on the upper hemisphere of that glass and concrete globe the current occupant of the presidential suite, Madame Feng, stepped naked from a salt water bath. Precious little good it seemed to do her. Prometheus kept her young and alive. No one would have believed that she was 105 years old. But the program did little for Oriental skin. Inherent chauvinism in the minds of the Prometheus scientists? She didn't know. She smiled bleakly. Salt water was supposed to help it though.

She lay down still wet on the pre-heated table. Soft skilful fingers began work on her neck and shoulders.

The headset built into the massage table's pillow bleeped urgently.

'Yes,' she said impatiently.

It was becoming impossible to relax. It was important to relax. To forget for a while even the most important affairs of state. To act as though they had never existed. Madame Feng had a lot to forget. For example, the fact that without any consultation with other world leaders she had decided unilaterally and illegally to break an international agreement. The Declaration of Bogota. It was hard to forget too, that she had used personnel from a supra-national security agency, namely Shadow Command, to do this, and without the knowledge of the head of that agency. It was hard to forget that the reason she had done this was because of rumours, leaks, call them what you will – about a space station hub. Cipola 7. There it was possible to believe very strange things indeed were happening. Things she wanted to be the first to know about. Because she was going to win the next election any way she could. And if what her scientific advisers said was correct, then the Hub could help her. No matter that her I Ching reading had just said 'Arrogant dragon has cause to repent'.

'Mme Feng?'

'Yes.'

'This is Edwin O. Goodrich.'

'Please continue Mr Goodrich.'

The voice at the end of the phone was breathing heavily. She enjoyed it. She enjoyed being awe-inspiring.

'Lady President Chair Person – I have bad news. Shadow Command operatives under United States auspice have lost a Mordell's Conjecture Probe! It is now believed to be in the hands of the nihilist surrealist terrorist group known as the Pranksters.'

Madame Feng's slim compact naked body became rigid. The soft skilful fingers went on probing gently but firmly for the chua k'a vortex points.

'No!'

Madame Feng sat up and spun angrily away from the head set and put Goodrich on hold. Her face was contorted with fury.

Looking suitably intimidated, the demurely clad pretty Japanese girl masseuse backed away bowing politely. Her face was heavily made up, eye shadow almost like a mask.

'Sorry Madame Chair Person. Did I . . .?'

'Foolish girl! Leave me!'

Still bowing, the girl left backward, bowing at every third step. Present ruler of the World, Madame Feng was naturally its greatest Democrat, but she expected Oriental ways from orientals. When she heard the door close Madame Feng returned to the head set. Fighting to control her anger.

'Naturally we're moving heaven and earth,' Goodrich was saying. 'The whole continent is virtually sealed off.'

With a huge effort Madame Feng sympathised. Then she complimented him on his efforts so far. She agreed to hot line liaison with him night and day, at every stage of the crisis. Her body was shaking. After a polite interval she said goodbye.

As soon as Goodrich was gone she reactivated the

head set, rapidly opening links to her chiefs of security.

'The idiot Americans have lost a probe. I want you to be ready if necessary to conduct door to door searches of every dwelling in the CENTERCOM region.'

'But Madame – with respect, you're talking about 689,750,000 homes.'

'No matter. Get ready! Begin by having the FTPA make sweep searches of every major city.'

She got up off the table, reaching for her dressing gown. She hated to be naked when she knew she was defeated. There was enough to worry about with that wretched Hub. Now this! Only the inscrutable synchronous workings of the Tao could save this situation.

Outside the girl masseuse sat demurely, her knees together, waiting to see if she would be recalled.

Her hands were folded in her lap. Lightly her fingers drummed on her stomach. Exiting from her vagina a miniaturised retractable antenna linked to a powerful transmitter implanted in her womb. It was belting out morse code.

'Feng is notified,' the message said. 'The shit is about to hit the fan.'

## DATE: LOCM 727 – 5835 J
## LOCATION: SPACE

**5**

> *'There is a similarity between thought and matter. All matter including ourselves, is determined by "information". "Information" is what determines space and time.'*
> PROFESSOR DAVID BOHM

They stared from the Scoot Ship's open exit hatch at the world that confronted them. Shadowy, intangible, nothing to home in on. It waited at the end of a white runged ladder, ten feet down. It was like descending into a dream, or a hypnogogic trance. Overhead stars, silver, bright. Beneath, a greenness sensed to be solid by complex machines. It was only as their boots hit that they could feel sure that they wouldn't fall through into limitless space. Swamp? Plain? Prairie? Steppe? Ice-locked ocean. You couldn't describe it. How come an atmosphere? Was it trapped by layers of unsolidified gas overhead? No data from that region. Thanks a lot.

For a while Morgan had theorised that the gas cloud had in reality (huh!) formed around them as a sphere, some parts of which were translucent, and that they were somehow on a solid belt on the inside. Kind of like the 'Hollow Earth' theory beloved of the nutty Nazi Copernicus, Hans Horbiger.

But it couldn't be. What the sensors indubitably did show was that in spite of the slightly concave appearance, (probably an optical illusion – like a fault in a windshield) they were not on the inside of a globe.

53

They were sitting on a 2.3 thousand by 2.3 thousand kilometre flat, which was at least a kilometre and a half thick according to the last information in. A huge chunk of solidified gas 5,290,000 square kilometres in area, with somehow an atmosphere, and somehow a gravity field. And Morgan knew. It was gonna get weirder.

They packed EVA suits, scientific equipment and nutrition in a voice-operated robot hover truck.

'C'mon truck!' they called. It bobbed along behind them. It was about two metres long and a metre wide.

The gas had solidified into a hard, smooth surface which was tactile rather than slippery. More like velcro than onyx. All around them it emitted faint light. Greenish, like reflector buttons on a highway sign.

In spite of the firm surface their feet rose and fell slowly like people wading in a swamp. The gravity had a positive sensatory muscle-pulling effect.

'The force of gravity here is remarkable,' Datsun said. 'Like sometimes on a mountain top on Terra. Very strong.'

'Yeah,' Angela agreed. 'My ass is really on the ground.'

'On Terra – I feel only the balls of my feet in contact with the surface – here toe to heel!'

Platinov was panting slightly as he pushed his big body across the plateau. 'Oppressive' he said. 'You need much energy to move.'

Morgan said nothing. The laws of physics told him. He knew. How far did the others realise? He stomped grimly ahead pausing only to check on the progress of the hover truck. Occasionally he whistled it up like a dog.

'Hey – phweet! C'mon lil' truck.'

The island spread out ahead of them broad and slightly curved. After half an hour had elapsed, the Scooter Ship – for a while a white saucer-shaped blob – was no longer visible.

Directional bleeps on their beltworn Personal Communications Centres (PCCs) would keep them vectored in on its ground plan location.

One hour elapsed EVA. Morgan stopped. Back at Base Camp, as they had now named the Scoot's landing place, the robot sensors and grabs would be collecting whatever information was available. Out here it might be different.

'Stay,' Morgan told the hover truck.

'Let's try to dig up a little piece of this turf,' he told the group. It was strange. Application of a shovel blade by Datsun disturbed short flaky shards of material from the smooth surface, which crumbled into fine dust as soon as they were placed in one of the multi-purpose sample containers clipped to the wall of the hover sled. Through the clear sides of the container they watched, gently stunned, as the dust vanished. Datsun smiled.

'You know I think, is gone back to gas,' he said quietly.

'We're walking on air,' Morgan said. His mouth smiled faintly. His brow creased into a frown.

'What happens if you put it back again.' Angela's voice was more like an instruction than an inquiry.

'Put what back?'

'The gas – dummy! You know, complete the experiment.'

'Go on ahead.'

She uncapped one of the containers and opened it – the neck pointed downward. A meter from the ground a small dust cloud appeared, and grew. Flaky green shards clattered quietly on the deck.

Gingerly Platinov picked one up. It fitted into the slot cut by Datsun's spade. It merged into oneness with the surface. Complete again.

Morgan's mind was spinning back to the training programme, to the deep space mission hypothetical environment simulator located on Cipola 5. They hadn't come up with anything like this.

There, the thinking had been: 'get people used to this – wave function collapses – new probability eventuates.' Surprise. Uncertainty.

Here, wave function reversed. In perfect order. Reality had undone and remade itself, he realised, before their very eyes. Maybe there were hundreds of quantum models to explain why but –

Morgan flashed suddenly.

'We can think of the degree of order in a system as the amount of information in it,' he said, addressing all of them. They turned, poised in various attitudes of frozen activity. Angela's long ringlets hanging straight down in the windless atmosphere – Datsun, every muscle controlled, crouched by the vanished shard which had lain for a split second on the ground – Plat hunched bearlike over him.

'Or *vice versa*. So dig – this is the FIRST COMMUNICATION! The cloud is demonstrating that it is sentient maybe!'

For a while he had known. The laws of physics told him. Now he wasn't sure. No use. Got to keep positive. Got to keep moving.

'Wow!' Angela said slowly, dropping her mask of cynicism for a moment.

'Very good' Datsun said. 'An interpretation seemingly great in its correctness.'

'You mean – this inconsistent, baffling behaviour ... 3,000 kilometre gas cloud – followed by island – followed by ingress of measurable, reversible event – is communication?'

Angela smoothed back the fronds of hair from her face.

'Why not? We don't know what we got here. Maybe it doesn't know "hello"'.

'We didn't measure it yet,' Angela said 'except through our own neurones. We should have filmed it.'

'Just make a note,' Morgan replied. 'And let's see what happens next. Come on. Let's keep moving.'

'Wait Morgan, please'.

Platinov's worried voice spun Morgan back around. The Russian's normally tranquil face was anxious, even afraid.

'Look Morgan – you're Organizer. But what we've

just seen. What if something else like this should happen without we've even done anything this time? "Density variable, wave motion irregular," the instruments said. Morgan, if it changes – maybe we could step right through this thing. Infinity is a long way to fall.'

A babel started instantly. A babel of three.

'Hey let's talk about it,' Morgan said. 'Sure we can suit up. But then you are in a problem. Got to recharge air and that stuff. Or we could jury rig some kind of canary system, tell us if we gonna need air. We could carry cold jet packs on "Ready" but this gravity already weighs a ton.'

'I couldn't make that,' Angela said. 'All suits so far designed work best in weightless or light gravity conditions. Toting a jet pack too? No way. Maybe I could jet pack the whole thing.'

'No,' Datsun said. 'We already decided. Save the jet packs in case we need to get back in a hurry. Who knows how far we have to go. Like oxygen in suits our fuel too is limited.'

Morgan pushed his hands into his pockets.

'Over to you Plat,' he said. 'Cipolan Parlay. Whatever you decide goes.'

Platinov looked back at Morgan his face still troubled. Then suddenly he grinned.

'It's okay,' he said. 'The feeling has passed. Let's walk.'

'So really – without film or something how can we prove we communicated?' Angela seemed in a talkative mood now as she walked beside Morgan. Trying to get next to him. She had to figure him out.

There was something sad and funny about the way the heavy gravity made her walk.

'We can't.'

At first Morgan was kindly but distant. But his creativity and interest in life were insuperable. He began to talk with quiet enthusiasm to Angela.

'See – like Datsun says – the whole pattern hasn't

unfolded. Who knows what may happen next? This could be just the beginning. We have to figure out some kind of analogue – more involved actions which will enable the cloud – if it is truly sentient – to communicate with us again at a more complex level.'

In the moments of silence his secret feelings of depression and foreboding showed through – when he moodily whistled the hover truck,

'C'mon, git along there lil' truck.'

The landscape – or gasscape spread out, long, green, slightly curved, forever.

One hundred years is a long time. Morgan flicked through his past careers. Bus driver (pre-automat era), carpenter, musician (that bebop band he'd played saxophone for in Detroit Mich. Terra) record store manager New York City, then as his life span accelerated realising somewhere around the year 2001 that he didn't have to die because he was seventy plus. Rejuvenation. Life extension. The Prometheus Programme. Decades of prophecy becoming suddenly reality. Then, teacher, engineer, physicist. Wow, you know just a little more time there ain't nothing you can't do!

He knew he was lucky. Fantastically lucky. That first year of euphoria. Prometheus available to all mankind. He slipped through, then the net closed. Projected side effects. Mainly environmental. Riots – Prometheus riots – like at the time of the Gregorian Calendar scam over four hundred years before. Only this time the rip-off was for real. Prometheus faded into rumour. Top people. Politicians. Scientists. Epopts of the world of business. Goodrich with his fleshy smile.

Mass populations of Planet Earth cheated of Immortality? The *Daily Facts* asks why? Programme rumoured to be freely available still at the Orbital Locations. OCTAVE auspice. Millions ask – why not me?

No use to worry, no use to cry, Morgan thought. So I'm one of the lucky ones.

A few little personal/emotional problems. Excessive use of 'Drive' – that powerful amphetamine effect neurotransmitter that allegedly increased I.Q. as it forced you on to ever greater heights of achievement. A serious neuro breakdown was heavy for an eighty-year-old man. Lead to voluntary relocation on the Seven Cities of Cipola. And there – peace as an energy supply physicist. A beautiful home on Cipola 3 – the latest style of dome surrounded by real trees. A forest nearby. A beautiful Dyadic partner. Two healthy intelligent kids. A meaningful life's work and an option on three years sabbatical per decade. Nice. So why had he volunteered? Why was he here? He couldn't decide.

Boulevard Ultima, through its encasing translucent tube, its gravitation computer controlled, its temperature set at 65 ambient, its solar filters equipped with Day/Night Effect and the most realistic Twilight Simulation anywhere on the Seven Cities, ran for ninety-six miles in a great curve around the northern perimeter ring of the Cipolan city complex, comprising the two largest industrial units Cipola I and Cipola 2 and the favourite residential zone, Ultima. That's why they called it Boulevard Ultima. Everyone was always headed for Ultima. Nobody liked to think about leaving it. Even to go to work.

Platinov liked Ultima and he liked the tubular highway and he thought about it now as he strode across the cloud. A special light fell into the tube, extra to the simulated day and night. Starlight leakage from the Deep. You couldn't see that light from Moscow. He loved to drive fast through it, beside the tall elevated magnetic freight train tracks, in his small wedge-shaped personal transport module. The most efficient and cheapest transport was by 'Jumper', big motorless two-hundred-seat shells free falling from cylinder to cylinder by force of centrifugal spin, but it hadn't taken the Frenchmen on the colony long to figure out a way they could still drive cars. Hence the little PT modules. Platinov was pretty glad about that.

He thought about his job at Galcom on Cipola 2. He thought about his lab in the little blue-bricked flat-topped office/warehouse building rigged with orange painted platforms and steps where he worked designing bearings for use on Terra. Super high efficiency bearings that could only be moulded in the weightless conditions available on Cipola. It was his job. He loved it. Always thought about it when he was away. His favorite fantasy. So why had he volunteered? Why was he here? He couldn't decide.

Like turf, she thought – wet heavy turf on the farm unit (Cipola 4) – though this was dry. But that's the nearest. Wet heavy turf after rain.

Angela remembered the last planting. When the first scheduled downpour came she stared out at the deep dark of the universe from her living room – played Beethoven's Pastoral at full volume. The fabulous storm scene with it's lightning and lashing rain. Veer had gone by then to his new post – supervising a germination experiment – Farm Project Luna. She had never felt so alone. Or so exhilarated as she listened to the deafening roar of the music hurtling from the Tetraquad speakers and watched the rain pour from seeded clouds under the translucent arched roof of the vast farm cylinder. In a few short months – harvest and shipping. Afterwards a big hoe-down. Guitars, violins, dancing – moonshine and earthshine liquor – right there inside a huge transparent cylinder at a Lagrange Point in space. With starlight pouring in from the deep dark she would sneak away warm, woosy and drunk – she'd call Veer on the sun phone to tell him she still loved him and yes everything was cool and yes she'd get her bi-annual now and yes, yes, next shuttle out ... in fact the first thing smokin' babe ...

She loved her job as a biochemist on the farm unit so why had she volunteered? Why was she here on this goddam chunk of velcro? No idea.

Datsun moved easily across the gas cloud. Every effort conserved. Every breath the right depth. Every muscle controlled. He rocked his feet as he walked, from heel to toe using the heavy gravity to help him move. His mind was a clear crystal. His thoughts were silence. No questions.

The gasscape spread out – long and green and slightly curved. Forever.

```
INTERJECT - ARCHIVE - ENTRY - REF:
```

Cipolan Parlay:

    Cipolan Parlay, a social custom peculiar to the Seven Cities of Cipola. Despite its reputation for anarchy, Cipolan society was in many ways as highly organised as that on JEFFERSON, with its touching recreation of early post-colonial American democracy or the Soviet built MIR Y DRUZHBA where theocracy and liberalism made strange bedfellows. It was not just the vast distances involved or thorny international disagreements such as those enshrined in the Declaration of Bogota that made the L5 communities virtually ungovernable from Earth. It was the fact that once 'out there', people let their fantasies rip.

    The Cipolan fantasy was to make 'The New System' evolve to its end point as prophesied by Lautrec. 'The highest form of government is no government at all'. Hence, the concept of the non authoritarian *ad hoc* Organiser – or the various societal 'games' such as 'Cipolan Parlay' (Effective Discussion) In this situation Platinov was the aggrieved party. Thus, after careful consideration of the issues by all parties, his decision is final.

DATE: 23.00 FEB 2 2031 TCT
LOCATION: LAS VEGAS,
NEVADA USA WESTWORLD
CCR 436

*'The more rational the polity, the more
blurred the difference between the sexes.'*
C.G. JUNG

The running man stopped. Back against a door of rusty
green metal. Dark-lintelled shadow blocks hid him. He
watched the flat yellow shafts of light from sodium
lamps strung overhead on wire cables spread out across
the concrete. He listened to the echo of his footsteps
die away.

Silence but for the distant hum of autos on an
elevated highway. Moaning through the bricks –
muffled drone of industrial machinery. Machines for
metal. Machines for meat. Reflecting onto the oily red
walls of the dark alley – shadow play images of the
neon sign across the street. Silhouette outline of two
copulating males and the words 'Gay Paradise' in
garish colours.

A cat strolled up the alley. It stopped by the doorway staring up at him, its eyes a huge overlapping
yellow glitter. It cried out Mnkgaow! once, and arching
its back padded round his feet rubbing its whiskery
cheeks against his trouser cuffs. With a soft hiss he
shooed the cat away. He felt the psychic fear of mice
and birds. Cat climbing powerfully up – bough by
bough into the luminous green beauty of a tree.

Tonight he was not the hunter. Tonight he dwelt in the global web of fear felt only by the prey.

Acrid stench of anit-personnel gas teased his nostrils. Every muscle ached. Not far away, they were out there. Every face a snouted mask. Every hand a weaponed robot limb. He felt their minds probing for him. Grey minds driving sightless eyes, sniffing him out. A close run thing. The transfers were getting harder and harder as the sweep and search intensified. This crisis had inspired them. The FTPA were probing deeper and deeper into the nebulous system of Prankster cells. Time to move to another country — under another name. He took the object from his pocket and looked at it. An oblong of black plastic maybe six inches long by four wide with an addition at one end — a short conical tube.

He knocked on the green metal door — a rapid, soft, complicated pattern.

A contacter clicked, and an electric motor began to whine. The door wound slowly upward. A pool of fluorescent light spread across the oily tarmac.

He was looking into the barrel of a flechette gun. Behind the gun, a white-gloved hand. Behind the gloved hand, the bright rednosed face of a circus clown. The tearful eyes registered recognition. A white-gloved hand pulled him inside. The ludicrous head ducked out, tiny bowler hat rotating as he looked quickly either way up the alley. Then the motor began to run again. The door descended till it sealed off the outside world, crashing onto concrete with a heavy clang.

Warehouse interior. Crates stacked high. Produce of the Central Communities 0706409. Truck this side. Use no hooks.

The white-gloved hand took his hand — led him at a lope through passage ways between the towering crates. They stopped in an opening where two office chairs were arranged by a high metal table. The ludicrous red lips with their permanent painted smile moved. A woman's voice spoke.

'You got it?'

'Yes Mormo. I had a hard time getting here. They've good as sealed off the whole West Coast, and inland as far as Texas.'

'I know Zany. It's getting hard. But the cell system will survive. And triumph! Not long now and we'll get it right out of the States!'

Zany laid the object on the table.

Mormo looked at it in awed silence. Zany broke the silence asking,

'You know what it is?'

'Sure,' Mormo said, the bizarre clown's head nodding, 'MCP.'

Zany said,

'It put all the lights out in Fort Worth a few days back. Plenty panic! Somebody must have touched a button by mistake.'

Mormo laughed.

'I know about that. Not so easy. Got a safety. Somebody pulling pranks! You didn't hear about the currency? Two thousand billion dollars taken out of UNIMED and paid as food stamps in Venezuela. Cancelled of course, mandated CENTERCOM. Serious though. Nearly de-stabilized a Bogota Signatory. Feng was set to invade.

'Little knowledge a dangerous thing. Had to wipe the cell did that. No one uses this – yet! Or else they're gonna trace us.'

'Yeah I know' Zany said. 'It's got a special destination.'

They fell silent again. Once more Zany broke it.

'What is this place?'

It's a warehouse for machine parts,' Mormo said. 'Mostly tractor and harvester machinery. Over production. Surplus. If Gold wins the election it will all be dumped, or left to rust. If Amalrik wins it will go to gather the Russian harvest. If Goodrich wins it will go to the Third World. Probably Africa. If Feng wins again – it will probably go to India to appease the New Moguls. Who knows? Yet still they leave these decisions to the electoral choice of 2½ thousand million Zombies with wrist watch radios. And they call *us* deranged!'

'So what.'

Mormo shrugged. She gestured to the object lying on the table.

'So we keep on trying.' She picked the object up. 'Somebody has to get to the Hub – with this!'

DATE: 17.30 MARCH 29 2031
LOCATION: THE STACK UK
WESTWORLD CENTERCOM
REGION 1010

*'A monstrous town more populous than
some continents, and in its man-made
night as if indifferent to heaven's frowns
and smiles; a cruel devourer of the world's
light. There was room enough there to
place any story, depth enough for any
passion, variety enough for any setting,
darkness enough to bury five millions of
lives.'*

JOSEPH CONRAD

G.T.V. GLOBAL TELEVISION. GRAY METAL
TELEVISION. LOCAL 409. CHANNELS 18/19/7/4/18/
8/19/21
　　MUSIC Music of Ravel
　　VOICE Details of four previous incarnations
　　IMAGE Shelves of food
　　MUSIC Pop synthesisers
　　IMAGE Supermarket trolleys
　　IMAGE Statues by Michelangelo
　　MUSIC Sales girls chirruping (funk bass)
　　VOICE dial 911
　　VOICE Like zombies and the sanitation man
　　VOICE Russian scientists new discovery
　　VOICE becomes totally conservative
PICTURE vast darkness of space ... six white plastic
like cylinders of enormous size rotate around a
central hub. MUSIC funky waltz time. PICTURE
young man with short blond hair and a big mous-
tache VOICE Hi, I'm Gary and I'm gay. That's why I

emigrated out here to the Seven Cities of Cipola. Because out here the New System really works. There really are *no* prejudices. I work in construction, moving solar panels in weightlessness conditions, and the pay is good ...

Turner lay back in his armchair hefting the television control in his hand lazily, professionally, like a starship commander with a new and marvellous beam to play with. He quit channel hopping and switched off the television.

RECLAIM AND DEPROGRAM. A simple mandate. Harder to do. Any point in contacting Security? Not a lot. Membership of INK is not illegal. FTPA? Why should they care. No known links with terrorist activities.

Have to investigate the hard way. There ought to be an easy way.

Hard, possessive love of parents. Censure of society. All kinds of freedom to be different kind of slave.

Difficult question, like;

Q: what did Eve say to Adam in the Garden of Eden?

Monogamy's millions of microhavens of reproduction Megaproductive organisation. Interaction. Freedom? No dice. Why didn't she opt for Leisure? It's okay if you've got money behind you. Because her folks encouraged her? Get ahead?

No way is Fisher going to turn her loose. This is going to be a grab job. Can't avoid it. Too bad.

I'm looking for a robot here. At this stage. Obedience to the structure.

Somebody that has sprung the coop, and chosen to become a new kind of person. A new kind of nonperson. Into a micro herd. Headed for the top of the mega herd. In secret.

Moksha? What is the price of it?

Leads. INK work on a cell system. She could be in any one of dozens of squats – or in a supervised INK haven anywhere in the city. Lap of luxury or perdition's pit. She could be in a damn brothel. It's been known. Keep up the payments. Sex slave egghead gave head to get ahead.

Yes.

Okay. Robot. First-stage initiates pound the beat. Ice, snow, hail, heat – it doesn't matter. Gotta be dedicated. Leaflets.

Let's check the gig lists. Channel 6 I think ... Recreation Information.

Click, buzz. Gray metal television.

'Wealth is fun but not for Leisure People it seems. Since the increase in credit allowance last autumn the incidence of Stack riots has increased a hundred fold in West World. We ask, does a little taste work up a big hunger? After this ...' Music of Bach – image of alcohol. Flip flip. Picture of Egypt. Pharoah! The deodorant perfume that's a gateway to another world ... Flip flip. Music of Haydn – image of cigars. Flip flip. Music of Bartok – Apaches in a desert. Flip flip. 'Your new book – Groove Juice or Ignorant Oil? A Social History of Alcohol – which you wrote while serving a life sentence for armed robbery, but taking part in a new scheme aimed at re-orienting misdemeanants.' 'Yes sir. That is correct.' Flip flip. '... hard time making it as a single girl.' Flip flip. Heavy music – image of a girl. Or is she a girl? Yes, Constance Appollo – lead singer with Heavy Period – isn't your name a little gross? – even for a sex change band? Yes I guess so but it's a history thing. What we are living through now *is* a heavy period.'

Hm. Coincidence. Come on. Say something about your next concert.

'The Savage perceives the Concrete Light – that's the title of the new album.'

Oh well I guess it's more likely the venue not the group – as I thought anyway.

Channel 6. Yes. Let's see. Lyceum – The Shuttle Band. Saturday. ... Funhouse. Shows five nights a week.

Hm. Well okay. I guess it's tonight.

An investigation. Yes. Counter kidnap maybe. Grab job.

Leaving the apartment. Dogs growling next door. Hate that. Fear. Seems less somehow. Less to worry about? Keth tranquilising me? Long thin needle. Don't like to see the stuff going in. Paste into my leg. But the instructions are very good.

Keth tranquilising him? Or was it loss of habit?

Why should they be out there? *Hier triffst du 'sie' sicher.*

Who's telling me they're out there.

Habitual sex thoughts. Below visible level. Hover in mind haze like a cold emotion. Naked forms of sex ghosts. What is a man? What is a woman? What are people anyway? Animals have four feet.

Goin to the Stack. Got to go to the Stack. Stake out that parking lot. Its got to be easier.

Turner had put on jeans and a faded Space Drifter jacket. It looked good. Faded, as though burnt by solar flares – pocked by laser battles. 'Suregrip' Astronaut boots. Good for running. Didn't alter his hair. Too old to convince any one he's a ganger. No gun. Turner didn't like guns. Mace cannister in back pocket plus Personal Defense Mfg 'TrankPak' with rapid assimilation molecules. A capsule of bright red dye. Half a plan in his mind.

The motorway fed into the Stack. Creeping and winding through towers of grey. Buildings like radios, like transistors and microchips. Atomic buildings with funnels and ducts from deep shelters. Buildings like machines, buildings like abstractions of pure thought.

Sometimes it took hours to pass a single intersection.

Traffic like reptile scales. Reptile asleep. Sometimes the traffic zipped and glittered and looked designed, the way the modern world was supposed to be.

Into the Stack. Layer on layer. Tier on tier. Dark shapes of mass. Plares in a yellow glare.

Old houses crumbling at floor level – never cleared. Concrete blocks – apartments. Offices, factories, works. Platforms built on top of that. No way to spread out.

Need every inch of soil to farm. Beat the soil erosion. Maybe orbit farms will fix it. Maybe not.

Lights and signs in the sky. Stack up, layer after layer. Boom and bust cycle of Upwave and Downwave. Boom! Move in. Get workers, get jobs. Bust! Pull out out. Leave to rot. Layer after layer, stjil after stjil. Pitched roofs and red brick of 1910 (level one). Concrete high rise (level two). Fortress cottages (fear of urban insurrection – level three). Effect architecture – level four. (Boom buildings now left to go bad).

Repetition of entire scam, less pitched roofs and red brick, levels 5,6,7.

Mighty high now. Very dense. Lights in the sky.

Warrens, caves, machines for living. Parts where no one but the natives ever go. Tribes who've never seen the outside world, or scarcely light of day. Think meat is from a factory.

Never had a job, never had a home. Living in the concrete caves. Piped for food maybe. Wall T.V. Some got blank bricks and gang fights only. Cookers made from oil drums. Car tyres for a sofa.

Going to the Stack. Kids go there. Kids from outside. For example, to the Fun House Auditorium. Reflected an entrepreneurial phase. Let's clean up the Stack. Now it was in one of the parts where a semblance of normal life went on. Officially designated: 'A sheltered area'.

The streets had a coffee bars of 1962 feel about them. Square office blocks with tile mosaics on concrete. Shops with glossy windows fading, glass and chromium doors that read PUSH/PULL. Urban rain fell bluely into the streets through disused vents and air ducts reflecting like faint romance from neon and grey sidewalks. Modern style. Echoes of twist/twang, shades of beehives and sleek cars.

The Fun House named for an old 1980s horror movie, had been one of the first 'Effects'. Product of a leisure-oriented enterprise zone that didn't last too long.

Laser lit auditorium, with energy field roof. Outer walls are vid screens that rotate. Hologram cashiers. Robot security.

Kids went to the Stack for kicks. The ambience. Sense of danger. Defiance. Gang fights, robberies, FTPA vs Pranksters, stuff like that.

Don't be there if you're over twenty-five and you don't belong.

Turner was over twenty-five but he knew how to belong. He nosed his old car through the battered traffic slowly, towards the Fun House parking lot where the girl Ellene had last been seen.

His car radio played softly – by synchronicity – '(This Time) I Wanna Be The Bitch' by Heavy Period. It jarred on his nerves.

The parking lot was at the base of Level 4, under a complex of overpasses and fortress flats. Trouble in the Stack as on Radio and T.V. reports. More rumours. FTPA Troopers in gas masks, carrying stubby UAP weapons patrolled the walkways. Ugly glimpse among the bricks.

The kerb was lined with No Waiting, No Loading, electro-magnetic repulsers. Turner felt them nudging his car as he eased towards the kerb.

Cars behind began swerving and honking. He circled the block. Till Doomsday if necessary. Just caddy around and caddy around. He didn't want to enter the parking lot. Sneaking up on it from the other side, he saw a van pulling out from a permitted stationary location. Stroke of luck. He pulled in and stopped.

Four credits. Turner punched his personal debit number into the meter.

He left his car, and began moving easily through the crowds.

It was too early. He paused by a flat oblong anodised metal dispenser set deep into the concrete of the sidewalk. The crowds had begun to thin a little but he instinctively clutched the grab handle bolted to the side of the dispenser in case the pressure of people should drag him away.

He tapped in another credit code. Out slid a wide greyish sheet of Releyon.

Funny how newspapers wouldn't go away. Their

death had been prophesied for over fifty years.

But you couldn't stop them. Even eco threats like deforestation hadn't stopped them. Now of course the bastards printed on synthetic paper – Releyon. Yet another wonder product of genetic engineering. So fuck the trees. You couldn't stop them.

Two businessmen carrying those briefcases styled like a space technicians' weightless zone tool box dashed from the flickering insubstantiation of an IITS transfer booth waving printouts. Some kind of big deal come through. Gray fla.

Gangers wearing vinyl knickerbockers with clear plastic fly to display their dyed and patterned pubic hair strolled by. Bloody ought to be arrested. Once upon a time they would have been. Now they wouldn't be. Where would they go next for fashion? Mass nudity and body paint? Got sillier and sillier. Nobody minded a bloke with green hair in a mohawk or something. But this? Fashion. Probably Leisure People. So – fuck you, fuck me.

He opened the newspaper.

Oh Christ.

'FTPA Battle Pranksters – Motorway Holocaust.

Charred bodies took hours to clear after a freeway battle between FTPA troopers using helicopter gunships and napalm ... Prankster raid on hairdresser salon in Luxury City ... new heights of bestial cruelty ... centre page picture spread ...

Gorgeous Kim has no inhibitions about revealing all

Sex Sex Sex

Horror rites of the Death Cults

Geneticists may "seed" new hearts.

44 Dead.'

Maybe people still needed something to hold onto. Not just to watch. Less of a headache. The word you read ... the world you read ...

'... the Milano supporters are well known for their private arsenals as readers will well remember after last year's Euro Cup Final Massacre in which

2000 German and Italian fans were slain. Fears that the conflict may spread along the linear corridors and engage eastern French areas of the Belt Metropolis (Ville Périphique) have been allayed by the arrival of an FTPA tank unit. Security forces are baffled as to how the British fans came into possession of so many weapons especially nerve gas mortars and lasers ... FTPA director Clon Moshmerl believes ... planted ... Pranksters ... subversion ... chaos.

'FENG INITIATES REIGN OF TERROR Welfare claims.

'British Prime Minister and CENTERCOM candidate Simon Welfare declared at a meeting convened by EESP members in Bremmerhaven on Friday that Madame Feng's decision to allow FTPA troops to use tanks, gunships, and firearms as well as UAP weapons had lead to a "veritable reign" of terror out of all proportion to events ...

'The pendulum has swung into our court ... the ball is firmly in the pit.'

In response to an inner craving, in response to a full page ad ...

Turner pulled out a slim white cigarette.

'Scientific research has determined – a hotter puff is a safer puff ... each of our revolutionary filters contains a microcomputer ... first developed to monitor tiny temperature changes in gas transfer controlled instruments on spacecraft ... tiny heater elements instantly kick into action ... you don't burn your mouth because the heated smoke passes through our patent AquaCrystal cooler bed, built into the mouth piece of each filter ... cheap enough to throw away each time you stub.

'... crystals are pure crystals synthesised in a weightless vacuum chamber where perfect crystals are formed ... at the Jefferson Orbital Location.

'Libration Light 100's from Western Gulf Tobacco –

"Dedicated to the quest for a safer smoke" (The

UNIMED World Director had determined . . .

'Gay spacewomen refuse to fly with sexchange Tony'

Turner's cigarette smouldered between his lips as he folded the paper, to a new page.

'Which way will you vote in the CENTERCOM elections? Here's your guide to the people and the policies that make up this crucial election campaign.'

Talk about laugh. Most people couldn't decide the sex of their first born let alone who should rule the flaming world.

'Calvin Gold, running for a second but not consecutive term, most commentators believe – single handedly invented the concept of the "Leisure Option" in the face of world unemployment. But – are too many brains going to waste in front of wall to wall T.V.?

'Gold is adamant that the Orbital Locations should be free of Earthian control. He has stated that the 1976 "Declaration of Bogota" was the thin end of a pernicious wedge which may eventually paralyse the entire galaxy under a dead hand of thinly disguised socialism. However the pendulum has swung into his court.

'Failure by the US still to ratify the UN's so-called "Moon Treaty" – classifying all heavenly bodies under the common heritage of mankind fifty years after it's inception is largely a result of Gold's persistent lobbying.

'His openly declared first act as President of CENTERCOM would be to disband it. A "return to nationhood" on Earth and a new free for all frontier in space are his priorities. The ball is firmly in the pit.'

Glancing up – a giant 200 foot holo-enhanced billboard. Cal Gold – gleaming hair of moulded aluminium – and a billion credit smile. He's planting the flags of earth's nations on a huge globe. Across his lapel – 'Return to Nationhood – Vote Gold for CENTERCOM'.

'Madame Feng's chances of re-election are

slimmer than ever, global pollsters are claiming. Her policies of "All Earth for Earth's peoples" and "Space – our right to a worker's paradise" are running out of steam as the Feng administration digs itself deeper into authoritarian measures designed to curb urban unrest. Feng's inability to adjust to Western attitudes prevailing in most CENTERCOM countries is a root cause of this. The mustard has fallen off the hot dog.

Her severest critics, especially Russian leader Gregori Amalrik, while praising her social ideas – for example the adaptation of the barefoot doctor scheme to the most desolate parts of the Beltburg Stacks – have constantly attacked her for failing to realise in Amalrik's words that – "the workers of Russia, Europe and America are not Chinese peasants".

'Her rigid attitudes on the Earthian control, and collective people's ownership of space, are setting up vibrations which are being felt at least as far away as L5.

'President Goodrich of the USA, currently running for a second but not consecutive term as CENTERCOM supremo believes that "strong unbreakable links" should exist between Earth and the Orbital Locations, reinforcing the "unshakeable social driving force of the New System", which he inaugurated. The Goodrich "Life Support Plan for Everyone on Earth" (a living wage regardless of employment status) is still stirring up controversy and campaign managers are believed to be urging him to drop it.'

Usual mixture. Sex. Horror. The lies and jokes.

No wonder people are so confused.

'Right Royal Moonshot!

'Cadsby Heppenstal reveals why these days the Royals prefer to craters to castles.

Fat Tramp: When is a river bankrupt?

Thin Tramp: When it has burst its banks!

Fools rush in while Angels gather moss.'

75

Time to make a move. Turner threw the paper into a nearby wastebin. It flew out again with a loud 'beep!' A sign illuminated on the side of the bin. 'This bin is for biodegradeables only.' Yes, they'd made a mistake with Releyon. Hard to get rid of it. He'd have to find a handy roadside synthetic degrader to toss the *Daily Facts* into.

He took a photo of the girl from his pocket. Strolled among the street people, speaking the fast fluid language, WestWorld English of the Stack.

– Hey wanna check ya –
– Uh? –
– scan this –
– no way –

Rays of streetlight pool through piers of concrete. Turner knew he should have got help. Reclaim heavies. But he didn't want to. He wanted to handle it alone. Either way one OCTAVE snooper would blow the whole scam.

Just a routine. Security at the corner. Rounded helmets and flameproof suits. This won't be so easy. Avoid them. And the Keth dealers. And the robbers. And the gangers. And the pimps. No one would see her. Obvious. Still it had to be done.

Tall man, dark skin – long deadlock hair. Wrap-around shades. Stands in shadow doorway. Presence like a tall morbid plant grown from beds of concrete. He leans from the doorway as Turner passes –

'Hey baby – wanna buy some 'ash?'

No?

Stares through green plastic at Turner's photo.

'Noway. Never check shi pan dis alley. Why fe shi come here man? Too savage!' Laughs.

'Got to fin' her guy. Over in that parking lot.'

'Huh! You never go fin' shi now!' Laughs. 'Man, you jus' go 'ere about you know. Too savage!'

'She's a girl in trouble. I have to find her.'

'Lissen snowflake – you go fetch shi parents down a dis alley. Hask if shi is fi dem chile. Dem let you know seh – Raas!'

Turner spun around. There was an off licence across the street, burning with seductive neon colours.

He came out with a quarter of scotch – took a long slug – there on the doorstep of the shop.

Turner moved through the concrete light toward the parking lot. He hung back in the darkness by a pier of the giant overhead motorway, scanning. The parking lot began to fill.

Turner's head was aching. He felt a strange emptiness. The medication drugs taking hold of him? He saw the eyes of passers-by assess him. Threat? No threat. Pass near – pass further away.

He watched the forms of girls and women. Bio forms only. Prints from the mother plan. No sex meanings. No attractions. Tall old woman – striding. Like a hawk, she looked to him. Small fat woman. Knew instantly – child vessel. They all passed through the concrete light.

Tall, thin girl. Sinisterly glittering with hard glamour. Plastic box and mirrors. Instinct would have attracted him. But no. Her gloss looked stale and rusty. Watched eyes of men scanning women. Attraction. Indifference. Repulsion. Desperation. Kids walk by with radio playing popular commercial ... 'hard to make it as a single girl ...'

Then he saw Ellene. Jeans, anorak, wool hat down over her ears. The boy from the film trailed behind her.

He watched her closely. She was the material but not the product. He'd never thought this way before. Turn on or turn off. But now seeing differently – her body and face capable of sex and glamour but – all that squashed, in climbing boots and wool hat. Shapeless clothes.

As she passed by him, handed him a leaflet. Checked him. Eye contact. Sudden flash in her eyes of attraction. Why? He was middle aged – getting fat. Like her father – or course she's eroticised that. Hm. Laser eyes into deep structures. Sudden repulsion. Ah! Reality. Alcohol breath? Tobacco. Big man things.

He nodded thank you for the leaflet and her face broke into a big childlike smile. Innocence. She passed on by, distributing to the slowly building crowds emerging through the parking lot.

The boy and Ellene took up a station four piers further down towards the entrance.

'GAIN ABSOLUTE KNOWLEDGE' the pamphlet read. 'Stop being a victim. You have infinite resources within you. If only you could learn how to use them.'

Reclaim and deprogram.

Turner watched until the crowds began to thin. Shift of schedule? This time the crowds going in, not the crowds coming out? He shivered. Overhead, giant temperature control units long in need of adjustment, blew blasts of freezing air into the humid smog-laden atmosphere trapped down by Stack layers above. Condensation dripping from countless square feet of roof area fell into the gusts like rain. Turner pulled up the collar of his jacket. Would they stick around in the chilly rainy breeze until the show was over?

Slowly sauntering the girl and boy began leaving.

Turner fingered the Trankpak in his pocket.

He paced slowly after them.

The streets had almost emptied.

Eerie light from the Fun House vid screens and lasers washed the tarmac.

'Excuse me,' he said brushing past them at the entrance. This would have to be fast.

FTPA up on the flats' balconies. Security could be anywhere. Turner got into his car. The car had one of the haute couture 'Designer' body shells that had been popular a while back in the last boom (Upwave) and was asymmetrical. Hence, any passenger sat uncomfortably but elegantly in a narrow compartment slightly behind Turner. He checked the equipment. The Trank-Pak. The Capsule of red dye. A thin gauze mask. He pulled it over his nose and mouth. Ellene and her companion were walking slowly, abstractedly, lost in conversation. Silly in the Stack, Turner thought, but what can you tell kids. No sense of danger.

He cruised up behind them. The sidewalk was broad here. The street almost empty, and an entire bank of the baleful yellow street lights were out on a temporary fault. Good as it was going to get. Turner accelerated suddenly and shrieked to a halt a cars length behind the meandering couple.

Turner hit concrete. Still a gamble. They might run. No. Check first. As they spun towards him he popped the cap of the TrankPak in their faces.

Ellene dropped as she opened her mouth to scream. The boy followed her downwards in a stone trance.

Turner coughed behind the mask, eyes watering, head going muzzy in a rapidly dissolving cloud of sweet cloying gas.

As the girl crumpled, he dragged her awkwardly into the car's passenger seat, cursing the moulded space module style buckets. An old Mercedes – gas burning, that's what you wanted for a grab job. Bench seat ten yards wide in faded greenish black leather. Not a 'Tracy's delight'.

He turned the boy face down to the sidewalk, breaking the capsule of red dye under him as he did so. He ripped off the mask, as he leapt into the car.

People had come from the nearest building. Passers-by had mysteriously gathered out of nowhere, all stopped in their tracks by the awful red pool oozing from under the motionless body of the boy.

By the time the little crowd had stopped staring at the horrible fascinating red pool, Turner and the girl Ellene were an unfocused memory of shrieking tyres and the howl of an electric turbine. Turner spent his whole life getting people what they wanted. It was only fair sometimes to make it work for him.

Turner raced through the Stack. Through the dark blaze of sodium discharge lamps. Dodging headlights, like blips on a Space Invader screen. The girl, pale-faced and breathing heavily, lolled beside him. Past the anodised snouts of a thousand security cameras. Recording him. Video star.

Beneath the platform layers overhead, traffic control robots, nuclear powered helicopter rafts loaded with scanners, radar and mikes, whirred and clattered in the massive shadows.

He motored on relentlessly, crouched across the wheel. Half expecting the harsh challenge of electronic voices overhead.

The Stack was thinning out. He should have been speeding towards Reclaim's deprogramming centre to which he had A7 access, day or night. Instead he put his car on the motorway.

Last vestiges of functional organisation. On metal plates. Route numbers. Town names. Turner selected.

Night lay draped like a grey shroud edged with black across the soft contours of the dreaming country. Ancestor ghosts slept in low mounds untroubled. One day they'd wake and claim when all else had passed away. When the soil was rich and dark again.

Concrete ribbons. Buzzing metal insects zipped and swayed. Turner among them. Human in his motor shell.

Wide valleys under deep darkness. Shadow masses of industrial formations, mechanised farms. Harsh matter in the midst of a silent dream. Distant yellow-blaze of far off towns. Purplish glare rupturing the smoky sky. Speed. Untouchable.

Turner scanned it, but his mind plotted numbers. Conscious autopilot.

Vanished flashing from the motorway, roaring slowly into narrow lanes.

He was heading for Dodman's Ley.

*'"Lord," said Pryderi, "I will go into the
caer to seek tidings of the dogs."
"Faith," Manawydan replied, "it is not
good counsel for thee to go into the caer.
We never saw this caer here. And if thou
wilt follow my counsel, thou wilt not go
inside. And it is he who cast a spell over
this land caused the caer to be here."'*
 'TALE OF MANAWYDAN SON OF
LLYR,' – *THE MABINOGION*

The dream always started pleasantly enough. He was
watching hundreds of beautiful blonde and brunette
drum majorettes in gleaming white boots and immacu-
late tunics working out to a nifty arrangement of 'When
the Saints Go Marching In'. The band was a group of
healthy virile teenage youths – crew cut and clean in
their crisp uniforms. The band leader was a happy
smiling negro with puckered lips and a red coat who
beamed happily at everyone. Here the uneasiness
started. Those girls shouldn't have been working out in
front of that nig. But then this was a dream. He felt
warm again. But the dream began to change.

At first all the drum majorettes would be hatless, the
elegantly coiffured blonde and brunette hair losing its
laquered shape and sheen and becoming gentle and
natural, blowing softly and wildly in the wind and he'd
know then that the girls were getting high. Then they
would be braless, and then the short skirts would fall
away and vanish, and the girls would be naked. Their
bodies swaying freely and sensuously, their expression
ecstatic, and on the bandstand was no longer the

flower of America's manhood or even the happy smiling black – but two hideously degenerate-looking Englishmen, one who looked like a syphilis-ridden eighteenth-century rake – and the other a Saxon savage – and the third, a barbaric Scot. Instead of pure trumpets, they brandished drumsticks and guitars. And instead of 'The Saints' – at a thousand decibels, they were singing 'I feel free ... I feel free ... I feel free ...'

At that point he would step in to stop the entire disgraceful proceedings, and then it would get horrific. The music would become a deafening cacophony and the girls would turn snarling, their middle fingers outstretched, and they would begin to chant 'Off the Pig ... Off the Pig ... Off the Pig ...' and for a second he would be back in the middle of that hellish Watts riot again ... Los Angeles is burning ... Chicago is burning ...

And then he would be awake – eyes still closed, his thoughts racing – an anxious confused stream.

'... give them their freedom ... and if that doesn't work, give them a drug. And it went wrong. The whole damn thing went wrong. Who would ever think we'd use those methods against our own kids? And they survived it! Most of that stuff drove my own best agents insane! Up there on the bridge – seeing monster automobiles. Jesus! And then they all took it and for a while we couldn't stop what was happening. It had gotten into the atmosphere and the whole thing spread like wild fire. Europe too. We only intended to hit a few trouble makers – conspicuous examples. Kill the head of the thing. Pop culture would have taken care of the rest. But they went berserk! All over the Free World on every level. Intellectual, artistic, spiritual, political. Plan 13. Thank God for it.

'Boy that was close! Phew.'

Fully awake now, Marshall Peredur sat up in bed – sipped ice water and lit a Pall Mall.

He looked at the display on his watch. 6.30.

'Jesus!' he thought. 'Because of that ghastly dream – I've overslept.' And cursing his wife, still asleep in the next bed, for not waking him as she usually did (a woman, even a neurotic woman with chronic insomnia has her uses, if only as backup to an alarm) he leapt out of bed. Maybe that's why he persuaded them to take her on Prometheus with him. Maybe he still loved her. Because, after all these years, a habit. Maybe because like the psycho-orientation report said – a stable Dyadic unit is preferable – yeah yeah yeah. Jesus! She'd complained!

'Marshall – why? Oh God – I wanna peg out like everyone else around eighty.' But no, here they were, ninety-eight years old, looking and feeling not a day over sixty. Goddamit!

Donned a towelling bathrobe and leather slippers walked to the dressing table. Stellachlorazine A/Stellachlorazine B. Goddam that Organ Implosion! Suspected in the arteries around the heart. Bound to spread to the liver. Goddam lab built oldster – now this! Christ! That isn't angina! Opened up the box of amylnitrate, broke one open and sniffed hard up each nostril, and then, still puffing on the Pall Mall, he strode into the bathroom.

Like the dedicated servant of CENTERCOM and the United States Government that he was, he had been completely resigned to the fact that his eighteen hour day year in, year out in the public service would probably kill him at some time around 55-60 years of age. It hadn't. Now, on a life extension programme, each day was really a bonus. Even without a sex life. Stellachlorazine A/Stellachlorazine B.

Marshall Peredur's wife slept on. She was dreaming about her doctor. He had prescribed her some new pills and new pills always worked at first. For at least a week. That first week of new pills she could close her eyes and sleep and dream of her doctor smiling kindly at her. In real life, he was never kind. Just hard working and bored with no time, like everybody else. But in her dream, her doctor had a voice like Billy Eckstine and he sang softly to her, tho' she never could remember the words. And his eyes, those beautiful deep eyes twinkled kindly and sexily at her like Marshall's once had when he'd been a young soldier in an Eisenhower jacket, waving goodbye across an endlessly blue and hopelessly sad Pacific Ocean. Now Marshall's eyes never smiled or twinkled. Army. Army Intelligence. CIA. FTPA, and now this new thing he was into. Shadow Command. His eyes burned like cold blue fire. But she never dreamed of those eyes.

By 7 o'clock Marshall L. Peredur, smart but relaxed, wearing a dark formal suit, white shirt, dark tie, and another Pall Mall, was at the wheel of his Lincoln Picasso on the Washington Belt, mental autopilot zeroed in on the sign which read 'Intelligence Boulevard, Next Right 2/3 km.'

He was thinking about his appointment with the President later that morning. President Goodrich. That Motherfucker. Something bad going down in The Hub. Cipola 7. He tried to imagine it. Plenty times he'd seen it on T.V. A big plastic cylinder in the middle of six more just like it out there in space. A mini world, quarter of a million miles away. At that distance it shouldn't be a problem. But it was. Because CENTER-COM had leased the Hub to SIS, Space Industrial Services, at a very handsome rate of remuneration. It shouldn't be America's problem. SPACEK handled the deal under a CENTERCOM auspice. The whole damn thing was European. But, the Rumours. America's problem? It might be the whole world's problem. Bad timing, because a whole batch of Green Echelon rankers had gone missing from a training centre in Peking and he had just about been ready to tell Mme Feng he knew damn well what she was doing with them. His personnel! One small worm . . .

The word processor bleeped and clicked. A pianist's slim fingers triggered the keys gently but rapidly – in a fire of inspiration.

'Population growth, aided by the development of Orbital Locations – "Space Cities" as some people romantically term them – is actually contributing to economic success and raising the standard of living. Per capita income is likely to be higher with a growing population than with a stationary one, and the long run impact of additional people will be to make possible an almost inexhaustible supply of cheaper energy. The evidence suggests that food will be less rather than more scarce as the population grows.

'Pollution is not so bad now as it has been in the past. If proof of a cleaner environment is longer life expectancy – then considerable progress has been made because people are living longer, not only in the developed countries but in the world as a whole.

'For too long we've been caught in a see-saw motion of inflation/deflation – push/pull – poussez/tirez – mish/mash. We have to bust out.

'Precession – Not Recession. A pooling of the sum total of human knowledge.

'Remember the first program most of your ever learned?

K = O
K = K + I
Print "K"

I+I 2+I 3+I 4+I – Yes, the computer starts counting to infinity.

Now try

K = I
K = Kx2
Print "K"

Even on the most primitive 16k computer you get 8.50705917E37 "too big at line 20" almost instantly.

'Expansion folks – expansion into infinity.

(GOODRICH TO LEAN FORWARD LOOKING SERIOUS, ON DESK. HANDS MAKE A NEAT FLAT PYRAMID ON DESK TOP. BACKDROP TO SUGGEST A LAB)

'Come with me now to the Creation of our own fabulous Universe . . .

(BACKDROP GOES TO SCREEN – WITH COSMIC MUSH FLICKERING ACROSS IT. SOUND TRACK. FAINT HINT OF STATIC.)

'Out of quantum indeterminism came the cosmic

seed. Colliding with anti-gravity, it exploded in an instant to something like its present size.

K = I
K = Kx2

(BACKDROP EXPLODES. DRIFT TO BE REPLACED BY STARS, PLANETS, GALAXIES, QUASARS (you name it). AT CENTER STAGE – MUDBALL EARTH AND HER SATELLITES. FADE UP THE STATIC.)

'The colossal energy generated went on to power the Cosmos.

(BACKDROP – GALAXIES START TO SPIN REAL FAST AND GROW AND MULTIPLY. EARTH FADES UP IN CENTER. ZOOM IN THRU ATMOSPHERE TO SURFACE DETAIL – POWER STATIONS, CABLES, SSET RECEPTOR BANKS ETC. SOUND TRACK: The Count Basie Orchestra.)

GOODRICH TO RADIATE JOY. GOODRICH SAYS:

'The Inflationary Theory Of the Universe wipes out all information about its initial state. Just like today! Who cares if a new automobile costs $100,000 (4,000,000 Credits) when it used to cost only $6,000, if you're riding on a wave of inexhaustible commodities, materials and knowhow?

'Precession – Not Recession. The effect of one body in motion on another body in motion.

'Precession and Space Exploration – Mandated by CENTERCOM under the Great New System have created a new industrial base for humanity of potentially unlimited wealth.

'There's no limit to the possible combinations.

(SHOULD LOOK SERIOUS AT THIS POINT)

'John Stuart Mill once wrote –

"I was seriously tormented by the thought of the exhaustability of musical combinations. The octave consists of only five tones and two semi-tones, which can be put together in only a limited number of ways of which a small proportion are beautiful."

'The fears of John Stuart Mill are unjustified. There are 479,001,600 possible combinations of the twelve tones of the chromatic scale. With rhythmic variety added to the unbounded universe of melodic patterns, there is no likelihood that music will die of internal starvation in the next 1,000 years.

'Nor life on this planet as we continue to expand into the Universe with

GOODRICH – CENTERCOM – AND THE NEW SYSTEM!'

The speechwriter fell back exhausted. Not since his Harvard days has he worked so hard. Goddam Einstein and his pygmys on stilts. This boy needed a crane. Worse still, he had to work right by the Oval Office in case Edwin O. suddenly got a bright idea for him to include. The pressure!

He wasn't too sure if the public would grasp the difference between thinking in terms of a five tone octave and chromatically – but what the heck. He had an eight foot Steinway at home, and every night he worked through a page of Slonimsky's Thesaurus. He was even more worried about the 'Quantum Seed Explosion'. Goodrich had to get the Southern States behind him and millions of other Fundamentalist Christians world wide – not to mention Jehovah's Witnesses and Catholics.

Maybe a subtle but passionate rewrite to suggest – no, *imply* in a way any fool could take for granted, that quantum indeterminism *was* in fact God.

'Come back with me now to the mind of God.'

Nope. That was even more blasphemous.

Okay.

'Look folks – Inflation is the way God planned it. It's our only hope. We got to abolish the gold standard, the petrodollar, the SSET token and everything else that gives value to money. INSTEAD the WEALTH OF THE SUN! SUN CREDITS – Not Money, and finally – FREE DISTRIBUTION!'

He wondered if even Goodrich realised that.

That that was the bottom line. The final conclusion of his policies – policies that were the result of applying the Inflationary Theory of the Origins of the Universe to economics.

Goodrich was a funny guy. He believed that Franklin D. Roosevelt, presiding over the art deco and breadline 1930s with his cigarette at a funny angle, had been the greatest US pres. A visionary. A prophet of a New Age. But unlike Roosevelt, Goodrich was basically honest. I mean who could ever forget Frank's great gag which ran 'American boys will never be involved in a foreign war'? Goodrich would never fun like that. Goodrich was unusual. 100 per cent sincere. 100 per cent beef. No worms. Got to hand that to him. No one but Goodrich could deliver this crazy speech. And be right.

Goodrich was an Aquarian. Intelligent. Encyclopaedia minded. Declamatory. Persuasive. And frequently incoherent. You had to sift through hours of tape to get a forty-five minute speech to put before the people.

His socialism was the result of ideals and beliefs, rather than a shrewd assessment of necessities. But he was also a realist. The vast welfare state inaugurated by FDR could never and should never be dismantled. The revisionism of the 1950s and vicus ricorso that followed had been a tragic mistake. And as for Calvin Gold! Oh boy. Global corporatism reduced to four major companies, and 10 billion unemployed. The Leisure People! Food dispenser apartments? Welfare brozene? Wall to wall TV? No matter. All Goodrich had had to do during his first term as CENTERCOM PCP was to take the whole thing over and reshuffle it as GALCOM, SCICOM and UNIMED and apply his economics based on the Inflationary Theory of the Universe. Unemployment halved in the first year.

Goodrich realised that centralised socialism, however you dressed it up – and his campaign managers dressed it up fancier than a Sunset Boulevard transvestite – was an inevitable stage of evolution.

New threats had arisen. Possible extinction from overcrowding and famine was the perennial one. But 'More for less technology mandated by war, if applied for peace, makes war obsolete.' That's what Bucky

Buckminster had said, and Goodrich placed the long-lived twentieth-century inventor as Ace #2.

But it was as a social theoretician rather than as an inventor that he admired him. Goodrich had no wish to drive a Dymaxion car or live in a Dymaxion house, or be washed by a water-saving fog gun. But he did believe in the slogan his campaign managers had distilled from the thought of his two great mentors. 'Precession – Not Recession'.

Precession – the effect of bodies in motion on other bodies in motion. Sum total of all minds at work. 'For every plant closed – a school opened.' He hated to see human minds permanently shunted off to the 'Leisure Option' drooling by a cold vid as Calvin Gold had planned. No. Precession – and himself, Edwin O. Goodrich as symphonic sportsman conducting and refereeing it all.

The script writer looked up, still thinking precession-ally – out of his office window – to see Marshall L. Peredur striding processionally along the corridor toward the Oval Office. He bent back to his work. There had to be a way to counter Madame Feng's claim that the triumph of the leftist reformist wing of the bourgeoisie in West World did not mean that the people's struggle was over. Boy, how did she ever get elected?

Marshall Peredur straightened his tie as he proceeded. Ran a careful hand over his moulded aluminium hair. He reflected upon past events, with a bearing on the present and the future.

They had originally organised the FTPA as a US landmass-based rapid deployment force, with dubious extra territorial powers. The Federal Terrorist Prevention Agency, which he knew (regrettably) some thought of as 'Fucking Thought Police – Aaaaaaargh!' The aim of the FTPA was to counter what the media had with their usual gift for literary invention and double entendre dubbed the 'International Terrorism Explosion' after the governments of America, Europe, and Russia had, in another eloquent phrase beloved of global politicians, 'moved together' and built FWC – the 'Federation of Western Communities'. The FTPA had become an official arm of the FWC, linking CIA and KGB agencies. The name 'Federal' had remained the same. Now it referred to the transcontinental federation of FWC countries, alliances and dominions. Then China had joined, and CENTERCOM was formed. The CENTRAL COMMUNITIES. A good name, Peredur thought, supra national – despite the states that had refused to join. India, Pakistan, Libya, Norway, Switzerland and those accursed Equatorial signatories of the Declaration of Bogota.

Even during his first term, when he had been nuttier than he is now Goodrich had foreseen the need ... and before that Cal Gold ... and Tsarchovsky ...

It had taken Madame Feng, Politics' Mistress of Mystery actually to get down and state that there was a need for a central, supra national, and if necessary, secret force that far transcended the old powers and scope of the FTPA. So CENTERCOM decided. Decided to invest in the research and development of Shadow Command.

Shadow Command, with its phalanx structure rising in layered echelons towards the top of a pyramid, mirroring the organisation of its greatest enemy – the chaotic profusion of Prankster cells which looped around the world in ever widening circles, based on the concentric circles of the circus ring ...

Shadow Command – 'Global Authority with a Human Face'. Or so they claimed. But was it? Marshall L. Peredur knew. He was President Chair Person of the Shadow Command Committee. Despite his primary allegiance to CENTERCOM, he was also an American Citizen and now Edwin O. Goodrich, President of the United States wanted to see him. He knew why. A 'private job' for Shadow Command. Espionage. A few carefully selected operatives spirited away in secret, and no one in CENTERCOM any the wiser. It happened all the time. It was the only way the world leaders could keep tabs on each other. Even before the door of the Oval Office had closed Goodrich was saying,

'Marshall, we gotta find out what's going on in that frigging Hub! The rumours are getting stronger and stronger. One month to the Election. If anything in that Hub can help my campaign ...'

'Yes,' Peredur agreed. 'But ...' He didn't get to finish the sentence. The famous crew-cut ball-like head was talking again.

'OCTAVE know. They *know* goddammit! You know that Society for the Advancement of Psychic Politics convention I had to address in Miami last week? Four guys from OCTAVE there, two days Earthside from Cipola. Two days! You know what they said?'

Peredur shook his head slowly and lit a Pall Mall. The plants fight back. Once you knew that it was safe to smoke.

'Here's what they said. This is a quote. "The advances SIS scientists are currently making at Le Centre Industriel – Cipola right? – could change the input patterns of human consciousness for ever. But it's only a rumour". Marsh I'm counting on you.'

'You got it, Mr President,' Peredur said, thinking 'You asshole' but knowing that if Goodrich got to be CENTERCOM PCP again there was no limit. 'I can get the right people, but they'll need disguises. One because the world must never hear of this. Two, because that dadblamed Declaration of Bogota inhibits the jurisdiction of Terran security forces beyond Geosynchronous orbit.'

Goodrich laughed.

'The world! *Feng* must never hear of this!'

Peredur smiled grimly and crushed out his cigarette.

'What makes you think she isn't already up there, Mr President?'

The President's genial features hardened. He became solemn.

'Crazy isn't it,' he said. 'Because of the legal interpretation of a Declaration signed nearly sixty years ago by a bunch of tiny Equatorial countries we have an area in space we virtually own, and can't jurisdict. So what do we get? Dirty tricks. Maybe Feng is right you know,' Goodrich mused, resting his head on the palms of his hands, 'Maybe we – or somebody – should invade those Bogota signatories . . .'

'Say the word . . .'

Goodrich looked up, shaking his head and smiling sadly.

'Marsh – let me tell you a little truism . . .'

Peredur cringed inwardly. Some of Edwin O's little truisms were two hours long.

'Disguises,' he said quickly, to deflect the conversation.

'Yes sure,' Goodrich said distractedly. 'That's necessary, naturally. You know Marsh, Space is becoming a headache. Gays are protesting at their exclusion from the Dyad Space Mission system.'

'Not my problem,' Peredur said quickly.

'No. They won't get far with Feng on that one. I'm sure she thinks homosexuals are degenerate. They're bound to turn to me. I must get a report from OCTAVE about this. Dyad programmes are our future.'

'Really. But you know sir, this may be an unpopular view – but if McArthur had gone around the periphery of China with A bombs in 1954 . . .'

Goodrich held up his hand.

'Marsh – please. Let's talk about disguises.'

Peredur produced a sheaf of designs from his briefcase. Goodrich looked at them with half a mind only. Inside he remembered. Only too well. The awful years of Super Power confrontation. Marshall and those like him had been formed by those years. Privately it still coloured their thinking. To them – strength vs strength. To people on the ground – vivid dreams of death by incineration. At times you could feel the waves of terror all around the world. And it had all been based on a false philosophy of scarcity, that was only slowly being eroded.

It was a good thing that the Arnold Effects had come along when they did.

First there had been the 'Lase the Nukes' theory. Orbiting laser stations capable of destroying ground-based Russian missiles. It was claimed that the strategy would save the surface of Planet Earth from nuclear bombardment by destroying the missiles before they flew. Dubious. Anyhow the Russians went one better with the OMEGA system.

They went higher than the lasers, into Geosynchronous orbit. But they didn't use any fancy lasers. Just good old fashioned bombs. OMEGA was – Orbital Missiles Exiting Geosynchronous Military Arena.

Then Lockheed developed a solar-powered kite-shaped military wing. Light enough to be capable of being delivered to space arenas by shuttle – tough enough to carry a big payload. They were computer programmed to drift in eccentric orbits outside the geosynchronous military arena, floating on the solar wind. They could be directed to their OMEGA targets by military personnel in earth orbit way stations. This system was known as ORK. Orbiting Re-Entry Kites. Or as others would have it – Orbiting Russian Killers.

The Russians then began to develop the Fission Ray – a ray containing the informational structure of a thermonuclear explosion up to several hundred megatons, targeted on US and NATO (as they were then) planet-side strategic centres. This they planned to locate at L5 – beyond geosynchronous orbit. The beam would instantaneously travel over a quarter of a million miles to Earth and – you know – explode.

In later times Goodrich, in bad moments would remember his sense of despair the day a Pentagon chief told him – 'you know if they deploy these rays – uh – this guy at Lockheed has come up with a great idea. We mine parts of the asteroid belt with nuclear land mines and attach computerised rocket motors to them – and if it looks like they're gonna use the ray – we trigger the motors – the asteroids fly off toward the ray projectors and . . .'

Oh boy. Where would it end?

By this time, the EESP – the European Evolutionary

Survivalist Politics Party were leading demonstrations that took days to pass the military bases they were protesting against. Some women from the party had hijacked a shuttle and were on hunger strike outside an orbiting laser station. There were plans to stake out the asteroid belt if need be. In America – peace protestors were once again encircling the Pentagon chanting 'Out Demons out' in a heroic re-run of the late 1960s. The only difference this time was that a definite horned shape could be seen materialising above the roof of that august edifice. Dissidents infiltrating the Soviet industrial structure had brought the entire Soviet Union out on strike. And they were all linked up by CB radio.

Europe and America faced famine for the first time in hundreds of years as food supplies backed up behind nationwide protest marches. Right wing elements of the civilised world led by Calvin Gold were calling for the deployment of the then infant FTPA. The crowned heads of Europe had decided to visit the first American Moonbase for an indefinite period. The only light relief, when Goodrich came to think about it. Funnily enough, they were still there.

Where would it end? Pretty soon someone would find a military application for Jupiter, Neptune, or even Uranus. Possibly the Sun itself. Why not attach gigantic rockets to the sides of the Earth? If the Ruskies cut up rough we can threaten to fly the whole planet into the Sun.

Mercifully, Arnold effects changed all that. They penetrated the heart of high level military coding and destroyed it, with the infinite variety of numbers between 0 and 1. No more secrets anymore. Any signal could be transmitted, but any signal could be jammed. Like the Shadow said – 'I know what you're putting, before you put it down.'

Rapprochment followed. The FWC was the first step.

Brilliant negotiations by a certain Senator Edwin O. Goodrich produced Japan's application for membership. Some saw the handling of the 'Japanese Application' as the shrewdest political and economic move Goodrich ever made, solving America's trade deficit problems by combining the economies of the two countries under the CENTERCOM auspice. It made him smile even now as he studied the Shadow Command disguises dreamed up by Marshall L. Peredur, which were enough to make you smile on their own.

It was hard to concentrate, as the recent history of the world circulated and recirculated in his mind. CENTERCOM, with its President Chair Person selected from among the leading politicians of several dozen countries by 2½ thousand million people. The first PCP had been the Russian Tsarchovsky, then an electoral swing right – Calvin Gold. A swing centre – Goodrich himself. A swing further left – Madame Feng (Politics' Mistress of Mystery).

And the whole thing was the result of discoveries in the field of information. Diaphantus locks could thwart the insufficiently equipped systems engineer, but nothing could resist the Mordell's Conjecture Probe. Classic Games Theory with no ifs or buts.

Diaphantus locks were a necessity to safeguard the privacy of individuals and the workings of finance and business on a day to day basis – but someone had to know what evil lurked in the hearts of men. And of course as comic book freaks realised – 'The Shadow Knows'. Shadow Command – White Echelon were the only Global government agency authorised to use a Mordell's Conjecture Probe.

Nobody – not GALCOM
      or     SCICOM
      or     UNIMED.

Not private agencies like SIS or academics like OCTAVE. They weren't allowed anywhere near one. Of course they could and did use Arnold Effect mathematics. Especially UNIMED in its quest for the secrets of life – SCICOM in its physical and chemical researches – OCTAVE in its search for new models of the mind. They could operate Diaphantus locks – but in general they didn't need to.

But it wasn't just the still powerful and persuasive need for global security under the auspices and veneer of CENTERCOM that gave the Mordell's Conjecture Probe its awesome power. It was the power of the Probe itself. It exceeded necessity, transcending the rules of the game. Because not only could it crack any code or access any system – it could reorder any program, however complex, however arcane. It could alter any electronic reality in an instant, at the will of the operator. Some kinda potential. You didn't leave them lying around.

No. Things were not a bed of roses. There was the legacy of Calvin Gold's President Chair Personcy. With the immediate military threat removed he had nonetheless progressed every possible lead towards the possibilities still left for building a Nuclear dictatorship. He back pedalled on the SSET programme – and built more nuclear power stations on Earth. He disenfranchised from the economy millions of industrial workers and left parts of Europe Russia and America in a state of virtual civil war as union members fought to retain their rights against the new breed of deunionised A6 classifieds – workers cleared to operate nuclear energy. Those who gave up the struggle were classified as Leisure. Welfare credits coined as phoney brozene – food dispenser flats – Wall to Wall T.V.

The entire population coded Leisure, Private, Security Cleared A1 – A13. He disbanded all the national police forces of the world and replaced them with SECURITY – a supra territorial police force under the control of CENTERCOM. And the fuckups! Leaks, burnouts, meltdowns. There were parts of North Britain you couldn't even go anymore.

The Prometheus scam. Life extension programme hushed up. Reserved for top people only. Original selectees relocated in the Space Cities. Very embarassing. Got to leak it some day. Prometheus unbound. Or there'll be more riots in the streets.

And of course, no one had decided how to dismantle the now useless weapons (the man or woman who did that would go down as a big name in the history books) and Cal Gold was talking about a 'return to nationhood'. Also a Mordell's Conjecture Probe was missing. Believed to be in Prankster hands. Theoretically a Mordell's Conjecture Probe could penetrate the Diaphantus locks on the silos. Made you shudder to think about. He stopped thinking about it.

'Sorry Marsh? You were saying ...'

'Yeah. I can get them into L5 through contacts inside SIS.'

'I don't like that Marsh. You know I plan to grab SIS under a GALCOM auspice when I'm re-elected as CENTERCOM PCP.'

'Mr President. Do you want to know what's going down in the Hub or don't you?'

'Yes, Marsh. I do.'

'Then leave it to me. I've had – gee – seventy or more years in the intelligence business.'

'Marsh – you got it,' Goodrich said, stretching out his hand. But he didn't look particularly happy. 'I'll tell you a little truism' he said as Peredur was leaving the office. 'One little worm can spoil a big burger.'

The door clicked shut behind him and he started walking, but Marshall L. Peredur never made it back to his Lincoln Picasso. Halfway down the corridor a terrible pain seized him in the back as though his liver was being pierced by the beak of a giant bird. He crumpled floorward – body-worn neural-system-linked alarm bleepers sending paramedics on standby running from all over the building. Bio-system Defcon One. Organ Implosion.

The Duty Surgeon knew. Only one thing could save him. The PMH programme. Within hours, Peredur's sedated, near lifeless body was on a DLV zooming spacewards. Orientation vector – Lagrange Point 5. Destination – Cipola.

DATE: LOCM 727 – 8435 J = 11.40
MARCH 27 2031 TCT
LOCATION: SPACE

*Then he was told:*
*Remember what you have seen*
*Because everything forgotten*
*Returns to the circling winds*
NAVAJO WIND CHANT

They all saw the new feature at once. It appeared at a point where the curve of the surface appeared slightly more pronounced. At about 500 metres. None of them could decide if it had suddenly appeared or if it had been there all along. An elongated cube with rounded corners – 15 metres high.

No one said anything. They all exchanged glances. Morgan's face was grimmer than ever. Dark. Smouldering. Determined.

As they approached, the ground under their feet, while still quite solid, began to exhibit a dim translucence. Through it, faint outlines like features of a vast distant countryside – all gray green. Or was it more like something bio-organic – like tissue – veins?

'Don't speculate,' Morgan said, reading the outline of their thoughts. 'Let's get the facts.'

The feature seemed like the surface on which they now stood. Thinner, lighter, but unlike the ground surface – opaque rather than see-through.

'It's a bubble,' Platinov said.

'Say what?' Morgan stared at him puzzled. Thinking 'I'm the physicist around here' and realising how practical Plat's engineering made him.

'It's a bubble,' he said again. 'Spun off the surface.

This one I am convinced is in liquid state here like glass – see the ground – gas bubble or better – envelope. Come, the atmosphere inside is breathable.'

Morgan flashed on paranoia – one brief instant. Where are these people coming from? he asked himself. First of all Datsun – so inscrutable but knowledgeable. 'The whole pattern has not yet unfolded'.

Then Angela – she knew to put those shards back.

Now this. Plat has grokked this feature out. How do they know? Are they in league? With what? Or is IT – whatever IT is – already off and talking to them?

Morgan moved over to the feature. His mind flashed again.

'Look! An opening!'

The structure seemed one with the surface like Plat had said. But one side had looped up about two metres high and was bevelled around the edges, frosted like thick glass.

Morgan ducked inside.

Darkness. He had not realised how subtly strong was the light outside, despite its dull greenish hue. His eyes and brain made rapid adjustment. He saw. He gasped. He called the others inside.

'Hey wow!' Angela said. 'A control room!'

She instantly glanced at Morgan, her eyes furtive and naughty. His face was a blank mask. But transparent. She could see behind it smouldering anger, despairing humour, and cold scorn.

People from Cipola didn't use words like 'Control'. People from Cipola had outgrown authoritarian hierarchical structures and the words that went with them, but amongst the young – and Angela was old enouh to know better – such terms were growing in credibility for their shock value and novelty. Older people felt sad to see a younger generation – which should be even more enlightened – come on so square. But on Cipola you didn't condemn or order. You could only teach – direct – guide.

'Oops,' she said. Her slim hand gagged her mouth. Baby doll lashes shaded her eyes. 'Mm......operations room......communication centre?'

'Yeah. Something like that.'

Morgan concentrated on the scene before his eyes. Everything was vague and misty, but tangible. Built for a function.

'Like a computer room for ghosts,' Datsun said.

'What have we got here Plat?' Morgan's voice was tired. A soft smile crinkled the corners of his eyes.

'This whole wall,' Platinov said 'is a K Line computer.'

Morgan waited, watching him.

'You know K Line computer? This one is very important to any autonomous consciousness, advanced robot, artificial intelligent complex, take for instance an automatic city ...'

Morgan fought to concentrate. The problem with Platinov was – stupidity. Compared with the average levels current in the previous century, he was already super intelligent. But like so many good operations people he had this denseness – lack of subtlety. Also he had some kind of dysfunction in his brain that impeded natural telepathic backup to his conversation.

Cipolans were already evolving a language. Very simple but very rich. Many people, of many races, close together on a new world in space. In a few short years shared experiences have made communication deeper. A few words carefully chosen, layers of meaning. Something was starting to trigger. One day maybe there would be huge subconscious packets behind the verbal drift, telepathy assisted. Like a thesis in one sentence, backed by holo drama and special effects. But even now in this primitive stage, less words had more meaning. Eventually, some challenge or crisis and they'd make it and be free. Psychic link up, mind to mind.

But Plat would always have a problem. No good. Morgan couldn't concentrate. Too much hominid grunt. It wasn't Plat's fault – too bad about the impediment. It was wrong to call him dumb but even if he had been a Mah Religion Adept No1 he would still have been dumb. Plus, being from a remote part of Russia he spoke English real weird to boot. American Basic? – forget it!

Morgan fought for focus.

'K – line computer works like this,' Plat was saying.

'K – Line is like spider – inside the brain – monitors everything – all the senses – audits – compares, refers to banks of stored experience – breeds – makes new spiders as required. So, and can operate at many levels – one thought process may be monitored by another – while the monitoring process itself may also be monitored at a deeper level. In this way parallel processes operate in – a kind of counter point ...'

'I can get to that,' Angela said. 'That's a nice analog, Plat.' She glanced at Morgan as if to say 'Don't be so hard on poor Plat.'

'Okay,' Morgan said, a little testily. 'We know what a K – Line computer is. It keeps all the balls in the air at once. Works something like the E.Z. Coder. So, this is some kind of nerve centre. Okay. We are in the cloud's brain – right by a nerve centre. So what?'

'So this,' Datsun interpolated. 'Is it natural to believe in this in this place? Or is it a construct? Is it autonomous (i.e. self programming) or is it a very sophisticated tool?'

'Plat?'

'I suppose either is possible.'

'Angela?'

'You tell me.'

'Okay. Datsun?'

Shrugs.

'Guessing time is over people.'

They knew that soft spoken drawl. Perfect vowels. Carefully articulated consonants. Light burst in the middle of the room. A pale but well defined holo flickered into visual form in the centre of the floor. 5/8 scale and twice as natural. A long robe. High pointed hat. A flowing beard.

'Dralon!' they gasped. 'Chief High Magic Man of the Seven Cities of Cipola!'

Dralon – in holo form projected from his voodoo crib on Cipola 5 didn't waste any time.

'Option No 2 is correct,' he said. 'It's a very sophisticated tool – or instrument. Though "system" would be an altogether better word. This little "gas cloud", as you call it, is my invention.'

'Oh what? – Dralon – what is this?'

'This – is a test of your intelligence, and will to live.'

'Huh? That sure sounds heavy Dralon.'

'Out there somewhere – on the surface of this world of illusion (he chuckles momentarily as mists of gas swirl up from the surface of the plateau) is your Scoot Ship now miraculously free of all malfunction. The trick is – can you get to it? You see I control the composition of the gas cloud anyway I want to.'

Morgan pushed his hands deeper into the pockets of

his jacket. His voice was tired, long suffering.

'Do the Council know about this, Dralon?'

As he said it, Morgan knew that what he was saying was pointless. The Council had no power. It was merely a forum for discussion and guidance. That was the whole point. On Cipola the New System had already flowered to the end point of its evolution. Or so one was led to believe.

Dralon didn't answer immediately. There was time for everyone to speak at once.

'What kind of garbage is this? You can't impose your will – or your mind games on other people. And these mists are really camp, Dralon!' Angela yelled.

'This isn't clever living Dralon,' Datsun mumured reflectively.

'Yes – what is happening?' Platinov asked, scratching his head and gesturing to the world around him.

The holo spread its 5/8 scale hands.

'Hush children. Peace. Let me pull your coats. Things are not as they appear. That "Council" (he accented the word heavily) you want so earnestly to whip on me is devoid of power. The Seven Cities of Cipola – that technological anarchist paradise you love so well, with its smaltzy high tech minarets and beautiful gooey plastic tube elevators and glittering mini skyscrapers under translucent domes with lasers playing rainbow patterns in the sky both day and night is er – up for grabs.'

'Grabs Dralon?' Morgan said quietly, his eyes half lidded, his shoulders hunched. 'By whom?'

'Well ...' Dralon smiled knowingly, infuriatingly. 'A struggle is about to ensue. Between the Council and ... The Federation of Initiated Neophytes of Knowledge. Of whom I am one.'

'Federation of Initiated Neophytes of Knowledge?! Dogdammit Dralon, that spells FINK! What kind of jive is this?'

'I'd hardly call it jive, dear boy. Top people at GALCOM ... SCICOM ... SIS ...'

'SIS! Those space pirates! I might have known it!'

'PLUS ...'

'PLUS? Who the hell are they?'

'No ... let me rephrase that – IN ADDITION – a *select* few of us at mm ... you know OCTAVE ... really the freaking cosmic *spearhead* you might say ... Well kiddies, the thinking is that CENTERCOM, The Central Communities or Centralised Command, as some believe it stands for, has mismanaged the entire Cipola operation for long enough and we're going to stop that. We're coming out and we're taking over!'

'Dralon – you jeffing con ...'

Morgan had started to shake his fist but realised that in the face of a shimmering holo it was pointless. Instead he said,

'Folks Cipside are solid man. They're all hip to the New System. You can't fool us!'

The holo smiled a 5/8 smile.

'Listen. What we have developing here is an infrastructure/superstructure situation. Blasphemous? Maybe. Immoral? Probably. Who's to judge? Here are the fax. The "New System" in which you all so naïvely and touchingly believe is possible for you mass of plebos due to the very existence of bergs like Ciptown out in space which ship all that good Lo-Cost Energy back to Terra. This means wealth for everyone – Education – Life Extension – a groovy existence. So it's easy to let you people think you live in a technological anarchist paradise. But in the long term you don't. You're nothing but a shill for CENTERCOM, man. The whole thing is going to waste. The potential out here is unlimited in the right hands. CENTERCOM and the New System are through. We Initiated Neophytes are going to see to that, and the first step is going to be – to seize the Space Cities. So for your protection we have begun to direct you in a million subtle ways. This is one of the less subtle ways. Reason? Emergency.'

How long has this been going on? Morgan wondered. The New System had been the best break he'd ever had. How could it be a mere charade? Yet if what Dralon said was true? Okay – but then why so many people using keth now? Folks burning up on drive? And – the weird control freaks trying to order people around and talking that strange language of authority. Like Angela just now. Grooving off on 'Control'. And what about those rumours? Couple of Exits found in a waste container orbiting 6. And – what the heck was going on in the Hub? Unit leased by SIS ... yeah everyone knows that. But those laser shields were a violation. Flagrant violation. Para 4 do clearly state ... 'free and unrestricted access to all ...' I got to get back to Cipola – find out what's going on ...

'Okay Dralon.' Morgan's voice was controlled. The fists were back in the SD jacket. 'Personally I think you are one crazy deviant ...'

The holo smiled blandly.

'But supposing all you say is true. What emergency? What is all this in aid of?'

'Defence.' The face of the holo was expressionless. Emotionless. Calm.

'Defence? Are you out of ... well we don't have to ask. You ARE OUT OF YOUR MIND, MAN! Defence against whom? Defence against what?'

Dralon said,

'Cipola vs. Terra'

Them: 'Oh NO!'

Dralon continued blandly.

'The emergency – of which I spoke. Let me remind you of history. 1976 to be precise. The Declaration of Bogota. Signed by eight Equatorial countries, claiming that the Geostationary Orbit (GSO) – 22,300 mile above the Earth and of course directly over the Equator was not "space" in the accepted meaning of the term but, and I quote "a natural resource" of the country or countries directly underneath. Their aim was to give the Third World, as it was then, a stake in the High Frontier. Remember that this problem of definition has never been solved. Remember that it has survived the old UN and the formation of CENTERCOM and been applied by extrapolation to include Earth's claim to the – and I quote again – "heritage" of L5. Remember that the whole question has never been formally ratified by any treaty or constitution. So it's lapsed into a kind of common law, which global legal experts have ruled "inhibits" the use of Terran security forces beyond GSO.

'Calvin Gold wants to clear up this mess once and for all, in our favour. In the meantime, the Signatories of the Declaration of Bogota refuse to join CENTERCOM. A thorn in the flesh legally speaking. A constant reproach. We can't take a chance on Calvin Gold being elected. He may be, he may not. He didn't do so well the last time. One thing's for sure – the old guard at CENTERCOM, Goodrich, Amalrik, Feng – naturally want the Space Cities to remain sympathetic to their interests. To remain under their influence, serving their needs. The Council stays. It all goes on as before. We Neophytes don't see it that way. We want to loosen our links with Terra. Break them, even. Maybe develop our own Space programme. You know, take off somewhere. And there's no chance "the old guard" will let us do that. They'll tear up the Declaration, incorporate the Equatorials by force – then they'll come after us! Which is why you're here. This cloud is a weapon – see?'

Angela pulled nervously at her hair – then spread her hands in desperation.

'What do you mean? It explodes like some kind of terrible *bomb* or something?'

'No – more subtle than that – more humane. This is the first example of a VPMBM. That's Victim Programmed Mind Blowing Maze. Technically – you should never be able to get out of here. If it works I aim to build a whole bunch more. To trap up the Terran invasion fleet.'

ALL: (except Dralon and Datsun) Invasion fleet? There is no invasion fleet!

'Oh yeah.' Dralon smiled a sophisticated blasé smile.

'You know how Terrans are – all that funky nature around them. They go ape at the drop of a hat. They're not like us Cipolans in our super civilized artificial

106

environment. But I'm not all bad. If this little VPMBM doohickey works – Cipolans can go on being gentle peace-loving anarchists as much as they want to. But first we've got to overcome the Terran threat.'

Morgan thought –'ain't so long since you lived on Terra yourself, bub.' But instead he said,

'Threat – there is no threat. We don't have that type of *word*, Dralon.'

'Okay,' Dralon said reasonably. 'You don't have to believe me. Check this –'

A vid screen like everything else in the place seemingly only semi material, flickered into life. It showed what purported to be an army, mustering somewhere on Earth. Looked like a Mid Eastern location. There was a commentary, crackly and faint. The commentator was heavy into manpower, weaponry and Megadeath.

After about a minute and a half, Morgan said

'No thanks Dralon. That's old stock. Early twenty-first century at the latest. In fact I think that's the United Nations Global Police disbanding ceremony 20II.'

Dralon shrugged, zeroing the screen.

'Anyway you want it man. Look I can't hang around here any longer. This 5/8 scale is cramping my style.'

'One more question Dralon,' Morgan said. 'Why us?'

'Why not? Don't mess around with superdeterminism. I'm cutting out. Guess what? In a puff of smoke. But first I've got to shake this little old Island up a little bit . . .'

The holo vanished in a puff of green oily smoke.

Mists swirled and drifted outside the doorway of the structure like snow on the tundra – fog in an old film of London – like memories in a tired old mind. The four companions sat huddled on the floor like doomed eskimos.

The mists cleared. They moved over the floor and looked out. Outside as far as the eye could see, horizon to horizon the ground had cracked open. The surface was crisscrossed with a titanic sunken maze. Huge, long, regular gashes crisscrossed each other for mile after endless mile. The gashes were deep and wide – tactile – ugly. The landscape looked forbidding and horrible.

To retrace their steps, with the aid of bleeps from their PCCs would now be impossible. The trenches were too wide to jump. Great dark green channels, maybe twenty feet deep and twenty feet wide reached out everywhere, suggesting in their vectors and points of intersection the design of a bizarre, malign, surrealist painting.

'Dralon – that son of a gun!' Platinov's voice grated between anger and despair.

'Yeah,' Angela quoted softly, 'Einstein disguised as Robin Hood, his memories in a trunk.'

They stared about them. Lost. Totally devoid of inspiration, thought or hope. Only Datsun seemed free of the despair that gripped them, sitting crosslegged on the floor he had withdrawn into a trance state.

A panel on the wall of the structure glowed suddenly into life. Morgan leapt up and ran over to it. He stared at the keyboard beneath the screen for a moment and then instinctively pressed a button marked 'Run'.

Patterns flickered across the screen. Plans, diagrams, intersections. Morgan realised instantly. He was looking at maps of the strange grid. Morgan turned around.

'Over to you Plat,' he said. 'Calculate a way out.'

Platinov lumbered over to the keyboard and screen.

He peered at it for a while mumbling to himself in Russian. Then quietly he murmured,

'I think I can do this.'

The others returned to their various meditations. Silence fell again inside the structure, punctuated only by the clicking of keys.

Platinov worked, it seemed, for hours. Waves of thought filled the room. Silence and the clicking of keys.

'THIS IS IT!'

Plat had spun around from the computer console to face into the room. He was smiling – a broad deep tired smile.

'This I have been dealing with man – so compli-cated!'

The others looked up eagerly. Platinov began to speak rapidly and for him, coherently.

'It looks like the co-ordinates are Cartesian. But they aren't. They are spatially complex and shifting. There is a time factor and various random factors. I can see that as soon as we enter this environment it will undergo changes – like a wave ... but look, see – I have constructed a model to comprehend what is happen-ing.'

Platinov had calculated four possible ways out. Complicated but rapidly comprehensible. Morgan remembered with a jolt that there was nothing wrong with what went on inside Platinov's head. His only problem was trying to get it out. Deficiency, maybe a chemical, in the telepathic circuits of his brain. Like a person in the past with a speech impediment.

Here he had diagrams, calculations and a screen. His system gave them four routes back to the ship. Four chances as a group and a possible escape route each if separated. That was how the logic of the maze worked apparently, and Platinov had capitalised on it.

'Nice!' Morgan said. 'Figured like a true Cipolan!'

The computer screen went blank. Then faded from the wall as though it had never been there.

They grouped by the door. At that moment, real depression, an emotion normally so alien to the Cipolan mind seized them. They were really lost, trapped on a strange shifting world designed by a madman, with only a map plotted on an instrument that no longer existed. Platinov clutched the print out as though it were reality itself.

No way forward but into the maze.

They stepped outside and stood staring at the strange green surface crisscrossed with the deep straight channels as far as the eye could see.

Platinov was busy by the trusty hover sled, bundled printout grasped in his hand, transferring information to the sled's inboard computer. Platinov stared at the patterns he had formed on the sled's screen, then back at the channels.

'I have this all mapped out,' he said. 'Channel I is here, okay?' He pointed down into the wide ditch opening at their feet. 'Okay. Channel I alternate – Channel 4 via Channel 2R – see? Right and left channels IR 2R 3R ... IL 2L 3L etc. Ahead Channels 1234 – got it? From Channel 4 alternate Channel 12 via ...'

'Cool it Plat' Morgan said. 'How far do we have to go? Where is the ship at?'

'Channel 4000 and Channel 3694L.'

Morgan sighed.

'Oh boy. How long?'

'Who knows? I already told you Dralon has fixed time as well as distance. Everything here is very, very relative as our friend Datsun says. How long have we been here already?'

'Too long,' Morgan said. '*Vamos, hombres y mujere* – LET'S GO!'

The gravity was too heavy to jump without the risk of injury. They lowered themselves carefully down into the murky depths of Channel I using rocket packs on retro. Morgan had proposed they walk as far as possible. Rocket packs had only so much fuel and who knew when they might really need them – like getting out of the channels again? Vote weary, but unanimous. The hover truck floated down after them coming to rest bumpily a foot above the surface of the trench.

Platinov's voice echoed and re-echoed eerily through the canyons 'Channel 10R or via Channel 2 ... alternate Channel 12L' ...

'How are we doing Plat?'

'Good. We are already nearly half way.'

'Good. How long has it taken? I feel like I have been here for a hundred years!'

'Maybe you have. Channel – hold it! We have to get this right. This is crucial. After this we are sailing ... Channel I008 – alternate Channel 200IR and turn into

Channel III7 via Channel 2002L. There are just four co-ordinates we have to cross, then it's simple.'

They all agreed,

'Plat – we like what you're saying!'

Out of nowhere – new input. At first a quiet sound. Singing winds, crying beasts – night forest elusive, out there, somewhere up ahead. Morgan held up his hand. Pause signal. Deep in Channel I008. Murky green walls rose high on either side – even higher it seemed – perspective warped as in a vivid dream. Ahead, clear light in faint rays, and with it more sound, building higher and sharper with every second passing. Four seconds more it would be deafening. The crescendo arrived, cascading down the channel, an ear splitting torrent of terrible, beautiful sound.

Angela screamed. Inaudibly.

DATE: 11.00 MARCH 2 2031 TCT
LOCATION: CALIFORNIA CITY,
CALIFORNIA USA WESTWORLD
CCR 437

*'Now the freeway rolls where old man
   Knowles
Used to graze his sheep in the meadow.'*
                    THE NEW RIDERS OF THE
                              PURPLE SAGE

California City ran two miles high from San Bernardino
in the south to San Luis Obispo in the North. Like a
huge inverted pear it looped out east around Bakers-
field and tailed finally like a stalk around Santa Anna.

It was two hundred miles long and at its widest
point, nearly a hundred miles wide. Once there was an
old song which went 'home folks say "Los Angeles"
and strangers say "L.A."'. Now strangers said 'That
California City sure is a BIG mothafucker' and home
folks said 'Really!'

Calvin Gold ran California City like Boss Crump had
run Memphis, and Tom Prendergast had run K.C. He
ran it the way he had run CENTERCOM. Tough.

'High unemployment is the natural consequence of
high technology' had been his watchword, and it still
was now. He invented the 'Leisure People'.

All unemployed people who couldn't be AI classified
(credit worthy status) were required to allow a food
dispenser automat to be installed in their homes, and a
wall to wall T.V. From then on they received a weekly
allocation of 'brozene' – welfare tokens based on the
value of the dollar, which they drew from a local office
in their immediate neighbourhood. These tokens could

only be spent in the dispenser machines.

A separate economy funded by the government and based on the world's most basic commodity – food. It was possible to make it sound quite philanthropic in a crude kind of way. Except for one thing. Calvin Gold was not only an ex-President of CENTERCOM. He was also an ex-president of that vast corporate conglomerate combine collectively known as US Food. He had been forced to relinquish that post when he had been elected President Chair Person of CENTERCOM, but had kept a hand on the reins and a finger in that enormous pie through the person of his son Richard (known as Rich) Gold. It had been disapproved of. It was illegal. It had been exposed by crusading media people. But Calvin Gold had gone on ahead and founded his dynasty. And, once out of office, he had it all back again.

For years that soft pinko dirt bag Edwin O. Goodrich had tried to deprivatise US Food under the GALCOM auspice, through CENTERCOM mandates. But he had only partially succeeded. The Eastern seaboard and Mid-Western divisions he had caused to languish under the rule of the CENTERCOM syndicates. Yet still Cal Gold's lawyers had managed to keep the Western operation free. 'Let's face the facts,' as Cal Gold was wont to say, '50 per cent of something is better than 50 per cent of nothing'.

Once upon a time in California, the novelist Raymond Chandler reports, old men with faces like lost battles sat on porches reaching their cracked shoes into the sunlight. Now there were young men doing it too, but Cal Gold didn't have to see any of that. He lived in a fortified high tech mansion of gleaming white neo-crete, glass and tubes set into the hills above Big Sur. From the swimming pool or sundeck or library – or from the communications console, you could see California City shimmering in the heat, shrouded in smog, or just there. From that vantage point, it looked like a vast wall.

It was a fine day, a warm day, a clear day. Calvin Gold lay back on his inflatable pool recliner, floating gently on the surface of the pool. A little quiet rock music burbled from the house where they'd left the radio on. Indiana Boys School 'Good time on the County Farm'. Reflected glare from the brilliant white walls of the house caused him to narrow his eyes. A young naked female Japanese masseuse knelt behind him on the raft working her fingertips into his shoulders. Anything Henry Miller could do (or rather had done) in Big Sur, Cal Gold could do. It was just that he preferred to be massaged by naked Japanese girls than to play table tennis with them like old Henry used to do. His wrists were weak. Arthritis. Silicone crystals, synthesised on the Jefferson Orbital Location were regularly flown in to shore up the joints.

There was a cure for arthritis. Had been for twenty-five years. If they knew it was incipient Organ Implosion, why the hell didn't the doctors say so? Goddam Prometheus programme. Extended his life by forty years. You weren't supposed to get sick and, if you did, they fixed it. As we get smarter, nature gets smarter too. Kali-Shiva Syndrome the freaks up in Berkeley called it.

Black specs in the deep blue water of the pool. The corpses of flies. Must have Priscilla speak to that Philippino boy when she gets back from Ontario. Synthetic Fur Convention at the old Seal Palace. Godam that Greenpeace. They sure turned some heads around.

Scarcely disturbing the movement of the masseur's rhythmic hands, he reached for the recliner's built in phone. When the phone answered, Cal Gold said,

'Did you find it yet?'

'No,' the voice on the other end of the phone replied. 'But we still looking.' It was a dark voice. An Afro-American voice. A Brown's Mule and Jack Daniels type of a voice. Wayne Cruthers, California City's Chief of Security. You could hear the voice clearly through the earpiece of the phone at a distance of several feet.

'We've pinned down the neighbourhood,' the voice continued. 'Ground level. PB 21 02 92 between ADZ 63

704 29 and 43 29 04, SIR. I've pulled Security OUT and put the FTPA IN!'

'Good. No problem with LAPD?'

'No sir. They directin' traffic and helpin' ol' folks cross the street, just like they supposed to do.'

LAPD was one of the few regional or local police forces still in existence after Cal Gold's 'GLOBAL SECURITY' revolution. But, like the others that were left, all they mostly did was to get cats out of trees.

'Okay. Remember I want it found. Even if they have to tear the city apart brick by brick.'

'That's a lot of brick, but we'll do it sir.'

'No sign of the others yet?'

'No way. California City Ordinance do state that no Shadow Command personnel may jurisdict within the City Limits without reference to me. Sir.'

'I don't have to remind you Chief – to Shadow Command your ordinance ain't jack shit.'

'I know that sir. We sure got our eyes open.'

''kay. Let me know as soon as it breaks.'

'Yes sir Mr Gold. Sure thing SIR!'

Gold cradled the phone.

I have to know, he murmured to himself, I have to know what's going on in that motherfucking Hub. No use to worry Cal. Just kick back and – uh, be cool.

He reached up and touched the masseuse's hair with his jewelled fingers. She let go his shoulders and moved carefully around on the raft toward the naked midsection of Gold's lean, tanned, 110-year-old body.

The girl's clothes lay beside the pool. A parti-coloured sweat shirt top and baggy pants. Like clown pants. Fashionable casual wear.

Her mouth and tongue worked rhythmically around the head of Cal Gold's gnarled penis. Glub, breath. Glub, breath. She was calm, detached. A skilled professional doing a useful job. Cal Gold lay back, his forearm over his eyes, squinting up occasionally to glimpse her perfect body, with its small, hard, pointed breasts. He fancied she was talking to herself as she worked, soft mumblings in an unknown language. He liked that. Boy, she sure was a foxy broad. The vibrations of her vocal chords at the back of her throat sent chills up and down his spine. Glub, breath. Glub, breath.

Tiny microphones were set into her teeth and wiring inside her jaw ran down through the larynx – exiting behind her mammary glands. Brilliant miniaturised surgery techniques had built silicone cavities inside her breasts. The cavities contained long-wave high frequency Arnold Effect transmitters. Miniaturised antennae ran out into tiny tubes inside her dark purple nipples.

'Glub, FTPA, breath. Glub, ground level, breath. Between PB 2I 01 92 glub, fuckit, breath, glub. It's the neighbourhood they call the Black . . .'

But the last word of the transmission was drowned in what sounded to listeners deep in the heart of California City, like the gush of a glutinous waterfall.

Herb Davis lived in the Black Hole. But it wasn't a Black Hole in space. It was a black hole in dense matter. An area of the California Stack so deep, the sun had become a part of folklore. Every week Herb collected brozene and went home to eat candy bars and watch wall to wall T.V.

Today was no different. He walked along under the giant elevated platform that held the layers above him watching the dim eerie glow of the street light filtering around the concrete, feeling the soft updraft of the giant exhaust ventilator tubes that ran up through the higher layers, sucking at the top of his head. Distant thunder of electro magnetic trains in the Mass Transit tunnels. Never knew who rode the trains. People with lives. People with dough. People with AI status. Abandoned cars rusting at the kerbside by NO PARKING repulsers that had long since ceased to function.

Davis had once worked at Nuke 17, California's biggest power plant, as a clerical VDU operator. He had a Nuclear Zone permit and A6. Two days before his 25th birthday, a Prankster attack using high level code breaking equipment, had nearly caused a major melt-down in the central pile.

After the narrowly averted disaster, the Governor of California, Senator Calvin Gold, had decided that all Nuke 17 personnel should be re-registered A8 – that included Global Security trustworthiness rating.

No way Davis was going to make that. Davis was an orphan. He'd come up the hard way. As a kid he'd run with the wrong crowd. Ran with gangs like the Omnis, the Chevettes, the Eldos, the Toyotas. He'd run through Watts and White Fence raising hell and tearing up heads. Petty larceny. Larceny from the person. Auto theft.

Modern science in the form of Creative Custody put an end to that. For years harassed city dwellers and suburbanites had used surgically fitted Mood Monitor implants to even out their rattled emotions. In the hands of the correctional authorities they were the ultimate probation. Corrections staff doctors put two way Mood Monitor implants in Davis' head. They monitored everything. Incidence of anger, incidence of greed. Penile erection. Incidence of grief. When he stepped out of line, little electric shocks nudged him around. No need for jail. His jail was the street. A total inmate of his culture. Behavioural Conditioning at the touch of a button. Instant salvation, instant reform.

Davis came through an exemplary candidate. A reformed misdemeanant. They all did. They had no choice. Davis' time was up on the fifth anniversary of Project CC. The authorities were so pleased they decided to make Davis a special case. By special arrangement they got him the job at Nuke 17. The Prankster meltdown scare put an end to that. A8 rating – no police record. Goddam that Calvin Gold. He wished the Pranksters had made it. Melted that goddam thing down like a thermonuclear icecream cone. Davis had had the last available job in the south western United States that year.

Now he was a Leisure Person. Piped for food. 50 credits brozene and wall to wall T.V. in a basement under a block of bleak old walkup apartments at the bottom of the L.A. Stack, where no one much had lived for fifty years but roaches, rats, and Herb Davis. The whole scam put a hole in his soul.

The ghost of a long dead tenor man lived in the door of his basement and when the door creaked open to admit its long shaft of damp acrid light that made a roach highway on the oily floor, you could hear him play the first four bars of 'Easy Living' for Herbie. But Davis didn't know what the noise was. He didn't give a fuck about jazz.

This morning the food vendor unit in the kitchen had read NIL – REORDER IMMEDIATELY when he touched the stock status request button.

Red letters. Bad news. CREDIT UNITS NIL. CREDIT UNITS NIL – 10. Probably just pushing those buttons would record a false vend and he'd be debited for some shit he hadn't even had. No credit. No food. They'd make up the overdraft by not supplying allocated food to the equivalent value, next time he pushed his tokens in. It was all on computer at US Food.

He'd flipped the refrigerator scanner on. SOS – his tired eyes staring into the small icy tunnel that seemed to run back forever behind the pale squelchy screen that flickered in the sealed steel wall of the vend unit. Same old shit.

Must be time to go to the Welfare Office on Yorba Linda Avenue. Yeah. Hard to keep track of time. Get some brozene. Brozene buys credit for cats like me. Davis lit up his last Libration Filter. Ran his fingers through his long thinning hair. Stepped outside. Headed out.

The Future Incorporated, Cal Gold called it. Saw his face on T.V. Last traces of a Southern accent. Long, lined face. 'Remember, even though you are not a part of the production process, which is mostly handled by computer and robot with the minimum of human intervention, – you Leisure People still have an important part to play in the Future Incorporated. By claiming your welfare tokens each week and spending them in

your energy meters and vend units you help to create
that all important cash flow in a credit oriented society
...'

Blah blah and blopdebloo. Nobody understood that
shit. Not even Calvin Gold.

The Welfare Woman looked at Davis a long time.
She thought she remembered him. If she did he'd sure
deteriorated. Her eyes were plate glass in a perfect
plastic face, moulded into a neat shape, smoothed at
the edges, paint to hide the surface defects. Lathe
turned legs, breasts pumped with compressed air. Her
uniform fitted like an aluminium shell.

She scanned the emaciated face, the nearly waist
long matted hair. Well, it could be worse. On Syndi-
cated Satellite News this morning – in the Beltburg –
twenty miles south of the Cadiz Stack, they'd got
leprosy breaking out. But that was Europe for you.

'Just one moment, sir,' she said. Better do a records
check. This guy could be a sub-leisure unclassified with
a stolen number or even –

She flipped his number through the records
machine. Oh dear. It was really too bad.

'Young man,' she said. Her voice was carefully
modulated to project the right emotions – official dis-
approval, official concern.

'You've missed two appointments! All this time your
allocations have been waiting for you. You really
should come in to claim them Mr Davis. All that food
you've wasted, and of course the cashflow! Well it's too
late now. You'd better catch up as soon as you can.'

She glanced down at the checklist on Davis' registra-
tion form.

ATTITUDE:

Hostile ☐ Friendly ☐ Wise guy ☐ Apathetic ✔

MENTALITY:

High ☐ Low ☐ Defective ☐ Borderline ✔

There was no point in checking the rest of it. She looked back at Davis, her face calm and businesslike – her eyes hopeless.

'Here's your allocation Mr Davis. Please try to keep track of time. This isn't even your day you know.'

Davis walked slowly. 'This isn't even your day you know.' That echoed in his mind. This isn't even my lifetime.

Out there somewhere there was a world that was a glittering crystal. Someplace where the surf broke on hard rocks and you could push your fingers into the warm sand and know that the sand had once been rocks too . . .

He kept walking, trying to imagine what was out there. But his mind cloudily filled with tons of empty brick and concrete and the stale smell of crumbling mortar – the hardness of iron fire escapes in dripping condensation rain that fell from the higher levels – the stickiness of blacktop stained with leaked acids and thin oil – oil seeped into his heels – choking acrid air opaque with heat from a million power plants.

Nothing out there but things in the distance. Couldn't see in his mind even as far as the peeling frame houses with parched lawns where tattered flags flew above the hulks of rusting cars. He saw the Mass Transit surface tunnels on Central Avenue, heard the rushing sound inside of the electromagnetic trains – like a giant was in there tearing up sheet metal with his bare hands. He feared now the people who might be in there. What kind of people? Saw cars in the distance. Clusters – dark sliding shapes beaming out heavy shafts of red and white light.

A Disposall garbage sack spilled out ahead of him across the sidewalk from the mouth of a dark alley. A hard shiny cannister gleamed in the trash. Automatically he stooped to scoop it up. Could be something he could use.

'Gelon Miracle Cleanse – shifts all stains however tough. Even shifts those biochemically bonded stains you couldn't shift before. Manufactured by Fresno

Genetic Engineering Co. Fresno Calif. 17478. US Health and Safety Dept. warning: Skin contact causes cancer in rats and mice. Wear protective clothing. LD50 Human Adults 0.7 liters/1.23 pints.'

'Hey don't fool around with that! That stuff is poison, man!'

Shocked at the loudness of his own voice echoing under the vast bulk of the city, reverberating around the desolation of dense tons of concrete, glass and brick – hardness of iron fire escapes – oil stained black top –

Then his voice was drowned in a thunder of weapons and running feet. Sudden movement down the alley. He saw snout faces. Jesus! FTPA troopers – gas masks! Acrid smell choking his nostrils. Gas! Something bounced past him hard and ricochetted through a plate glass window. Rubber bullets! UAP Weapons. Then gunfire, real hard and loud. He cowered into a doorway and pulled his coat over his head. Troopers rushed out of the alley into the street. They fanned out, and started running away across the parking lot opposite.

A crunch of caterpillar tracks on blacktop. Clatter of booted feet. A military half-track came out of the parking lot with FTPA troopers cling to the sides on footplates and grab handles. The half-track accelerated away up the street, exhaust billowing from an olive drab stack.

Silence. Davis eased out of the doorway. Down the alley again he peeked.

A huge mound of uncollected Disposall sacks had crashed down onto the floor of the alley. Some were split open by the impact. A pack of stray cats – their eyes bright and glazed in the darkness stared back at him like so many pairs of mirror shades. As he pushed into the alley the cats jeeped up over the sacks and away with a chorus of high pitched yowls. Something was stirring in the garbage, feebly among the sacks.

Davis pulled his T-shirt over his face. The stench of gas put acrid fire in his lungs, rancid, cruel and thick. He could feel his sinuses beginning to freeze as tears ran from his eyes. He pulled one of the bulging sacks aside. An old man – to Davis he looked old – maybe 40 years old, was lying in the garbage. The upper part of his body was naked. His face bore traces of smeared makeup – the face of a clown. Ripped and dirty, a pair of baggy pants clung around his legs. The face was greenish under the makeup. Lungs too full of gas.

'Prankster,' Davis said, smiling through chemical tears. 'Real live one – but not for long.'

Davis could sense the old man's death circling around his head. It was cold and long and white. Under the stench of gas he could imagine the smell – the sweet choking smell of organs soon to rot inside the flesh sack.

The old man raised up on one elbow. Held out his hand. He held a long plastic block covered in buttons, switches and mini VDUs. One end of the block terminated in a long cone like tube. Insect probiscus. Probe.

'Here kid,' the man said. 'Control this.'

Davis took the object from the dying man's hand.

'Give it to my partners ...' The old man's eyes burned a pale flame. 'Lissen kid – Do you believe in Christ? ...'

The fuel ran out.

The smell of death. The chemicals and bio equipment still warm to Davis' touch but already on the rot. The smell thick, nauseous. Death was coming stone flesh rigid white.

Something turned on a light for Davis, looking down at the object. He didn't know exactly but ... maybe he could use it. But like very very heavy. Oh boy what a mess! Maybe I can use if I know what it is – Pranksters – oh my god!

The flechette flashed past Davis' ear as he stepped from the alley.

'Unngh!'

He gasped in pain and shock. Half an inch closer and his ear would have been off. A car had drawn up silently across the mouth of the alley.

'*Que pasa hombre?*' a soft voice said.

A man in a baggy jacket and baggy pants – a big red nose and bald head with a silly thatch of hair over his ears held the flechette gun. He held out a gloved white hand towards Davis then groaned and slumped back against the side of the car. Blood stained the jacket shoulder darkly.

'Goin dizzy,' the man said in English. 'Mothafucker, you better drive.'

Davis stood, staring helplessly. Clutching the probe.

'Get in the car man, and drive.'

The voice was soft but very urgent. The Prankster motioned with the gun.

'Put that thing in the back seat.'

Davis did as he was told, dumping the object. He got in the driver's seat. The Prankster got in behind him.

'Now drive' the man said.

Occasionally Davis looked up. The man had removed the clown's disguise from his head. He had a dark sad bearded Latin face with staring hollow eyes. The face was lopsided with pain and shock.

He had taken the mask off to pass unnoticed as the car cruised through the city. Seeing his face Davis knew, for him meant recruitment or extinction. Very very heavy. Pretty soon he was going to panic.

The Prankster directed him out of the Black Hole in a wide loop. No road blocks. Must have moved too fast. Then they were heading steadily north, out of the 45kph zone – 65kph zone – soon they were cruising Level 2 on the freeway at 110.

So far north. Farther than Davis had ever been. Then they glimpsed daylight. Nearly blinded by the astonishing brilliant glare, Davis drove on. Sometimes gunships passed overhead. Security vehicles flashed past on the inbound lanes. Davis kept going. The Prankster sat behind him, the flechette gun held at his head. Sometimes the Prankster groaned. Otherwise he said nothing, but to direct Davis through an interchange or merge.

They came off the freeway as the Stack began to thin out. He sensed that the Prankster was searching, looking for something. Maybe a parked car, or a sign – something left in a window that would mean nothing to anyone else but would tell him that his cell were there. The city looked desolate. Nothing moved but their car. They roamed past sidewalks of emptiness, parking lots filled with acres of time. Faded pink buildings, faded brown buildings. Empty brick shells. And in the warm sunlight, saw beams of light reflected on old neon signs of the twentieth century that didn't shine anymore. Saw rats in packs among the empty trash cans spilled. Saw skeletons of hookers on street corners, whose tricks were ghosts. Boarded up stores. Bars run dry. Sign boards and route indicators flickered in his mind, but he didn't follow them. Only the Prankster's soft words behind the barrel of the flechette gun.

'Cut over,' the Prankster said. 'Nobody here. Cut over onto Highway One.'

They'd soon be clear of the Stack now – on the coast highway. First time Davis had seen God's good country since he'd worked at Nuke 17.

The girl rose early. She didn't have to, but she liked to. The kids were at summer camp. Her husband was in Minnesota. He was never coming back – except maybe to be friendly when he happened to be in town. It was Thursday. The last day of the working week. At 1.30 she would be through. She showered quickly, fixed her hair and dressed.

She switched on the screens, pushed buttons to arrange what input she wanted to record for later from the business, communications and entertainment channels, then she scanned the video mail while she fixed breakfast from Natural diet food. ('Natural' is a division of US Food.)

She had to make a trip – a face to face job. Bobby Kennedy, lead singer of the Indiana Boys School was in town and she couldn't interview him by remote screen. She had to get with this, make it real. The viewers had to see her and Bobby together, in the same studio, the same room. He was said to be like – WILD! She had to know why it had taken him until he was sixty-five to make it. Was it to do with 'Age Oriented Rock'? And how come he appealed to younger kids too. She had to know why he had himself shot at the end of his act and why one night it might not be blanks – it just might be for real. Was he merely trying to shock? Or really say something valid to Young America – all those kids out there from fifteen to fifty. She could figure all that out screen to screen, but the kids would want to see a face to face. She had to go downtown. In California City.

She set the laser operated Securi Eye precinct linked scanner as she closed the front door of the little stucco house. Checked all the double locks. She got into her US Automobiles Electrondrift car, eased forward the joystick, and headed out.

Neurosis set in as she glided in lane. Anxiety – a sense of meaninglessness, doubt. Fifteen years in journalism, and where was she? Three kids and four broken marriages. A crazy career in a crazy business. What did it mean? As she nose-dived towards despair, she felt a little surge effect in her temples. Preset one way Mood Monitor implants had begun to re-order her brain chemistry. She felt a little glow of joy. Began to think about her weekend job as checkout girl in the neighbourhood supermarket.

She didn't have to do it. She had all the credit she needed, and the supermarket was stock and credit automated from cold store to computerised robot till. But it was so much fun to work. So much fun to do one of those old timey jobs. Part of her recreation. Besides, it made her feel so useful, and all of her friends would be there, working their leisure time jobs or just fun shopping. Maybe she'd find out at last if Sylvia was really dating a dolphin, or if it was just another hype.

The implants were doing their job now. She felt she was so lucky, so blessed to be A1 classified. Maybe one day she would be Super Rich. She said a little prayer of thanks to Aphrodite – her ruling deity she had contacted through her spirit teacher at the Bixby Canyon Neo Pagan Vacation Complex And Eclectic Church. She said a little prayer of thanks to Jesus and Buddha too. Tonight she had a dinner date. She would dress in rags she had bought from the Po' Folks Store and make up her face to look haggard. It was the latest thing.

Davis took the coast highway for 30ks with a gun at his head. The freeway was silent except for the distant roar of inter urban magnetic trains rushing in the Mass Transit surface tunnels that ran along the median line. Davis and the Prankster were alone with the seagulls and the sea, the emptiness of distant cliffs, the ghost of pacific fog and the sharp tang of salt breeze.

A light flickered on the dashboard. 'You have ten kilometres left before recharge,' a soft feminine voice said. The car was old, circuits were breaking down. The voice was fuzzy at the edges. The car was an old US Autos Powaglider with the eight powerful batteries that gave you 400 kilometres cruising for the price of a litre of gas. Now the batteries needed recharging. Soon. There wasn't a re-energiser station anywhere in sight.

A car appeared as a speck up ahead.

'Get with it,' the Prankster said, his soft voice now a harsh weak whisper. 'We're gonna hijack that car.'

Davis felt the flechette gun brush his hair as he accelerated.

It hadn't been such a good day after all. The Mood Monitor implants grooved a cosy sad/happy self comforting mood. Never mind baby – more fish in the sea. That type of feel. Bobby Kennedy had split back to Florida. Decided California was a drag. Should have run a screen to screen while he was still there. Still never mind lil' baby, never mind.

The girl turned off into a narrow canyon road. Didn't notice the old car following her.

Clean low-rise apartments on the skyline, built from

stucco, plastic, neocrete, aluminium, glass. Doors of redwood – pretty, neat lawns. Davis had only seen these type of places on commercials before. But this was real. Beautiful homes. He could smell that good credit everywhere.

'You are entering Topengua Canyon,' the car dashboard said. 'Luxury residential. 35k zone. Please think of others and reduce your speed.'

'Force her over now – or the scanners are gonna range us,' the prankster said.

Davis speeded up. Pulled out level with the girl's car.

The electronic voice squelched with only a vestige left of femininity.

'IMPACT IMMINENT!'

Her assignment with Senator Gold completed, Yuki Yamamoto made quick use of the Senator's bathroom, briskly brushing her teeth and rinsing with Peptocin. (Peptocin gives fresh breath, Peptocin doesn't give medicine breath.)

Then donning her harlequinesque top and baggy pants she skipped smartly down to her little Toyota car.

Her outwardly calm, implacable appearance – the perfect mask. Inside, her emotions seethed. That fish-eyed, long-nosed barbarian bastard, was one thought. But more urgent – I hope my message got through. Must get down there and find out. This is the closest we've been to losing it.

She came down out of the mountains of Big Sur, past hundreds of surging sports cars. At a safe undetectable distance she rendezvoused, with two members of her cell. They were waiting in a scenic overlook in a battered camper van.

Their faces were blank, desperate.

'We've lost contact. We think that a cell was wiped out in the Black Hole. Our monitoring tells us that they've just set up roadblocks, which means the FTPA don't have it either.'

'It's serious,' she said. 'Shadow Command are on their way.' And as she spoke a huge supersonic jetliner painted olive drab hurtled overhead towards Los Angeles International, California City's second largest airport.

'That could be them,' Yuki said. 'Well we have no choice. We must head back into Concentration – I mean California City.'

The truck sped south.

'Wait – I'm reading something! A bleep – 2k radius. Topengua Canyon!'

Davis cut in ahead of the girl's car. They stopped in a squeal of brakes and dust.

On top of the hill a hard eye in black anodized lens holder recorded everything.

Davis and the girl hit dirt together.

'What he hell do you think you're . . .'

The mood monitor implants were getting slightly warm, allowing a 'justified outburst' programme.

'Lady, we're in big trouble' Davis said. He looked around for the barrel of the flechette gun.

It wasn't there.

The Prankster lay in the road, still and silent.

'Hold it, please hold it,' Davis said to the now scared girl. The Mood Monitor implants were working overtime. Quite without warning, they ceased to function. She stayed scared.

Davis was surprised at the strength of his own voice. This was the first time in like – light years – anything had happened to him and somehow, he was getting with it.

The girl stayed where she was, trembling inside her Senslon pants and 'Barelook' blouse.

Davis turned the Prankster over, and pulled his loose jacket open. He was no medic, but he could tell a bad one. The poor guy must have stopped a high velocity bullet a few inches below the shoulder at close range. He had all but bled to death in the back of the car. Getting out onto the road had taken the last of him.

'Dead.' Davis looked up from the Prankster's body.

Vehicles approached from both directions. Over the

hill ahead, two armoured half tracks like the ones he had seen in the Stack. Up the road behind the two stalled cars, a battered camper van. The camper screeched to a halt.

Overhead a huge helicopter clattered into view. From it a vast klaxon voice blared, but it was too distorted to be heard clearly.

Pure instinct snapped Davis into action. Grabbing the girl's hand he began to run across country, away from the road. She stumbled after him finally breaking into a run as three figures emerged from the camper with long slim shoulder-mounted tubes held aloft.

Three puffs of flame.

Davis pulled the girl down behind a bank of sand. Where the two half tracks had stood were two blazing balls of flame. Twisting and clattering the gunship was plummeting earthward streaming smoke and fire. Then it exploded in midair.

Two of the three figures were already in motion racing towards the cars. Davis held the girl down in the sand. They don't have time to look for us Davis thought, that's the only thing that will save us.

The figures raced back towards the van, one of them waving a short black object in the air. As they climbed aboard the van it took off like a supercharged dragster.

Davis and the girl stood up slowly, staring open mouthed at the blazing hunks of metal littering the canyon floor.

'Wow! Ground to air missiles' Davis said. 'All right!'

'Hey,' The girl was looking up at him full of apprehension. 'You aren't a Prankster are you?'

'No, not personally,' Davis said. 'But like – I hang out wit 'em you know? Sometimes they use me as a wheel man.'

'Hey!' the girl said again, looking up at him. After years of electronic medication her real feelings were gradually returning. 'Far out!'

Davis shrugged and kicked at the sand. Ran his fingers through his hair. He laughed suddenly.

'Could you give me a ride someplace?'

'Sure,' the girl said grinning cheerfully. 'I'd be happy to.'

At the scenic overlook, Yuki Yamamoto pushed the Probe into a brown paper sack and locked it in the trunk of her car.

'You better move fast,' she told her partners. 'When you went down to the car those scanners must have took a good look at you.'

The two men grinned desperately and patted their SMGs.

'We'll pull a few tricks before we go,' they said. 'Maybe we'll tip on up to Cal Gold's house.'

'Don't be stupid. You'll never make it,' Yuki said. 'Either way, don't get taken alive. At least not while I have the Probe.'

'You can depend on that,' they said.

Yuki drove slowly towards California City. The communications centres in her body alive with messages. Information exchange flickered rapidly back and forth through the Prankster cells.

Slowly, six facts emerged.

1) She was clean.

2) Shadow command had let all hell loose in the Black Hole. Two Green Echelon troopers had been shot by a gun happy LAPD cop (female) and now two Blue Echelon phalanxes were under siege in an abandoned cinema, penned in by three hundred members of the Eldorados, California City's toughest black gang.

3) Chief Cruthers was near to apoplexy, and refusing to direct FTPA troops or Security to assist the beleagured Shadow Command people a) because they had moved in without his permission (his jurisdiction wasn't jack shit to them just as Cal Gold had predicted). b) He was black too, and this time skin was heavier than duty. c) The doggone Probe was still missing.

4) The bazooka shoot out at Topengua Canyon had clouded the issue brilliantly (!) The FTPA vehicles had been there searching for South American terrorists

believed to be held up in that plush residential neighbourhood. They were now searching for a man and a girl (white, caucasian) believed to be members of the gang. The presence of a dead Prankster only confirmed their suspicions that terrorist gangs were interlinked world wide.

5) That despite Yuki's calming ministrations earlier that morning, Cal Gold was also now near to apoplexy. But Yuki would not be re-engaged immediately by the disquieted senator, as his wife had curtailed her fur buying trip and was even now winging her way south and west in a US Airlines personal luxury class jet.

6) A European Airways flight (no XYZ 123) was due to leave California City's InterWorld Rooftop Sky Port at 8.30 that evening. Three members of the cabin staff aboard that plane were also members of a Prankster cell. The two other members of the cell were ground crew servicing Euro Airways flights out of said skyport.

Yuki smiled happily. She thought about the parcel in the trunk of her car and remembered the childrens' party game she had played when she first came to the USA. 'Unwrap it – and pass it along!' The object was about to leave America. Hidden once more in a secret web of people.

Davis had forgotten how good a shower felt. Even that experience had been erotic. Now, beautiful soft sheets too.

For the third time that evening, the girl's hips were pushing up at him with an urgent passion that matched his own hungry thrusts. She'd forgotten all about her dinner date. He moved his mouth from hers for a moment and laying his head on her shoulder allowed himself a huge glorious triumphant smile as through the blazing currents of sexual delight coursing around in his brain words faintly echoed,

'This isn't even your day you know.'

A heavy white fog had blown in from the Pacific. The Philippino boy had lit a big driftwood fire on top of the breeze blocks built out from the wall of the sundeck. The fog was chilly and mysterious. Yakut ghosts stalked in it whispering legends of the ocean and the spirits of the other world.

Calvin Gold shivered as he sat by the fire. Not because of the Yakut ghosts. Because he was cold. Larry Hart had been right about California.

Goddammit! This morning that motherfucking thing wasn't but a cunt's hair away! And now the FTPA and those Shadow Command cocksuckers had slapped dogie's doos all over the cow byre!

He cursed again and reached for the Wild Turkey. He'd spent years trying to lose that old Texas way of talking – smooth his voice out into well modulated Walter Cronkite-isms. But under stress and with a little juice inside him, he always reverted.

Now he wished he could call that little bang-tailed nip back again. Boy, she could suck the chrome off a trailer hitch! But not even that would have taken his mind off the Probe. They've lost it! Those fools have lost it!

Lights below on the road moving westward. Probably Priscilla's limousine. Aw fuckit!

Lights in the sky moving eastward. European Airways flight No XYZ 123 out of California City's Inter World SkyPort. Calvin Gold would never know what those lights actually signified to him.

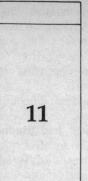

**11**

*'If the individual were no longer
compelled to prove himself on the
market, as a free economic subject,
the disappearance of this kind of
freedom would be one of the greatest
achievements of civilization.'*
HERBERT MARCUSE

The television set above the bar flickered dimly. Three
political commentators were discussing the policies
being bandied about in the forthcoming last stage of
the CENTERCOM elections.

Moncef Leclerc watched moodily as he sipped a
Paraquet. He was on his way home and, as he usually
did, he had stopped in at his favourite bar/restaurant
'Le Coq Sportif' for a couple of quick ones. Attitude
adjustment. His wife would be waiting when he got
home, and the kids. He preferred to feel mellow when
he met them. He was of mixed French and Algerian
parentage. *'Pied Noir'* some people called him. He lived
in the Marseilles Stack, which was connected by a vast
suburban sprawl to La Ville Périphique, the linear city
which stretched from Tashkent to Madrid. His apartment had an atmosphere conditioned bubble pack
garden, and on weekends he drove out to *'Le Parc
Naturel'* a conserved region of coast, which still had
sandy beaches and pines.

He couldn't make up his mind about the CENTER-
COM elections. *'Il de put!'* he murmured as he stared at
the screen, watching the talking heads.

'. . . of course CENTERCOM allows for local government at national level and from these governments the

CENTERCOM committee is elected. And from the Committee, the president chair person is elected. And I think we'll see a lot of votes in the western nations going to Calvin Gold – the strong man with the tough policies ...'

Moncef stared into the pale green depths of his Paraquet.

'From the Committee the President Chair Person is elected.'

If only it were that simple. Moncef had studied politics. At the moment, he worked in an electronics factory operated by GALCOM, but his real wish was to study politics further at university, and one day perhaps became an academic. He was only twenty-eight years old.

The ground structure of CENTERCOM had been based on the ideas of the influential French political thinker Simone Lautrec, a leading theorist in the revolution that had lead to the complete rethinking of politics in the Age of Information.

She began at ground level with '*la nation radio-phonique*' As she wrote in 'Le Système Nouvelle' – '*la radio montre comme Dick Tracy est arrivé!*'

Late twentieth-century satellite communications technology had made the dearest wish of human kind – the Dick Tracy style wristwatch radio or '*radio montre*' – a reality. Thus, '*les populations radiophoniques*' could ballot from any street corner, armchair or automobile in the world – straight into the vast banks of bussed computers that registered their votes.

They voted initially for two candidates – a leading national politician in the local government of their own country, and for a member of '*Les Etats Industriels*' (ie a member of one of the vast committees – in turn voted for by shop floor industrial workers) that ran the huge international publicly owned combines such as GALCOM and SCICOM. That was Phase One. Phase two ... but Moncef was temporarily distracted from his inner musings.

At a table across from the bar a couple had started

arguing. Snatches of their conversation drifted across mingled with the noise of the television.

'Madame Feng? *Merde! Quelle coutre!* A hard-line Chinese Communist in disguise! Our own candidate Yves Panassier would have restored true democracy to world government but the fools never voted for him. Now look at our choice! Two Americans – one a crypto fascist. The other a starry-eyed futurist with a baboon's grip on reality! Or Amalrik, the gloomy Russian bear. An ex-dissident with a ridiculous fawning attitude to everything Western!'

'No!' The other – a girl – rejoined loudly 'You misunderstand Madame Feng. She wants to bring the benefits of the People's Revolution to the whole world! By this means she can do it. Look at the "barefoot doctor" scheme she has started in the worst areas of Europe's Stacks!'

Her companion, a young man, responded with another volatile denunciation.

'No! CENTERCOM has perpetuated the worst features of the party political system! "The New System" was supposed to stop all that. Now look! People voted for Madame Feng in panic, after Calvin Gold's conservative excesses! Where is the much vaunted balance? *La Concorde Mutuelle*? The balance of forces? Party political ideas are getting stronger than the *Syndicats*!'

The girl began arguing back again. Moncef felt that the conversation had an air of theatrical artifice about it, as though it were a diversion. A small suitcase lay on the table between the two combatants. His attention wandered back to the television screen.

'President Goodrich of course has caused a lot of controversy with his "Basic Life Support Plan". This, as you know, is a device whereby everyone on the planet is given the equivalent of a decent living wage, regardless of their employment status.'

'No,' one of the other talking heads on the flickering screen said. 'I don't think he wants people to think of it as a wage. His view is that the bounty of the planet can now and should now be shared. This goes back to the fundamental roots of human society. Goodrich believes that modern technology and the SSET system are capable of making the earth a bountiful paradise again within our lifetime.'

The third talking head leaned forward.

'Madame Feng is claiming, is she not, that this idea will destroy the power of the proletariat.'

'Yes – while Calvin Gold who, oddly enough, introduced the "Leisure" system, says that it robs people of the incentive to excellence and achievement. Of course, it doesn't stop anyone from working – but it does prevent them from starving.'

'Quite. Amalrik on the other hand, would like to see a modification of the "Leisure" system devised by Gold.'

'It's certainly confusing.'

'Yes,' Moncef thought, and ordered another Paraquet from the neatly attired robot barman, who was really nothing more than a very sophisticated vending machine. At 7.30 when the restaurant began to fill up, he would be replaced by a human. The French family diners preferred it.

The final stage of the election was a pisscutter. After Les Etats Industrielles everyone voted again for a politician. I.E. someone elected to the CENTERCOM committee during the first round, and at the same time for a member of Les Administrateurs, who were in turn voted for by *Les Etats Industriels.* Les Administrateurs were essentially civil servants and experts drawn from the ranks of *Les Etats Industriels* and *La Population Radiophonique* in a different and preceeding and eternal round of elections.

By the time the computers had sorted out this complex melange into a list of single names, the third and final vote was left. The vote for *Le Chef* or *La Chefette.*

Moncef wanted to maintain his interest, but it got mentally exhausting. It was amusing to reflect that those not possessing or disdaining the wonderful wristwatch radios could always vote from their home communications centre – their privacy protected by a Diaphantus Lock.

Those who didn't own a home communications centre either, went to the local church hall and dropped pieces of paper marked

```
        X
    X       X
    X       X
```

into a sealed box. This had a strongly traditional ring to it, full of historical references.

The couple at the nearby table were still arguing. Suddenly one of them, the man, got up to leave. He picked up the suitcase. Moncef scratched his head. He was sure that the girl had brought it in. Nevertheless she said adieu, and swivelled her chair to get a better view of the television.

Moncef came to a decision. That he would vote for Goodrich. That 'Basic Life Support Plan' would enable him to quit the electronics factory and give the job to someone who really wanted it. Meanwhile he could continue his studies for as long as he wanted. *Viola! La Grande Libération!*

Much encouraged, he ordered another Paraquet. He'd have to talk his wife into it.

The man with the suitcase walked around the corner and got into a battered Citroen. Only then did he open the suitcase which Moncef had quite rightly noticed he did not bring with him. Inside – a small plastic oblong with a long nose cone. He smiled. Starting his engine he drove north. Soon the Probe would be in the UK.

*'He said, "I ain't 'shucking'.*
*It's cream puff work.*
*In fact 'Tender Dick',*
*    it's what you like to do best.*
*Want the run down?"'*


ICEBERG SLIM,
*Pimp – The Story of My Life*


The car nose dipped – into tunnel – shrieked among parked shells – came to rest beside elevator unit. Turner dragged the girl Ellene from his car, along the tunnel – into his home. Struggle with the dead weight. Struggle with the numbers. Then she lay snoring on the sofa, slightly askew – her green hat.

Turner felt pain. Harsh raw pain in the right side of his body. He had been a long time now without medication. And the girl had weighed some.

Checked her again. Still out cold. Snoring.

In the bathroom, the gun. Clean plastic. Loaded two of the pink ampules. Stellachlorazine A. One for the shot he had missed. Stella first. He was playing a game with his will. The gun pushed in, released, extracted. Dark red droplet amid black thigh hairs. Swapped the needle. Two pearly white ampules. Stellachlorazine B.

The pain went on, unceasing. He loaded again. One ampule only. Enketholin. Green spherical capsule. Four would be permissable but he played a game with his will. Had to stay clear headed. Because he had no idea what he was doing.

He stood up slowly, fastening his trousers. Keth creeping through him. Got to –

Mind flash white of hospitals. Suddenly no terror. Only colour. Blood red and bleeeeeeeech! of tissue in aluminium drainer. 'If we can restrict the implosion to one organ only – then a chance of a transplant.' Slice of scalpels. Surgeons replumbing layer after layer.

Scalpel dropped in tray clatter – surgeon turns from throbbing parts laid in flapped open cavities. Surgeon through to casualty, phone hand wiped on apron – 'Can you get me a liver – prime? Got an Implosion case here – my new customisin' project. When I get thru wit'im's gonna run like a Cadillac motor on a Model A frame!'

'Well – got an accident job. Might pull through but – he's sure got good liver – and he carries a donor's card.'

'Okay – let 'im slip but don't louse up that liver!'

Got to –

Turner came into the front room, his pain abating, stood by the door jamb staring at the sleeping girl.

No doubt about it. His sex drive was off. He saw a bio organism. A print from the mother plan. Built up right to carry and deliver children. Hm. Half and half makes one. Complete the circle. And in each a grain of the other. Hm. Not the product, but certainly the material.

Cool eyes soft surveyed the girl Ellene.

Turner checked her bag. Document. Keys. Tampons. Hang up. She may have the curse. This could take a long time. He felt no embarrassment. Bio function of the female species. Stellachlorazine. Detachment. She might. Cabinet. Bathroom. Old ones left by Tracy. Never got round to.

He added them to her supply, his mind scented with old thick incinerator smells of ladies toilets. Seven years in Security gets you to some funny places. Put all back in bag, except document. This might tell him where to start deprogramming.

'Test 25 – INK – Initiatory Achievement Program. LEVEL 4. Mental Flexibility – Alter Your Perception!'

He fetched a glass of water with ice in it. Placed it by the girl's limp hand on a low table. Then he slumped into an arm chair – bifocals on his nose. Always interesting to see the inside.

'Compare and contrast ... Give in your own words ... Refute the argument ... explain ... explore ... examine ... expand ... This part the easy part. 24hr examination ... due Weds. Today Tues. Lost deadline.

'"In creating the human brain, evolution has wildly overshot the mark," A. Koestler.

'In not more than 5000 words ...

'We speak with the right hand or dominant side of the brain. Music is on the left or non-dominant side.

'How far do you judge this fact to have affected the development of global culture during the past 2000 years?'

'We seek love, happiness fulfilment – and yet we do not yet know how the brain sees a straight line. How far do you judge this to be important in your life?'

'We each have 150,000 million nerve cells in the brain. You will have lost 256 by the time you read this sentence ...'

Turner scanned fast. Dead cells fell in dusty heaps in far corner of his weary skull, as his cerebral cortex glowed like a reactor going critical. Yes, she had been hard working in between stints in the cold and dreary car park.

Her opinion seemed to be that evolution was pre-programmed, unfolding. Interesting. That the brain's overcapacity indicated growth towards some magnificent destiny. That's why she joined INK – to get 150,000 million brain cells working before they too fell into dusty heaps.

Clever young woman this – see why she didn't opt for Leisure.

RECLAIM AND DEPROGRAM – simple mandate.

She seemed dedicated. If she stayed seven years she would graduate. Learn the first secret. Turner knew it already. It was his business to know it like he knew the mysterious 'awakening' at the 'first contact' with Ron Zultan, Epopt of the Holy Overmind Church was caused by a microdot in your cup of tea.

At fourteen years she'd learn the second secret. Then at twenty-one years she'd become a 'Seraph' – one of the fully fledged phytes. (Gk plant – denoting a vegetable organism.) With the other 40,000 Seraphs around the world – the mystic 40,000 she'd – light of light descending!' – adore 'THE KNOWLEDGE' – by television relay from the heart of INK's shrine at the Naptown headquarters – an ithyphallic uranium pillar enthroned on a lead plinth inside a glass pyramid. (Mythical linkup No 3.)

It was quiet. No psychic interference. Soft drone of dreams from brains in the bricks. Turner's eyes scanned on.

'. . . zombies and the sanitation man. Thus we see the final synthesis of . . . a green dragon in bay rum soup.

NO! That isn't right! WAKE!

He sat up and sipped cold coffee. Lit a cigarette.

The girl was still out. O.U.T. Out. That TrankPak must have been very strong.

Turner flipped the T.V. on. Tired mind. Chewing gum for the eyes. G.T.V. Global Television. Game show glitter. Teeth and red faces. Platignum and powder. Laquered brass from the band. Mohair suits and tight dresses. The folk in action.

'Your last question Sheila my love, – on the Bible – your chosen special subject – for 4000 credits or a new Electron Glider car –

'What did Eve say to Adam in the Garden of Eden?'

Pause

'Christ! That's a hard one!'

Turner got up and moved over to the inert form on the sofa cutting the T.V. off as he did so. He shook Ellene gently.

With a sudden jolt she came around.

Mumbling and confused she stared around her with fuzzed eyes.

Turner had the lamps dimmed low. Soft greenish light bathed the modern furniture. Beige designer three piece suite, simulated 'Weightless Couch' style. Cone-shaped glass-topped table. Kind of industrial abstract style. Orbital Homes shelving. The work station screens on rather dated 'high tech' frames. The one valuable old thing. An antique 1950s television stand. Curtains drawn across the display window, shutting out the yellow precinct lights and the dreams of the silent downs.

'Don't be afraid,' Turner said quietly. 'No one's going to hurt you.'

It sounded kind of hollow. And why should she believe?

She sat up and looked around, still a little dopy. She could panic any minute Turner thought. But maybe the Trankpak has fixed that. She pulled the wool hat from off her head and sat picking at it with confused frightened fingers. She smelled faintly of patchouli – funny how that remained popular with drop out types – and rain. Rain soaked clothes. Slept in. And campstyle living. Yeah. Definitely. Living in a squat. They were putting her through the hard way.

She looked as though she might stand up.

'Please,' Turner said. 'If you want to – it's okay.'

She stood and quickly folded again onto the imitation weightless couch. She dropped her hat in her lap and tugged distractedly at the imitation non-functional restraint straps on the arms of the couch.

She went rigid and pale.

'Oh my god' she said hoarsely. 'You're the De-programmer aren't you?'

'Yes,' Turner said coolly, aware of how his own words chilled the air.

'But why – what's happened to Roger? Have you hurt him?'

'Roger? Your team mate? No, he's okay. He's not my account. He's unhurt, believe me. We're experts.'

'But why – I shouldn't be here. Where are the others?'

'Deprogramming group? There isn't one. Just me. I shouldn't be doing this. I don't know why but, it's you versus me. I'm very sick. Got no time. Under medication. I have to sleep now. Long night. You know very tired. Drugs.

'There's a shower. Through there. Toilet. Everything. Food. You can't leave. Securilocked. You'd need the numbers. So's the bedroom. You can't get me. Smash the place up if you want to. I don't care. But it won't do any good. That window's toughened glass. My wife threw a vacuum cleaner at it once – it bounced off. Smacked her in the mouth. I'm going now. Goodnight.'

She sat staring. Her eyes frightened and blank.

He'd overdid. That had been one heavy Trankpak.

Late morning daylight when Turner woke. Air chilled by ventilation but still stuffy. He washed quickly at the sink in his room. Dressed casually. She had been alone a long time now. Probably eager to talk. To anyone. That was the plan. Phase I.

He released the locks and stepped into the front room. Would she be waiting with a kitchen knife? A broken high tech chair leg?

No. She sat cross-legged on the floor, anorak and wool hat both discarded. Piles of loose leaf A4 paper in front of her – in her hand, a pen. Vid screens buzzing. Books open. She looked tired. Drawn. And utterly absorbed. The exam was beside her. Finished, obviously, and though she could not now hand it in – she wasn't stopping. It was like these people had the key to some kind of natural benzedrine.

'Your name is Turner,' she said as he entered.

Okay, not hard to discover. She read from a list.

'This place is called Dodman's Ley. Dodman: Old English word meaning snail – quoted by Dickens in *David Copperfield*. "I'm a regular dodman I am," said Mr Peggotty, by which he meant snail, being an allusion to his being slow to go."

143

'Ley: Land temporarily under grass – pasture or enclosed field.

'Dodman's Ley: Primary meaning therefore – "Snail's Meadow" or – "Pasture Where the Snails Are". There is however a secondary, deeper, and far more fascinating meaning –

'Ley, secondary meaning: Prehistoric old straight track. Ley System: A web of lines thousands of years old crisscrossing the countryside linking the holy places and sites of antiquity. Mounds, old stones, wayside crosses, churches placed on pre-christian sites, legendary trees, moats and holy wells all standing in exact alignments that run for miles across the landscape over beacon hills to cairns and mountain peaks.

'The Dodman, secondary meaning: The prehistoric surveyor. The man who planned out the leys with two long sighting staves held out before his eyes – resembling the snail's twin horns. Hence, Dodman – "snail" Dodman – "surveyor".

'The route of one such old track – as you might expect runs right through this apartment house.'

Turner looked down at her papers – thought it was just an old name. Well! Notes headed 'Central Archeological Resource Library – Land Line Link No Arch o.93846/5 Pre.'

She motioned towards the screen of his work station vid.

Mapped out on it, Ordinance Survey grids.

'Look,' she said.

Bleeps appeared at relevant points. In a long straight line. Old church – Dodman's Ley Apartments – site of prehistoric camp – St George's Church in the centre of Burroughdown, a nearby village. She superimposed a modern map, justified to scale. The line continued through the premises of MiniComp Ltd – underneath on the history map you could see 'old tumuli' – now flattened to build some industry. On it went, strange eerie line, flickering and bleeping onto a geological map – Brendan's Tor – hillside, elevation 800 feet, at the edge of the downs, neural pathways of a silent dream.

'Understand?' she said.

Not altogether. Turner had not fully realised. Forgotten. Their minds worked like little information leeches. That was old Artie Grunewald's theory. Faced by an information deluge you assimilated it all. Got those 150,000 million brain cells working at optimum. Even after a short time, they started to get like it – and they desired to communicate. Wait a minute! Who's they? This was just a girl, a human girl – and what she had said – how interesting. He had to admit. Professional prejudice. Trapping him up. Mentality. Us. Them.

'You are Turner,' she said, as if recapitulating. 'Frank B. (Barrington) Turner.'

Yes. He blushed. Oh that middle name! Barrington. Some cult cricket hero his grandfather had admired years and years ago. Wanted to make the name a family tradition. Bastard.

Barry Turner. Eeeeeeeech! A nastly little salesman. F.B. Turner. Okay. Sinister anonymous policeman. Frank Turner. Better. Grim tough gumshoe deprogrammer.

'Turner. Your name probably has roots in the era immediately prior to the Industrial Revolution. Furniture manufacture. But more importantly –'

Christ! He should have taken her to a group. She was winning! Hands down, and he hadn't even fired a shot. Except for a few hours forced isolation while he slept.

'– you're suffering from Organ Implosion.'

His vid/comp controllers he noticed, were arrayed around her like an old time NATO field battery. She reached out and pressed buttons. His curriculum vitae and medical history flashed onto the screens.

Career ... ambitions ... less than totally successful ... fixation ... invasion ... clean fracture – healed completely ... fitness ... stress ... sexual profile ... latent ... hetero ... regression ...

'Turner,' she said smiling. 'I've got you down cold.'

Christ. He couldn't go on. She really worked fast. But how? Most of this stuff was under a Diaphantus lock!

145

'It's easy really.' She was smiling contentedly. 'Did you ever hear of Fermat's last theorem?'

'Yes,' he said, suddenly feeling very tired and very old. Oh yes. He knew about it. Anyone who had ever been involved in Security at managerial level knew about it. As did anyone who had a bank account, or followed politics. It started innocently enough. It ran something like this. In 200 B.C. the Greek mathematician Diaphantus, in his second book of arithmetic, had asked for a solution to the equation $x^2 + y^2 = a^2$ in whole numbers or simple fractions. It was obvious that the cunning old Greek had been thinking of Pythagoras, but for centuries ever since mathematicians had been asking – did the equation still hold true when the power (n) of x,y, and a is *greater* than 2?

She wasn't stopping for breath.

'As you probably know, the French mathematician Fermat claimed to have found a complete solution to this problem about 1637 but failed to write down his proofs. Fermat's Last Theorem. US mathematicians proved Fermat to be right for a range of powers up to n = 125,000. But the big question – the "ultimate" question you could say, was – did the Theorem hold good right up to infinity?

'Then – I don't really have to tell you this – in 1983 a cyberneticist called Arnold Arnold published a solution claiming total penetration of the problem. And shazam! Since then security coding and information have never been the same. It's what forced the governments of Russia and America to come to terms isn't it? The formation of CENTERCOM?'

'Yes.'

He knew.

IT BEGAN –

'Any equation $a^n = x^n + y^n$ where $x > y$ can be reduced by a factor 'w' so that

$$\frac{a^n}{w} = \frac{x^n}{w} + \frac{y^n}{w}$$

146

subject to the limit $_2 \left( \dfrac{x^n}{w} \right) > \left( \dfrac{x}{w} + I \right)^n$

if we let $(a - x)n$ be the value of ...'

Reaching for his cigarettes, he raced for the bottom line. Neurones frizzling. Dusty heaps mounding. Mind dazzling –

'... and that all values of $(a - x)$ irrespective of the values of n, a, x and y where $x > y$, must lie between 0 and 1.

'The majority of these values lie beyond present and possibly future computing ranges.'

Atoms, electrons, all floating and whirling in gray miasma, exhaled smoke from his cigarette. Numbers. Big numbers. Think of a number. For example – (2 to the power of 2,143,138,339) – I ... shown to be a prime ... contains 645 million digits in a base 10 notation. Might take centuries to print out. Too big at line 20. Jeez. It stuck in his memory, that pregnant last sentence in the study report. '... beyond present and possibly future computing ranges.'

Now those parameters had opened up. There were multi-dimensional vector techniques, general systems analytic computer program generators, ADs – Arnold Devices – and god knew what all. Just a few decades and mankind had gotten infinity under their fingertips at last, in the inconceivable variety of numbers between 0 and 1 hinted at by Fermat's Last Theorem. Gray flashing sheets of information gray flashing sheets of information gray flashing sheets of information gray flashing sheets of information gray flas

These techniques had reached to the heart of high level code breaking, leading to a new political rapprochement. No military secrets, no state secrets, no scientific secrets. No secret launch codes. MIRV ICBM VSOP RSVP PRICK all impotent forever in their silos until dismantled.

The SuperPowers were militarily paralysed. Only the terrorists and guerrillas now had a military option.

Small groups, operating cell systems world wide, kept the nerves of the mass populations of the globe on edge with the crackle of small arms fire and the blast of high explosive's livid flame, flitting elusively through the grey flashing sheets of information.

Other most complex codes cracked – like genetic codes. So bingo! Stellachlorazine A / Stellachlorazine B. Much vaunted cure for Organ Implosion. Only Turner wasn't feeling so well.

Cigarette smouldered between his fingers.

'All my personal information codes are under a Diaphantus Lock,' he said.

Ellene smiled.

'It's no match for a Mordell's Conjecture Probe.'

An infinity math fucker! But . . .

She was gesturing towards a small controller lying innocently amongst her own.

Turner frowned. Suddenly this was getting serious.

'No one outside of Centercom Shadow Command White Echelon can have one of those.'

'I do.'

She flipped a card onto the cone-shaped table.

'Ellene Novotny. OCTAVE. Mah Level Adept No. 1'

Turner felt like crying. But he had his manhood to think of. He got mad instead.

'For Christ's sake!'

Ellene continued smiling infuriatingly.

'If you invoke him one more time he may materialise,' she said.

Turner stared at her and back at the card and back at her. Yep. It was her all right. And of course she was older. Twenty-five years old it said here and now he could see that. Without the severe asexual hat – light brown hair softly falling; less the intense, drawn, neurotic teenager – more the rather tired young woman. Funny, should have made her look older. But – a nice jouba.

'Yes Mr Turner – we're investigating you!'

She pointed with her pencil as Turner's heart sank. Organ Implosion.

'That bastard EESP rap! All because I deprogrammed that kid with Real! You know by the time I was through he could associate the colour red with a sunset again instead of just blood? I've done six weeks suspension – no pay. Can't they ever forget?'

'Yes. I don't blame you Turner. You did a good job – but break the rules once and maybe – in your line of work – something inside starts collapsing. Like judgment. Ever read Fanon? No matter. He did some studies on what happens to people – professionals – who do bad things they don't really believe in.'

A little German in the accent now. He heard it. She was looking more like the product too. Somehow she'd found time to wash her hair, he realised. Made it look very soft. What's the function of hair? he thought. Not merely a sexual trigger. No. Like cooling fins? Some kind of brain case radiator?

'I didn't ... that ...'

Despite the keth he was raging on that raw spot.

She regarded him with a level stare.

'Turner, look what you did to me! You know Trank-paks produced by Personal Defense Mfg. are banned in France, Germany, Holland, Belgium, Sweden, Norway, Denmark and twenty-one states of America? Lucky I'm young and strong you know.'

'I'm sick. Short of time.'

He started coughing. Anger and despair choking him.

'Exactly. Turner, no one supervises you people on an attitude level. It's all business isn't it? Reclaim, deprogram, collect. Somebody has to be sure ...'

'So what about INK – was the whole thing rigged? I saw Fisher – at the office ...'

'Oh, I joined. But I can handle that. I have an I.Q. of two hundred forty-five. In any case that organisation is under perpetual surveillance. Two birds one stone eh? They have some heavy long-range objectives. Plans to canvas the Orbital Locations and so forth. Them in space we don't need. But that's classified.

'Boy are they full of crap! El segreto! Our researchers

know all about that. After seven years of mind busting study they take you to a little pyramid room and tell you $2+2 = 4$. Fourteen years $2\times2 = 4$. I mean – heavens! After that they take your calculator away – because the secrets have set you free! What's the third one after twenty-one years? I can tell you don't know it! I'll tell you – $2/3 \, \pi r^3$ – the volume of a sphere. Very mystical I must say. Of course to a recruit from the Stack it's like the lost knowledge of Atlantis.

'But they're dangerous people. They've gotten to me even after a few weeks.'

She gestured towards her pile of papers.

'But – I don't need deprogramming!'

Turner smiled bleakly and crushed out his cigarette. Lighting another he said,

'If the clutch adjustment of a petrol driven car should be set at 25mm ± 4mm at the pedal and the mechanic misread and set it at 25 thou instead, on the cable, at point of gearbox entry – what would be the differential in wear on a clutch plate with a total width of 12mm over 6,000 miles?'

She looked up frowning.

'I've no idea.'

'Shouldn't you try to find out and learn to play the violin at the same time?'

'No,' Her voice was a shade colder. 'I really don't want to.'

She paused, then suddenly looking up she opened the rough woollen hiking shirt deftly. No bra. The coarse material fell either side of two attractive breasts.

'Turner,' she said gently, 'would you like to make love?'

Weird business, breasts. Cones of flesh on front of woman. Obviously milk sacs. Pink/tan nipples. Designed so cleverly for. One way hydraulic valves for infant lactile ingestion by oral induction. Why/how sex trigger to adult male? Neural linkup to symbol system in male cortex? Who planned it?

He had an orgasm. Jennine – the giant holo girl on

the highway – billboard girl with magic vee who was just a pair of thighs – Ellene. But it was just a thought. A mere mental sensation. No pleasure. No physical sensation. Something was still there. But it had no meaning. He sat there whey-faced. Smoking his cigarette.

She buttoned her shirt.

'Just as I thought. Stellachlorazine. It's really got you.'

'They told me it would be like this,' he said abstractedly.

She stood. Tucked the shirt into her jeans and sat on the edge of the sofa.

'Turner, you're through as a deprogrammer. License revoked. Mental and physical health grounds. Mandated CENTERCOM. As of now. We're putting you out of business.'

She touched a button and it flashed on the screen. A picture of his license – red slash superimposed through it. Cancelled. Mandated CENTERCOM and date.

Oh boy. Goddam that Goodrich! No room for the little guy.

She continued relentlessly.

'You don't know why you brought me here instead of to a depro group? You bastard Turner! I know why. You were going to rape me! To prove to yourself you still could!'

'No – you've got it all wrong ... I wanted to help you ...'

Turner was no longer angry. Just desperate. It made no difference.

Who cared.

'I don't *like* those groups.' He'd never said it before, but he did hate them. So and so mindbenders like the cults themselves.

'Actually, I believe you.' Her tone was quieter now. 'But there could have been a subconscious sexual intent trace.'

'Trace! Dammit! Sometimes I think I really loved her. We could have worked harder. ...'

151

'How were you going to do it?'

'What?'

'Deprogram me.'

A hint of humour? Probably not. Bad taste to smile.

'Still don't really know. It sounds silly but – reason with you. Try to show you that knowledge is good but compulsion is bad. Einstein is good. Graeme Fisher is a shit bag. Stuff like that. Reason seems to be a very neglected value today.'

'Agreed. But you know what depro groups do. They chant either side of your head. They play strobe lights on the wall. They don't let you sleep. They show you movies. They guilt trip you with photos of your family. You didn't plan to do any of that?'

'No. Not solo. How could I?'

'Tapes. I don't know. What are these straps for on the sofa?'

'They don't work. It's to make it look like a weight-less couch in a space shuttle. Latest thing. Or so my wife thought.'

'Next question. Surface level. Why? Do I remind you of someone?'

'Yes.'

'Who?'

'The daughter I never had.'

'Oh God! You tough types are always and without exception so sentimental. You haven't been drinking have you?'

'No.'

'Do you know why you have Organ Implosion?'

'It's because it's a virus – nature's way? I don't know.'

'I sus you at Mah level. It's because of all this. Your whole way of life. Some men would have become cruel and vindictive by now. Instead some part of you wants out. Just like brother Tony.'

'How did . . .? Oh I forgot. Fermat's Last Theorem.'

'Turner, do you want to get better? Because if you do, I can help you.'

Turner buried his head in his hands. Who could say?

Maybe without keth he would have broken down completely.

'You see it's on all the records. You're through with this career. You may as well start looking after yourself. My mission is over, but for some reason I'd like to help you. OCTAVE have a base on Cipola – you know, the Orbital Location. They run a research programme there – 'Pyschometric Healing – the PMH Programme.' They're trying to find the natural repair centre that we know must exist inside each and every one of us. They treat the whole person there – body mind and soul. No need yet to quit your medication. So far the success rate has been 100 per cent. Your case is a very interesting one. I could get you on the programme. You want me to try it?'

Turner felt the temptation then to give in. It was all fixed up. Everything was gone. Wife gone. Job gone. Health gone. Yes, a good excuse, Organ Implosion. Chronic sick. He could stop worrying. Medication junkie, drooling by a cold vid. Wait like Tony, for the last whisper. He could say it with a little hint of bitter pride – 'don't bother me, I've got Organ Implosion.' Hell – people dropped out. Why go on? Nice Exit Ashram waiting. Anything you want till you go. Dr Sheer's voice echoed.

'Why when today man can live ninety, a hundred, a hundred and thirty years!'

Something snapped again inside him. A new level borne higher on the doctor's angry voice. That's why the Exit Ashrams were so full – rebellion against the possibilities of life. No, Organ Implosion was no kind of meal ticket. It would kill him, sooner rather than later. No no no. He didn't want to die. Cipola – out there at L5. The vast darkness of space. Six white plastic-like cylinders of enormous size, rotating around a central hub. For some reason he'd always wanted to see it. Ever since they'd run those commercials on G.T.V. A pipe dream. Just like to see it. A futurists' city in full working order – before he died. If he died. No! Fight it. Live, live! He didn't trust Sheer – any doctor.

153

He didn't trust UniMed but – maybe – maybe this other thing will work. At least he had a chance. Best of both worlds. And a space flight! Chance to live for a while at an Orbital Location. That would be a smack in the eye for the Graeme Fishers of this life. Yes he said suddenly to himself – I want to live.

DATE: LOCM 727 – 2335 N
LOCATION: SPACE

*'It takes pretty people to make pretty music, and there ain't a pretty bastard in my band.'*

LESTER WILLIS YOUNG

Datsun's face split back in a tense mask. He stood immobile – shuddering slightly – fighting the sound with his mind.

Angela and Platinov crouched, cupping their ears with their hands. Then Morgan moved – pushed them. Back down Channel 1008 they ran. The noise struck a lower pitch, less decibels but just as dense. A minute passed, or appeared to pass, very slowly. Carefully they began to edge forward. The noise began to mount. At a bearable level they halted and instinctively looked up. Ahead of them, above the level of the trench top four pale towers arose from the surface of the rutted plain. Four tall spinning narrow waisted turrets. Four turrets of sound.

'Out!' Morgan yelled. 'Onto the surface!' He grabbed a rocket pack, shoved a foot into each shoulder strap, hit the igniter and clasping the cylindrical body of the pack firmly to his chest, he 'pogo jetted' to the top. Landing in a crumpled heap with the motor cut completely, lest it scorched his legs and feet he crawled from under the unit and stood groggily upright, his bruised body and wrenched muscles reminding him why the dashing, but sometimes fatal, practice of pogo jetting had been banned at Training School. In a few seconds the others joined him zooming sedately out of the trench and pirouetting gently down, cloudside surface, on retro, jet packs strapped 'firmly and securely over the mid shoulder area' as the EVA manual laid down.

Morgan's face grimaced, somewhere between sheepishness and pride. Then he gestured yonder with his least numb arm.

The turrets were many metres tall. The nearest one stood about a quarter mile distant. The others were spaced around it forming a rough quadrangle, maybe a quarter of a mile square.

Huge and shimmering they spun slowly reflecting many colours in the pools of soft light that surrounded the base of each tower like an ethereal moat. Colours – some vivid, some pale and opaque. Light fragments, colour washes – patterns – cubes – chains of colour – crystals of light. Sound so intense it could be seen.

They stood and stared at the turrets for a long time. Their perception expanded – adjusted – decoded.

Each turret had its own sound. Each turret spun its own colours in the soft pools of light. They sorted the turrets and gave each one a number: The nearest turret they called Tower No 1. Behind that, back left, Tower No 2. Back right, Tower No 3. Front right, Tower No 4. Then they gave each one a name.

They called Tower No 1 'The World' because all the sounds of life were there. Singing winds and crying beasts, rattling leaves, rushing water, clatter of stone, tramp of feet, shout of anger, moan of love – whisper of tyres on a highway – clicking spark of electricity – proto music of machines – explosion's boom – blended into a tall whirling tower of sound.

Tower No 2 they called 'The Band'. A million types of tonal organisation whirled and sang inside it. Cadence, dissonance, strange scales and astonishing chords, familiar as folksong, daring and free as jazz, broad and great as symphonic form, rhythmic and harmonically arcane as raga, primal as the beat of a single drum, haunting as the echo of a lost refrain at the edge of memory – it droned and cried and sang.

Tower No 3 they called 'The Lab'. Here the sound was layered. Essential sound waves. They watched them oscillate and interact, harmonising sinuously or looping jaggedly away from nodes of dissonance. Designs in sound.

Tower No 4 they called 'The Galactic Orchestra'. To stare at it, to listen to it, took the mind far away to the remotest boundaries of creation, into the static crackling through space – sounds of interstellar radio – sounds of pulsars pulsing – bleep on/bleep off – messages the ear received but the brain failed to decode.

Inside the quadrangle formed by the turrets the sounds from all four combined to form a dense sonic web. Here too colours danced and floated, dazzling, enchanting and bright.

Motioning to the others to stay back Morgan edged closer along the surface. This was the best thing he'd heard since Calvin Calhoun. He made about twelve feet. Somewhere near the top of No 1 a light, jagged like lightning, flashed. A vast mass of notes spun off the shoulders of the tower at blinding speed and shattered around his head like glass bullets. Morgan sprang back.

The sound decreased again. It hummed at the edge of the aural perception field. A sigh – a drone – a rattle – a scale – a noise – a pulse – a song. Their ears ached with the memory of piercing pain.

'Location?' Morgan queried Platinov – dizzily – still hardly able to hear his own voice. Plat quickly figured at the hover truck's computer keyboard.

'1008 – 2001 – 1117 – 1889L'

The base of each turret appeared to stand exactly on each of the four intersections they had to cross.

'Oh my God,' Platinov said. 'WE'RE BLOCKED!'

INTERJECT – ENTRY – ARCHIVE – REF:
Calhoun, Calvin:
Origin: Terra. Harlem, New York City, New York.

Occupation: Musician. Saxophone. First to
    synthesise work of Charlie Parker, John
    Coltrane, Bela Bartok and J.S. Bach
Albums: Include −
$E = MC^2$ and Gone!
Red Shift Blues
Mr C.C. meets the Moscow Philharmonic
The Cosmic Sound of Calvin Calhoun
Calvin Calhoun − A Saxophone in Space
Weightless!
Et al.
Present
Space/Time
Location: Jefferson Orbital Space City
Notes: Calhoun is Mah Religion Adept No 1


Hands in pockets, shoulders hunched, Morgan stared moodily at the others through bloodshot eyes. Occasionally he withdrew a hand to scratch his beard. Pushed hand back in pocket deeper.

'For Plat's system to work − we've got to go this way, right? Okay then somehow we have to shift or even destroy these towers. Man, I can't handle that. They're beautiful.'

'I agree with you Morgan,' Platinov said, 'But how else can we follow the diagram back to the ship?'

'Agreed. We have to get off this crummy cloud.'

'Morgan,' Angela said, 'I agree the towers are beautiful − but they are also potentially very dangerous. And they are in our way. You're the Organiser. What are we going to do?'

'Okay,' Morgan said. 'I know. I mean what if they were to turn up the volume now? I mean right now! Listen they ain't even cookin' − but if they get hot! Phew! We couldn't even jetpack far enough! My head is still ringing. Angela − don't that No 2 tower sound to you a little like Cal Calhoun?'

Angela grinned. 'Yeah I guess − every now and then. But his music is the work of a sweet serious beautiful gentle guy. As far as we know this is the work of a nut who is also a FINK!'

Datsun stood up suddenly from where he had been

sitting on the green tacky surface. He said –

'Physics and engineering put the towers there – somehow – however sophisticated. Physics and engineering must remove them.'

'Good thinking.' Morgan smiled his slow weary smile. 'Maybe if we could work at the base of a tower – knock it loose – it would spin off or disintegrate.'

'Whatever we do,' Angela said, 'ear protection is mandatory.'

'Right. Space suits. And helmets. Radio contact only from now on.'

Angela watched Morgan suiting up, then taking his first steps. He looked funny and lovable in a space suit. He lumbered funnily about with nowhere to put his hands, like a great white bear, his lean frame suddenly bulked by the suit, brown face showing through the visor, comically unhappy.

'But this don't mean we can get any closer,' Morgan was saying, his voice now a semi-personalised radio crackle, 'this is just in case a tower falls this way or they turn up or something. Okay? Plat – what can we rig up?'

Platinov who had quickly suited up was already hunting through a tool chest he had lugged from the hover truck. They could hear him cursing softly over helmet intercom.

'Junk! Garbage! Everything bar thing I want!'

Outside the suits they could hear like a swarm of bees – radio static – a musician tuning up – the muffled menace of the four turrets of sound.

'This,' Plat was saying, suddenly waving a piece of equipment in front of Morgan's visor and pointing, 'sonic lance – for taking samples where you can't use pick or laser or heat – certain types of rock etc. Want to try it?'

'Yes.'

'We'll need to amplify it.'

'Hover truck has P.A.'

'Speakers no good man. I need a *beam* – something focused.'

159

'Well can't you rewire the amplifier somehow – back into the lance? I give you my full and total blessing as temporary Organiser appointed on an *ad hoc* non-authoritarian co-ordinating basis only, by the Council – if there still is one – of the Seven Cities of Cipola, to tear up that hover truck sound system to hell and gone.'

'Morgan, watch your air consumption honey.' Angela reclined against the parked truck. 'We may need these suits for real if the atmos goes funny.'

Morgan lumbered over and sat down beside her. He said nothing.

Datsun and Platinov were hunched over on the other side of the truck. Plat was the mechanic. Datsun was the wrench monkey.

After a while the two could be seen helmet to helmet, busy over a heap of plastic and metal boxes, printed circuits, cables and gear. A solder gun fizzed and smoked. Datsun's gloved hand squeezed crimp pliers. Plat pushed and shoved and pried and poked.

Pretty soon weird loud noises began to emit from the probe of the sonic lance which lay nearby on the deck, hooked to a tangle of multi core wires. It bucked and kicked, and then lay still.

Platinov straightened, took his helmet off and mopped his brow. Helmet refitted, and Morgan heard his speakers fill with the sound of the Russian's voice.

'Okay Morgan – I think we got about 200 decibels here. This amplifier is weak you know for what we want and the lance really is only for small rocks – but maybe – who knows? We are only guessing anyway.'

'Let's do it,' Morgan said jumping awkwardly up, suit and gravity heavy. 'Everybody back!'

They turned the hover truck sideways between them and the towers and crouched behind it. Platinov cradled the lance on the forward bulkhead. Aimed at the four turrets of sound.

'Take a last look – take a last listen,' Platinov said. 'After this – anything.'

They looked and listened to the wonder and the

splendour of the astonishing, awkwardly situated towers. No 2 'The Band' had become prettier and more harmonious than ever. Much of the obvious dissonance had gone. It spun at mid-tempo emitting an impression – no more than that – yet heavy and subtle as fragrant perfume – of a melody endlessly fascinatingly perfect and sweet – the beckoning semi-audible harmonies of a vision or a dream.

'If I hit No 1 and No 3 maybe I can calculate a new way through.'

Platinov hesitated.

'You know I can't stand to damage "The Band". They play so beautifully.'

'It's a mirage Plat,' Morgan's voice grew harsh. 'Just some freakish magic Dralon is trying to whip on us. Pull the trigger.' No one was looking at him. They watched the towers. No one saw the sadness in his eyes.

Sound ripped out of the sonic lance, a high piercing dreadful shriek. It muffled out somewhere in the moat of light at the base of Tower No 1.

Nothing happened.

The tower whispered on. Sound of wind, lap of water, rattling leaves.

The intersection remained blocked. Platinov fired a few more times and then he quit.

'Look, I got adjustment to make. At this rate the gun will burn out. Who knows. Maybe something – perhaps a shock wave will build up at the base eh?'

'Yeah, maybe Plat.'

Morgan crouched, staring and listening. The turret was whispering singing softly all the sounds of the world. Behind it Tower No 2 'The Band', played on. That unbelievable, unbearable melody. Emotion circuits null program, Morgan told himself. This ain't no time to cry. And as his consciousness jetted downward back to Kath centre, away from Oth region, away from Mah level he thought of Dralon and hoped that one day Al Sharbasi would truly teach how to forgive. And as he gained control he noticed, and saw that Platinov had noticed too, up on one knee alert, a cable loom hanging forgotten from his gloved hand.

Tower No 2, behind the one they had fired the sonic lance at, had changed. The melody was still there, strong, hypnotic, and sweet as opium – but near the summit, dischord. Nothing atonal or far out. Just ugly. Out of tune. Wrong notes. A tiny imperfection, but the lovely tower was spoilt.

'Say what Plat?' – There was noise and static everywhere they realised, faint but really irritating, everything blurred – like the onset of deafness – Plat?'

'It's nothing we've done I don't think – Tower is exhibiting malfunction – I got to fix –'

'Plat?'

'I can't do it Morgan – when it's running right maybe I can disperse it –'

Plat back at the sonic lance now craning for an angle. The dischord altered – otherside of the melody now – louder, but smaller spread of wrong notes. But it was worse. The dissonance was worse.

Angela got Morgan head to head – Tell him to watch his air!' she shouted.

An hour passed. Platinov was frantic now, rushing from computer to gun and back again. The tower was out. Really really out. And as huge and intractable as ever.

'Plat – what in hell is going on here?'

Why me? Morgan thought. Why me – Organiser?

'I've got to get it right Morgan,' Platinov's radio voice insisted. 'This harmonic pattern is all wrong – here!' His gloved finger jabbed at a pattern on the VDU. 'I know what these towers are now, man. In a minute I get it right. Then we can pass through here. It's "cool" as you say Morgan. Don't worry.'

How many hours now? They had lost count. Datsun had pulled his helmet off. He gestured to Morgan to do the same.

Angela watched from her fish tank. Silent but for dischords and static. The two men gesticulated, argued. Shook their heads. Agreed.

162

Plat still buried in his work, oblivious. Aiming his gun. Triggering ever more varied and complex collections of frequencies towards the towers. Angela flicked on her radio. Listened in. Tower No 2 was running better. The chords were sweeter again. But now Tower No 3 was out. Way out. Crazy vibrations were running through 'The Lab'.

Someone was shaking her. Morgan. Bare head. Lift! he was gesturing, hands waving up. She pulled off her helmet.

'He's flipped, Morgan,' she said. Her voice after all that time in suit, penetratingly loud.

'I know. These towers have really gotten to him.'

'He doesn't want to disperse them – he wants to fix them back up. Isn't that what Datsun said?'

'Yes.'

'Can't you reason with him? – grab the gun?'

'You do it. It could happen to you.'

The central web between the towers was leaking. Fragments of weird sound were jittering, echoing and jangling across the surface of the eerie plain.

'Look Angie –' It had to be serious when Morgan called her that. Her mouth drooped in a sad smile.

'Datsun has figured another route. Longer, but he showed me the calculations. Ol' Plat ain't so dumb you know, his system works – but not this one – not any more. Check it out Channel L2014.

'Alternate channel . . .'

'Spare me the details Morgan. Let's pack the truck. Who will tell Schoenberg that playtime is over?'

'I've been through it with him. He's staying here.'

'No Morgan –'

'You want to use coercion? Plat is a big guy.'

'I thought Datsun was supposed to know some martial arts?'

'New System Constitution do state –'

'I don't care Morgan. We can't leave him here with this crazy quad. Where is your humanity?'

'You tell him.'

Angela found Platinov much quieted. Dreamy.

Totally absorbed. All the sounds were softer now but still so very wrong.

'Plat –'

He smiled. His helmet lay discarded by the sonic lance. He jotted reams of figures on the back of the printout that had originally issued from the computer inside the strange 'structure', that was now many intersections away.

'Just leave me the sound tools,' he said, like a formula he'd been through many times before. 'I got to stay here. I can't leave this mess. When the system run right you know – it's so PERFECT – so perfect. I understand it now. I can pass through this block when I fix it. I know that now. Join you at the ship, location Channel 4000 and Channel 3694L.'

He smiled and squeezed her hand.

'Remember – PCC to stay in touch. So long.'

DATE: 16.20 MARCH 30 2031 TCT
LOCATION: DODMAN'S LEY
DEVELOPMENT SUSSEX UK
WESTWORLD CCR 1010

*'Among real men, there has always been
one simple rule.
Never settle with words what you can
accomplish with a flamethrower.'*

BRUCE FEIRSTEIN

G.T.V. – Global television – grey metal television –
Local 409 – Channel 18. (Turner packs a small airline
bag.) War film on T.V. ending. *The Heroes*. Boots clomp-
ing. Tromping martial music. Deep male voices sing in
rough harmony – 'Ain't no sense in looking down, ain't
no discharge on the ground. Ain't no sense in looking
back, ain't gonna see no Cadillac.'

Turner looks up from his packing in time to see the
credits roll up.

1st Corpse – Mort Slayne

2nd Corpse – Ded Bodie

Dead Officer – John Kilt

Ellene sitting on the sofa speed reads a thick Reley-
onback book. A fat book 1,000 pages long, about an
orchestra in the Second World War. An Orchestra of
Nazi spies. The book is called *The Enigma Variation*.

G.T.V. GLOBAL TELEVISION – LOCAL 409 –
CHANNEL 18. WEATHER REPORT. BELT OF RADIA-
TION COMING IN FROM THE NORTH. LIGHT
BREEZE. NO RAIN. ETA CITY 2323. SHIELDS EFFECT
CITY LIMITS 1927.

'We'd better hurry,' Ellene said, snapping her book

shut with a thump, 'before those shields go up. The monorail to Limoges shuttle base leaves from the City Port at 2120.'

They daren't be late. The Cipolan temporary immigration papers Ellene had arranged for him by computer link would be waiting at the shuttle base. She had some pull. He had to hand her that. Definitely. But – hang up – potentially. There was one and only one flight they could catch.

Turner picked up his bag and cut the scanners on. Like you always did. Habit. (The fear all urban people felt.)

This time they were out there. Four men and a woman. Masked like harlequins. They stood pointing, questing, glancing under the grey arch of the parking lot tunnel, ready to approach. They carried SMGs and UAPWs. The leader cast his weaponed hand aloft. Halt! His screened shadow phased across the concrete like a menacing ghost.

Pranksters – no doubt about it. Why here? Random terror raid on the SuperRich? – like G.T.V. 40 every other day? New heights of cruelty? Sick jokes? What motive? No one really knew that. But – murder, extortion or both usually.

Turner backed instinctively away from the screen.

'Roger,' the girl said.

Turner spun around feeling as though the screen had burned his face.

'Roger? You mean the kid who was with you at the Fun House? Why? – those are Pranksters out there – nihilist terrorists – what –'

'He's there – look – the leader. The one on the left INK is a cover for Roger. He is a Prankster – his code name in the movement – Pagliachi. I should have warned you. I didn't think he would trace me here.'

'This is getting crazier and crazier,' Turner said. 'You OCTAVE – him Prankster. What's going on?'

'He was my supervision guide at INK. Each new member is assigned a team guide. Someone a little more experienced. OCTAVE warned me before

166

infiltrated INK, that the movement was being used as a Prankster cover – unknown to the INK hierarchy. They warned me it could be dangerous.'

Turner's eyes were glued to the scanner screen. Two of the figures had moved into the mouth of the tunnel. Like tumblers – one had mounted the shoulders of the other and stood there swaying precariously. The figure raised its right hand. A short cylinder in the hand. An atomised cloud of mist drifting upward. High in the roof of the tunnel the scanner's camera lens ran with black spray paint. Turner's screen became a bright particoloured mass of interference.

'Now we're blind,' he said.

Ellene's voice raced on.

'I was careful, but I used the probe to pick Diaphantus locks that INK put on what they call "Privileged Information". No access for the lower orders. Roger questioned me. I let slip something that only a seraph would know. I told him my high I.Q. made it possible for me to gain insight into the higher mysteries. He didn't believe me. And of course I realised that he was no ordinary Neophyte. He suspects I have the probe, and he wants it – badly. For the Pranksters.'

'Why should they want it?' Turner's voice was tense, urgent. He looked around for some kind of weapon. There was nothing. Ellene and Roger had copped his last Trankpak twenty-four hours earlier.

'Think about it. With an MCP they've got a potential in to every bank account in the world. Access to the silos even. Can you imagine? Unlimited finance. Unlimited terror. Unlimited chaos.'

'There's no way they can get in,' Turner said. 'These hinges are lirium.'

'No way we can get out either.'

'Well we can get help. Landline to the FTPA.'

'Turner don't kid yourself. They don't.'

The intercom beeped. Turner opened the mike.

'TURNER.' It was Roger speaking through a voice box built into his mask. So the voice was harsh, metallic, non-human. A deliberate technique the Pranksters used for instilling fear.

'We know you're in there.'

Even horror can have its moments of comedy, but Turner was too tense to smile. Somehow he had to stall. Turner stood still. Tranked. Doped. Sick. His mind blank of stalling ideas.

She was right. By the time Security or FTPA got there – they would be gonners anyway. NFG.

'Shadow Command,' he said.

'I can't – no way. You're right. I'm not supposed to have that Probe. Also I'd better admit, I stole it from Roger.'

More bad news, but Turner was past caring.

'What the hell *is* going on,' he muttered.

'One day I'll explain,' Ellene said, putting her hand on his arm.

'LET US IN Turner!' The voice was louder, harsher. Volume up.

'What if I don't? These doors are lirium hinged.'

It seemed real dumb to open the door right now. If anyone comes out now – from one of the other apartments – if they don't check their screens –

'Wipe out,' Ellene said, answering his question, reading his thoughts.

The intercom crackled.

'Turner – there's a nuclear landmine in the parking lot. Re-tune your scanner. See it?'

Turner scanned. Away from the painted out camera in the tunnel. He picked up the parking lot lens. He saw it. Small. You wouldn't notice it. Looked like a maintenance fitting of some kind. Except for the Code 1 Nuclear yellow paint. Clever. It was attached to a roof support with carbide steel hoops and padlocked bolts. Bastards. Lirium or no lirium. Forget it.

'Turner,' Ellene's face was very tense – white. Till now she had seemed so calm. Mah Adept. But young. 'We can't chance they won't use it. Sometimes you know – what they call Coco Beans – suicide squads –'

'Yes.' Then his mind started working. 'The Probe. We have to hide it.'

Ellene flipped on the intercom.

'Hold it Roger,' she said. 'I want to get dressed.'

Subtle intimacy in her voice. Stoned out like he was Turner scanned her. Detachment. Sussed. They have been lovers. Now she taunts him. Hint of control through sex. Ha ha. If he knew. Even if she was nude I couldn't. But – hm. Could use this. Use this. Resourceful young woman.

'OPEN IT!' Angry klaxon tone. Anyone step out now – Finito. Muerte gringo. Adios. i Voto a dios!

'Will he be able to recognise it exactly?'

'No.'

'Or be able to use it without a manual?'

'I doubt it.'

'Then pocket it. Give him that.'

Turner pointed to his Reclaim Contactor Control. High access. Multi channel. It looked similar. He hadn't noticed the MCP himself earlier that morning, lying among his stuff. Ellene put the MCP in her pocket and grabbed Turner's controller.

'Somehow we've just got to stall –'

'Yes.'

'Kick the other controllers under the sofa quickly, except the one I need to operate the house –'

Ellene moved fast.

Turner released the locks.

The door opened.

Turner could almost smell the danger. They stood in a semi circle. Under the masks you could tell. Young. Intelligent. Fanatical. Desperate.

'GIVE IT BACK – YOU THIEVING SLUT!'

Ellene did a good act. Buttoning her shirt as she handed Roger the phony probe, white faced – begging him to please go away.

Motioning with his gun he said 'SHUT UP!' like snapping through iron jaws.

'We haven't hurt you,' Turner said.

Roger snarled.

'You sentimental old bastard! You think I care about that! See, you and your poxy red die. You should have wasted me in the Stack when you grabbed this girl. Anyway you're already dead. Got you sussed. Organ Implosion.'

Ellene glanced at Turner. He said nothing.

Then something suprising happened. Roger motioned again with the gun, and the other Pranksters left. Melting out into the corridor and vanishing towards the parking lot.

'Switch on your scanner.'

Turner saw. They were leaving in an old petrol-driven Japanese car.

'SIT DOWN.'

They sat. On the edge of the sofa. Roger sat down in an armchair facing them. Pulled off his mask. Face drawn, intense, pale.

He laid down his gun. Box from his pocket.

'Don't try it,' he said. 'This remotes the landmine.'

He held the box in his left hand. The SMG was across his knees. The handle near his right hand.

'These are keys to the bolts.'

He showed them.

His manner became less menacing. A light came into his face – of fanatical saintly enthusiasm, which dimmed rapidly to a glint of low cunning.

'Listen. I rap – you sus.'

He was talking an arcane form of West World Street-speak, local to the Stack. Turner knew it. Too tense to talk normally perhaps – or sheer force of habit.

'I sus you play go do man – head Cipola.'

(I know what you're going to do. You're going to Cipola)

'How come?'

'Has to be. She lik 'ead witchew. Sorry for you guy. Wanna fix you up. Got to be OCTAVE. Got to be Cipola.'

(It has to be. She's met up with you. She feels sorry for you. She wants to help you. The only way is through OCTAVE, which means Cipola.)

Roger paused, then –

'You gotta take me with you when you go dat.'

Ellene said 'Noway Roger. We can't do that.'

'Lissen – or I blow you away. I know. Sus you, baby. Double agent! Make your head smart, Turner. She take this probe to OCTAVE – ON CIPOLA. BAD DEAL GOING DOWN IN THE HUB!'

Ellene turned white as a sheet.

Turner said 'Hold it!'

To Ellene, 'You told me – fixing my disease –'

'Yes. I meant it. I *can* do that –'

'What is the Hub?'

'Cipola 7. The central hub. No access. Sealed.'

'I thought they were all anarchists up there.'

'They are. But it's not as simple as you think. Deals. Treaties. Links to CENTERCOM Earthside. Something is going on in the Hub, and OCTAVE are worried. Space Industrial Services are involved, and CENTERCOM. Whatever it is OCTAVE are afraid it's not good. We have to know what it is. That's why I was asked to "requisition" the Probe.'

'Check this – I sus the Hub scam.' Roger was making an effort – speech becoming clearer. 'See I *know* what's going on in there. Got to check it. I need the Probe bad as they do. And I need clearance. Got to take me with you. Clear me through OCTAVE Personnel. I got a ticket here as Turner's doctor. I can qualify. INK. Doctor, Architect, Engineer – you name it.'

'Yeah?' Turner felt baffled. 'What if I shop you?'

'Go ahead you 'ol cunt – shop me.'

Roger sneered. Motioned towards the screens and keyboards.

'You'll shoot me – blow the place up.'

'No – go on ahead. Do it.'

Cleared of the sneer his face was blank, chilling, insolent. Turner touched the keyboard. Roger nodded – 'Go ahead.' Turner fed in codes. Personal ID to Security Central.

F.B. Turner. Security. Ex B5422. Reclaim Inc. Citizen's Report.

His card showed on the screen.

CANCELLED.

Mandated 'CENTERCOM' and date.

He tried again – through regional.

F.B. TURNER. CANCELLED. Mandated Centercom, and date.

F.B. TURNER. CANCELLED. Mandated Centercom, and date.

F.B. TURNER, CANCELLED. Mandated Centercom, and date.

'See,' Roger said, putting the gun back across his lap, 'how fast, how cruel, how stupid the System is? You're fucked!'

Ellene looked across at him, worried. Yes, but really she had more in common with Roger. Age, outlook. New Generation. Suddenly he hated them. All of them. The boy, the girl, the screens.

'You bastards,' he said.

Ellene looked hurt, away from Turner.

'This is the deal,' Roger said. 'Turner it makes no difference to you. You're through anyway. Plus – you got Implosion. Cipola is your only chance. Sooner or later UNIMED is going to throw you in an Exit Ashram with a gallon of keth, if you stay here and you know it.

'Ellene – I've got the Probe. You need it. So you can't let go of me. While you're around me there's a chance for you to get it back. I need you to clear me space-side. I got long-range life signs indicators implanted in my lungs, heart and brain. I'm switching this remote box which triggers the land mine to automatic, and I'm leaving it here on this table. If those life signs stop – this place is blown away. What choice have you got?'

'We don't have much choice.' Ellene looked from man to man. A blank expression.

Turner said, 'We don't have to kill you to cross you up. Wait till you're asleep. It's a long way to L5. A reaction liner from GSO takes over a week.'

'Not if we ship by DLV.' Roger smiled a cunning smile. 'Before I came here I shot up three caps of Drive. I'll be awake and functional for the next 120 hours. That's plenty long enough for a Direct Lift flight.'

Ellene looked at Turner sadly.

'Yes. OCTAVE will ship us back DLV. But Roger –
DLV flights are exclusive. What if I can't get you a
seat.'

'You'll fix it,' Roger said. 'OCTAVE want you back
ASAP. They'll do anything to get you on that flight –
with your cover.' He flicked his thumb at Turner. 'Now
I'm part of your cover.'

Roger looked very calm and assured. Didn't care,
Turner supposed. That's how he did it. Tool of the
Organisation. So – in the midst of etc. If he lives –
good. If he dies – it's for the cause. So. I'm in the same
boat really. Wonder what sex would feel like? I think
I've forgotten. Got to stall. Soon – the shields. Then
we'll go nowhere.

He turned on Roger.

'So what's in this Hub? The last remains of Herlechyn or something?'

Roger's face registered hate.

'No,' he said, regaining control, 'it's a weapon. A
new, real, usable weapon. An information weapon.
There will be nothing we can't do with it!'

To Ellene Turner said, 'Why should OCTAVE be
interested in a weapon? I thought you were just a
branch of the thought police.'

'That's nice,' Ellene said, 'coming from you. Look –
we think it's some weapon that is controlled by, or
affected by, the mind.'

'Oh boy.' Turner laughed. 'Imagine when he puts his
soul to it!' He gestured at Roger.

Roger sneered and swore.

Ellene continued.

'If so – we must know. We watch over the minds of
countless millions in a way.'

'I thought OCTAVE was supposed to be pure
research.'

'So it is. But think of the significance of our findings.
We teach people. We guide the planet's future. And our
recommendations are mandated.'

Roger laughed.

'What is it with you people?' Turner asked him.

'What makes you hate everybody?'

Yes. Play for time. Remember the radiation polluted weather drifting in from the Northern power plants. The shields affecting city limits. Hoped now to delay both of them. Set them against each other. Two's company. Three's a crowd. Time. Get time to invent a strategy –

'There are four theories.' Roger's face was humourless and intense. Anger and contempt mixed with vision. 'There have to be. Dialectic is no longer enough.' Suddenly he was the coherent demagogue. No longer the street-fighting kid.

'Theory One. It's the people, not the system. Artie Grunewald, J.P. Morgan, Henry Ford, Madame Feng. The Rule of the Wicked. The Hierophants of Babylon.

'Theory Two. It's the System, not the people. GM, IMF, KBG, CENTERCON. Giant organisations out of control. Chaotic cannibalistic octopus of Global Capitalism.

'Theory Three. It's a conspiracy.'

'By whom?' Turner said.

'Your sense of outrage disgusts me. Your so-called decency. You know that?' Roger held the gun in both hands now, his face thrust towards Turner like a figurehead. 'Your so-called decency. Your deadliness. Your ability to be a normal member of a society like this.'

'Let's not get personal,' Turner murmured, lighting up a cigarette. He glanced towards the remote control box on the low conical table. Roger ignored him.

'Ever scan Ishmael Reed? "The history of the world is the history of secret societies". Remember Idres Shah? "Different sections of the community are to all realities 'nations' ... to imagine they are the same as you because they live in the same country is a feeling to be examined". Faction against faction. Plot against counter plot. Intrigue, Manipulation, Assassination, Private interests. Smartest get to Heaptop fastest.'

'Theory Four?'

Turner edged to the arm of a chair by an ashtray Casually he perched on the edge of it. Let's all relax and shoot the breeze. Hell, it's getting too late to go anywhere, anyway.

'It's all these – all at once.'

'Bottom line?'

'Our response!' Roger barked slamming his gloved fist against the stock of the SMG. 'Arise Dada Nihilissimus!'

'I still don't really get it,' Turner said, flicking ash. 'Corporations – CENTERCON as you so shrewdly call it – individual Mega barons – yes. But why ordinary people? Seems so pointless.'

'Because,' Roger snarled, 'you're the fucking backbone of it. Pigs like you. The Good People. NMS Faction – Normal Members of Society! Living here, Richville, Happy valley. You go to work and you come home to your televisions – game shows, psycho dramas, inter-active vids and soaps. All of you staring at the same stupid screen. Some vote for Goodrich. Some vote for Amalrik. Some vote for Calvin Gold. And you're all credit rated and Security A1. And all of you are like the living dead! Zombies! Well we hate you for all that!'

Turner stubbed his cigarette.

Ellene said, 'Yes, ordinary people. An anathema to Buddha, Mohammed, the Triple Goddess of pre-christian Europe, the Elder Gods of Norse Mythology, the entire Hindu Pantheon and our Lord Jesus Christ! My god, Roger. I sus you at Kath level – you run a riot. I sus you at Oth Level – a rage in your heart. At Path Level – a head full of faboids. At Mah Level – a silent endless scream! How do you live with yourself?'

Roger snarled. Anger born of too intimate aquaintance.

'Take you needles out of me, soul doctor! Have we got a deal or not?'

'Yes,' Ellene said glancing at the wall clock display, her voice suddenly urgent. 'It's a deal Roger. I'll clear you. Let's go for God's sake, before those shields go up!'

Turner's heart sank. Pain across his midriff.

Organ Implosion.

DATE: LOCM 727 – 1136 H
LOCATION: SPACE

'E quindi uscimmo a riveder le stelle'
DANTE, *INFERNO*

Datsun called gently through the channels '3050L alternate 3290'.

He had changed. His usual unknowable self-possession was gone. His footsteps danced. He seemed lighthearted. His face smiled. His eyes happy, skipping through heavy gravity and dull wall like a child.

Morgan and Angela trudged behind.

'You don't like Schoenberg?' Morgan asked. Her quip about Platinov troubled him. He dug that atonal stuff. He admired Schoenberg. Hadn't the man said 'One must believe in the infallibility of one's fantasy and the truth of one's inspiration'? Morgan went for that. Too bad Schoenberg had missed Prometheus, or he might still be with us today. But that was a long list, people who had missed Prometheus.

'No,' Angela said. 'Teutonic serialism scares me. You arrange twelve tones in a set of random numbers and weird things come out. Predetermined, forever.'

'It's not random.'

'Okay, don't let's argue. But what if the Universe were arranged as rigidly as that? And before you say isn't it ...?' She smiled suddenly and said, 'I like a pretty tune. See?'

She sang a few bars, 'She loves you, yeah, yeah, yeah.'

Very flat. She laughed.

'Oh yeah.' Morgan grinned, eyes veiled by heavy lids. 'Most people sing that wrong – she loves *me* yeah, yeah, yeah.'

His voice was deep and unmelodic but perfectly in tune.

'Say, what do you play on that Moog – you know when you're on leisure time?'

'Classics mostly. Mozart, Bach, Bartok, Glass, Weitz, Nikolayev.'

'Right – I see. I dig most of that. Nikolayev is great I think. The greatest composer in Space I guess.'

'Maybe.' Angela shrugged. 'Andrew Barton is just as good. Do you play, Morgan? You talk as though you do.'

'Uhhuh – used to be my job one time, way back when – last century – before the Premetheus scam.'

'So how come "used to"?'

'Angela – man, you know with all that extra strength and health and time – I found, wow! I could do anything, go anywhere – you know, new frontiers, new possibilities for REAL – not just some hype on the other side of the tracks. First thing, I went back to school. You know how easy it was back then when Goodrich was President of CENTERCOM. Remember, he was the first one that said "For every plant that automates or closes, a school opens" – right? So I took advantage of that and I found out – I was a better teacher and a better physicist than I ever was a musician. But I still play. They can't take that away ...'

'... from meeeeeeee,' Angela completed, still out of tune.

'How about you?'

'Oh Morgan, I was never a pro. Nowhere near it. Just the eternal student musically. And I'm much younger than you are. I was born in space – on Jefferson. I went straight into the scientific thing. I never wanted to do anything but agrarian biochemistry. It's my thing.'

'Minimum age for this Mission is 65 years. Jefferson hasn't been in orbit more than forty. How come you're on this mission?'

Morgan's voice enquired. Suspicion tone masked. No overt alarm. But she startled – quickly recovered. Said,

'Because no one else – biochem – applied. Of the right age group. So they waived me.'

'They? Or Dralon, personally?'

'They. The Object in Space Mission Committee. I was approached, Morgan. They invited me. Raoul Vaux – on vid. One evening at home. Bleep! "Hi sugere – wanna tek a leetle ride eh? To a weird rendezvous among the stars – maybe get to meet Azathoth and the rest of the guys?" You know? Raoul told me – "Be at SCICOM 12.30 Friday. We'll run the scam down then".'

'So you accepted, knowing it could be dangerous. A mission with three men. GLX OOXX – just like that?'

'Morgan, I was bored ... I wanted a chall ...'

'You weren't bored.'

'Morgan look – I love this boy, Veer. Domicile Dev. He's an Indian boy. Real good chemist. He's on Luna right now, supervising a silo base for the Farm Project. My bi-annual is due two weeks from today, and I should be booking a shuttle – Lunaside to see him, but ... really Morgan I know I don't want to go. When Raoul Vaux appeared on my vid with this proposal ...'

'You knew it was the right way out for you.'

'Something like that. Don't let's talk about that dingy emotional stuff.'

'Oth,' Morgan reflected. Emotion centre. Al Shabarsi had taught him to realise it. Warm centre in chest region.

Morgan's arms waved – his shoulders more hunched than ever as he loped along. His eyes thoughtful. Gentle, faraway eyes.

"Kay, so – look I'm not mad about this. With you. But Dralon sat in that Magic Man office of his – you know he asked me about my past lives!'

'Huh? – musician and so forth?'

'No. What the heck I did before I was born, for God's sake – this time around.'

'Heavens to Murgatroyd!'

'Yeah. He figured it had to do with the cloud being sentient and so forth like that. Needed fully conscious self-realised souls that had real in-depth experience – capable of real symbiosis. You know a cat that has maybe been a flea is heavier than somebody that has only ever been a person. That is – if you want to relate to a sentient non-human cloud, dig?'

'I think so. But now we know that Dralon built the cloud.'

'Uh huh. He's just another hype. Know what I mean?'

'A fink. But why us Morgan? Why our skills and psyche profiles?'

'Yeah why? Which reminds me – where is Datsun leading us? Datsun – hey man, what's goin' on?'

Because they had been talking they were not fully aware of what was happening around them. The labyrinth seemed to have shrunk in scale and become more intricate. Now all the angles were planed and precise, the tops of the trenches sharp like machined metal, though still tactile and green. And they realised, Datsun's route seemed devilishly complex. Trying to follow him through the last few turns had triggered Morgan to stop talking and start thinking. For a few seconds back there, Datsun had vanished out of sight and they had ducked into the next alley on voice trace only. Now Morgan saw him. Datsun had stopped. He stared intently at his chart on the hover truck screen. He still seemed unusually happy and Morgan knew that wasn't right. He should have been worried and confused.

'It's okay, it's okay,' Datsun said as Morgan approached. The cheerfulness in his voice sounded manic. 'But look – the thing is changing again. . . .'

'Yes it seems smaller suddenly – compressed.'

'Exactly so – but the same scheme still applies. All I have to do is adjust it. Please – you wait.'

Something in his tone made Morgan look at him funny.

'Okay,' he said. 'We'll wait. While you're figuring we'll call Plat on the PCC.'

'Good idea,' Angela said.

They unclipped the flat slabs of white plastic from their belts, dialled, and flipped the switches to recept.

Music they heard, soft sweet familiar music, but no human voice came from the speakers.

Morgan glanced at Angela.

'The song is you,' he said.

'Morgan – he's done it! We have to go back. Listen it's beautiful. We can go through now. I just feel it.'

Morgan flipped off his recept switch and grabbed Angela's PCC out of her hand. He silenced that too.

She stared at him, shocked.

'Don't,' he said. 'Don't fall into the Siren trap. Remember Ulysses? Heard the Sirens sweetly singing? I'm putting wax in all our ears. There's no mast around here to tie me to. If Plat has fixed the towers or started to disperse them or found a way through and gone – then his system is still valid – for him. Remember how he figured the options? He allowed a way out for each member of the crew if separated. If things is cool – he'll join us at the ship. If things ain't cool – then we got to keep on anyway. Once we have the ship, we can go back for Plat if necessary 'kay?'

He started to turn away fists in jacket pockets tightly clenched.

'Morgan, I was born in orbit. I have lived my whole life in orbit. During that time no one has ever offered any kind of physical violence toward me, or physically violated my personal space in any kind of way. 'Til now.'

Angela reached for her PCC trembling, her face flushed.

'I'm sorry,' Morgan said quietly. 'This whole thing is starting to crack me up.'

'Me too. I think maybe we should . . .'

But Datsun had spun around to face them.

'Come on,' he said. 'This way.'

INTERJECT - ARCHIVE - ENTRY - REF:

SUBJECT: Vaux, Raoul.
ORIGIN: Terra. Dinan, France. W. Europe.
SPACE ORIENT: Co-ordinator: SCICOM - Cipola 5 Co
    opt, OCTAVE
Committee - sci/managerial adviser.
PREV: Editor, 'Planete' Magazine. Paris, France.
Adviser, Societie Anonyme d'Exploration
    Astronautique. Rennes, France.
Lecturer, School of Imagineering, Jefferson
    Orbital Space City.
MISC: Raoul Vaux is Mah Religion Adept No 1


'Morgan!'

'uh?'

'Say Morgan, slow down willya. I only got little girl's legs and this gravity is puttin my knees in the dirt!'

'Sorry about that. I'm just trying to get there is all. Look Angie – I gotta ask you something. Have you seen the ship, up there somehow, on the surface, up ahead?'

'I'm glad you asked that Morgan. I thought it was me. Going crazy.'

'Yeah. Something strange is going on with the perspective around here ... say what?'

Datsun had stopped again, and was calling to them. They pushed forward as hard as they could.

'All lines reach back to point zero.'

His face was not calm. It was blank. They had never seen him look that way before.

'But Datsun – the ship is up there! We've seen it!'

'No'

'Yes! Let's quit fooling around with this dingy maze. Let's get up there and jet pack!'

'No Morgan. You are my friend. I'm telling you. You think Dralon will let you get to the ship that easily? No. You will end up like the guy in the myth of Tantalus. Check your PCC. The bleep says it's at least ten kilometres away. And when you have covered ten kilometres and your fuel is all gone the ship will still be ten kilometres away. Dralon is as well versed in the myths of your culture as he is in the philosophies of mine. This maze resembles both of them in various of its components. That ship we are all glimpsing is an illusion? Certainly. Cruel? Perhaps. This is where we are. Point zero. I wasn't wrong. I just didn't understand. Now I do. Actually it is very beautiful, just like our friend Platinov said when he began to realise . . .'

'Realise what?'

'How it really works.'

Above, Space. Star studded darkness. Around them, the eerie green of Dralon's VPMBM.

Cipolans were already evolving a new language, simpler than any of its root languages, but very rich. Many people together on a new world in space. Something was starting to trigger. Even now in this primitive stage, less words had more meaning. Psychic linkup – mind to mind.

For a second Morgan flashed – that he could see it all too. And his own chosen role in the specified location.

Datsun had jetpacked out of the trench. He sat high above them on the edge of the trench in a full lotus position, deep in meditation.

Morgan watched him. How to reach him? Datsun was tranced out. Untouchable.

He had to reach him. Had to find a way out of this.

Morgan concentrated, using everything he had ever learned from Mah meditation. It had to be possible. Reach him without words. Telepathy.

The 'self' he knew could be located in the brain at the junction of the frontal lobes and the limbic system. But in Mah training it was taught that the self could equally as well be thought of as an invisible field, extending for several feet around the brain. The trick was to visualise that field.

He stared at the foreshortened figure above him, cleared his mind of conscious thought and narrowed his eyes, fogging what he saw. His pulse rate slowed and he began to feel light headed. His mind blanked out and he lost all physical sensation.

The area either side of Datsun's head became a mushroom shape, translucent, twinkling with points of coloured light. Suddenly Morgan was floating, a pin point of consciousness. He was a point of light in a field of lights – some too brilliant.

Transmission. Reception. Mish mash. Psychic static. He was in there with Datsun.

*Trust me Morgan. I can fix it. I will get sudden ILLUMINATION!*

*Datsun, this isn't helping anybody. Least of all you.*

*Morgan – this is the most important thing in my life – to solve this.*

*No way!*

But Datsun had blocked him out.

Morgan came out of Path (mental level), back into Kath (manual/laryngal operational level) to find himself supine on the trench floor with Angela kneeling over him. He felt groggy and sick. Datsun had blocked him hard and before that he had caught a glimpse of the complications that were going on in Datsun's head. He pulled himself together slowly, and stood up.

Angela said 'Are you all right? One moment you were standing there – then the next moment – like, you just fell out.'

'I'm okay,' Morgan said. 'I reached him mentally. Momentary total interface. But it's no use. He's gone to the far far lands.'

They stared at the squat figure above them. Silent. Eerie. Unmoving.

'You know we have to go on don't you Angela?' Morgan said.

'Yes.'

'Okay. You're next.'

Morgan's feeling of weakness had passed. His patience was running out. He was angry. Very very angry. His whole face smouldered with repressed rage as he stared out into space. Angela didn't want to speak to him, but finally she said

'Why not you Morgan?'

'Figure something out,' Morgan said, 'or I may just cut out.'

'Where to?'

'Anywhere. Back to the ship.'

'You can't go back to the ship – can't pass go – can't collect 200 USONIAN CREDITS – you know that.'

'Okay – some other weird corner of Dralon's mind. Who cares? You know baby, I'm BORED with this ... scene! It's BORING you know?'

She looked back steadily at him.

'Oh I'm so sorry. Landsakes Morgan – you're the Organiser!'

He was hunched over, hands in pockets deep pulled his shoulders down. He looked thin. His knees were bent and knocked together. A strange junkie grin showed through his beard. His eyes were yellowish, remote, bloodshot.

"Kaaay. So figure something out' he said.


The pink glob was about 120 feet high, 200 yards wide, vaguely circular like huge blancmange or jelly. They were suiting up almost as soon as they saw it because the fumes it gave off were choking, acrid and obviously very poisonous. It lay across three intersections they needed to cross for Angela's system to work. Of course they tried jet packing over it but at close range the fumes were so acrid their suits began to rot. They boosted out of there with the outer layer of their suits blackened, smoking and tacky. No use going around the sides. The fumes became an impenetrable wall of fog. You had to fly so far that the co-ordinates Angela had calculated were no longer viable. The system became increasingly random. Increasingly warped. No doubt about it. They were totally and completely blocked.

They pulled back out of range of the fumes and removed the damaged but still servicable suits. They said little. Angela had begun work using the probes and sensors available on the hover truck, trying to determine the chemical composition of the blob.

'If I can find out what it's composed of Morgan maybe I can disperse it.'

Morgan said nothing. Nothing happened. After a while they went for a walk.

'Morgan – I got two caps of Desire. Let's do 'em. Get out of this for a while.'

For a second Morgan felt his body electrify. Desire was a compound of THC and genetic neural transmitters. It intensified erotic awareness to an incredible degree. It was used by the cults, psycho-sexual therapeutic agencies, and by the people for pleasure. It's most common use, in a controlled environment, was to bring people down from the long and intense periods of focused mental activity required by so many of the scientific and industrial professions followed on Cipola and re-integrate them into everyday life, sex being a universally popular and convenient avenue.

Morgan knew he shouldn't be feeling that charge so intensely but for two days he had missed his Stellachlorazine A shots. He had taken them at first to co-operate but after a while he couldn't stand it. Stella brought him down. Sure it was convenient, but after a while he'd sooner burn. He could always take a shot if the longing got too bad.

Now? With Angela? She was beautiful. Oh boy, imagine it – loaded on Desire! But the crew harmonisation chart had shown, too many interactive instabilities in each of the four personalities to advise sex relations of any kind. Hence; the Stellachlorazine. Another little gremlin that bugged the trip. For a job like this, Dyadic units would have been much better, but nearly all the experienced Dyads were flying deep space missions. Those that were available hadn't tested out very high on Dralon's requirement questionnaire. But then, neither apparently had Angela. Somehow that didn't really seem to matter anymore. One thing I forgot when I picked up my EVA kit Morgan thought, that cute little Stellachlorazine gun. It's in the frigging ship.

'No,' he said finally, his face and voice tense. 'I'm

playing this by the book. Anyway we don't have the time. The trick is to get back to the Scooter and the heck out of here.'

'Okay,' she said suddenly very quiet. 'It never entered my mind. You're only playing his game you know.'

'Maybe. How about you?'

'I'm going back,' she said, suddenly very childlike. 'I'm going to do some more work on the Blob. There has to be some way to dissolve it. I'm sure that's the way out.'

'Then I guess it's a race,' Morgan said softly. 'Me versus you and eternity.'

'Perhaps.'

She was in his arms suddenly. They held each other a long time, his brown hand darkly tangled in the light blonde of her hair.

She broke the embrace.

'So long Morgan.' Tears misted her eyes. Morgan said nothing. His body was hunched in a long shrug.

'Take the hover truck,' he said grabbing up his space suit and jet pack. 'You'll need it.'

She turned and started back towards the Blob, moving as fast as the heavy gravity would let her, looking tough and funny and sad. The hover truck slid along in her wake.

'Poor little plaything,' Morgan said aloud to the retreating out of earshot figure. 'Goodbye to the real you.'

'So long truck,' he said to the hover truck and shaking out of the shrug he pogo jetted downward, into the nearest trench.


INTERJECT — ARCHIVE — ENTRY — REF:

STELLACHLORAZINE A Synth. Dev Orbital Location,
    A.D. 2021
Ex Lab: Mohindra Kesh M.D. PhD. R.B.M.
Stellachlorazine A is used successfully in the
    fight against Meade's Syndrome commonly known
    as Organ Implosion.

Stellachlorazine A is a powerful genetic agent
    that strengthens internal tissue in the human
    biot. In small doses however it is an
    effective anti aphrodisiac with no other loss
    of functions or side effects.

Morgan walked a long time down the trench, his suit
and backpack slung on his shoulder. He had no idea of
the trench's co-ordinates or its number, either according to any of the three previous systems or any new
system of his own. He'd decided to stop playing that
game.

'If I walk long enough,' he thought 'something will
break. Me or Dralon. After all he controls the time and
energy around here. Let's walk.'

As Morgan walked, he practised. He was a Path
Level Adept, and likely to remain so for a very long
time. The first three levels of the Mah Religion were
hard but not impossible to attain. Morgan had gotten
into it while recovering from his neuro-breakdown. He
had made good progress. Mah helped him order his
life. It helped him in his work although it had never
been approved by SCICOM Admin, the way it had by
GALCOM.

On each of the first three levels, Morgan had
achieved. Visualisation and realisation of Kath (operational) level. Visualisation and realisation of Oth
(emotional) level. Visualisation and realisation of Path
(mental) level. But the final level – Mah (spiritual) level
– that was for a Mah Religion Adept No 1. On Cipola
they didn't use terms like 'No 1' but a person's religion
was their own business.

Morgan kept practising whenever he could make
time. Now he did it with a strong thought orientation,
because walking, he couldn't use the physical exercises
that were a part of each stage. Nevertheless Al
Sharbasi taught that Mah was a practical everyday
vehicle. Hence Morgan used every means available in
his present situation. He got his breathing regular and
deep. He got his pace rhythmic, listening to his foot-

steps over and over until they fell into the repeated rhythm of the trance music available on disc or tape from Mah Systems Music. He heard the echoes of his footsteps off the canyon walls as an overlay, complicating the rhythm in sophisticated ways. This was good. His footsteps and their echoes were a drum. Soon he could move his centre of consciousness from behind his eyes – becoming aware of the sensory robot walking. He realised this new consciousness first on the Kath level, colour green, located in his midsection. He moved higher to the chest, Oth – emotion centre – warm cloudy – colour orange. He moved higher to the head – Path, mental centre. He wanted to be there again. Datsun had shaken him up.

Soon his mind was bathed in blue light. Messages came in. He didn't know how people would bear telepathy without the blue light. But that was only one of the benefits of the Mah religion. He picked up strife, confusion, surrender, despair. At least he knew how the others were doing.

Above, the Mah Level. White light. He had glimpsed it. Sensed the flavour of it. But as yet he could not reach it. Path became his reality. He was out in the Deep – looking, searching, free-falling through starlight space, thousands of degrees below zero.

Through that unimaginable vastness, through that unmeasurable cold, he sensed a presence like mental rays of heat. His awareness focused. He was looking at 3C 273, two thousand million light years distant, not that that mattered or had any more than peripheral significance. For a few seconds Morgan was awake. More awake than he had ever been at anytime in his existence. 3C 273 was awake. As it had been for countless eons in the past. As it would be for countless eons in the future. 3C 273 spoke to him, in a split second of his spiritual dawn, in a voice of pure radio, just as Al Sarbasi had said it would, or one of them would, when Morgan was ready to make the leap. Morgan's consciousness accelerated into the golden fringe at the edge of white light. White light exploded. Mah Level.

Morgan regained operational consciousness. The green velcro was gone. He lay on a hard curved sheet of metal. High above him a translucent shell through which the Deep – dark and eternal – spread, and stars twinkled. He was in the end of a large cylinder – a shelf of unfinished space station built from moon-mined metal or recycled asteroid. Maybe it was a field waiting for crop matrix or more likely a base for lab or factory installations. Trenches and slots cut in the surface suggested foundations. Morgan's head was fuzzy but he thought clearly, 'how easy it would be'.

At the end of the sheet, maybe a quarter of a mile distant where the clear roof sealed the cylinder in a dome-like construction, the ship sat. A flat white saucer, in fact slightly cream in the synthetic daylight.

He knew where he was. Really he'd known all along. It had to be, the laws of physics told him. The Seven Cities of Cipola. This area? He didn't know but he could guess. High up inside the dome, colouring the universe outside – a faint, barely visible pink film. Laser shields.

Cipola 7, Central Hub. Unit leased by SIS. Purpose unknown. He was in the unfinished part where access was restricted, in direct contravention Preamble para 4 blah blah blah, or so they said. He stood up and began to walk towards the ship. The area operated at earth normal gravity. His feet barely rang on the surface after the heavy gravity of the 'Cloud'.

He walked as far as the ship – slowly. A ladder dropped away from the Exit/Entry hatch down onto the cylinder's floor. Just as they had left it, except that the floor had been like green velcro then. Morgan climbed the ladder – high onto the curved side of the ship and swung his legs up into the bioformed shape of the air-lock chamber.

Inside, the ship was just as they'd left it. Angela's private play headphones lay on the keyboard of the wall built Moog.

Silence.

Nothing disturbed.

But Morgan had a creepy 'tampered with' feeling as glanced around the interior of the ship.

His eyes scanned the wall mounted VDUs.

RANGE FINDER'S REPORT: SITUATION CONSOLIDATED

GRAVITY: EARTH NORMAL

ATMOSPHERE: BREATHABLE

Just as they'd left it except for the gravity reading which reflected the conditions of the Hub. So it should, now that the 'cloud' was gone. The instruments were still on, and functioning perfectly. Morgan's eyes traversed again. Above his flight console and seat the Mission Base Bulletin screen was lit. Green lettering on a dark ground — tank like and filmy — shot through with silver veins of static.

SUCCESS. CONGRATULATIONS.

PLEASE GO HOME.

Escape At Line 23

Morgan climbed up out of the scooter ship, down the ladder and onto the surface of the cylinder again. A coarse synthetic breeze, created by temperature adjustments in the atmosphere generators as the space city reached the Sunmost apogee of its orbit round the Earth, cooled his face and head.

By the cylinder's nearest external access point a big 110 seat motorless Jumper was locked in. He opened the bulkhead door and stepped through, looking back once through the transparent sealer membrane at the deserted silent ship.

Morgan cut the Jumper loose and floated weightlessly up and down the long echoing aluminium shel touching his hands on each of the worn, faded greeny-red bus seats as his body drifted by. The Jumper was free falling at 500 mph towards Ultima, Cipola 3. In ten minutes he would be home. He grabbed a seat strap by a window and stared at the distant outline of Cipola 6 home of SIS, noting its sleek efficient styling and the orbiting rings of garbage and junk. Were there reall Exits in the garbage? And if so who and why? Whe

vere FINK? Did they really exist or where they just
gments of Dralon's worst case negative programming?
Don't know. Maybe never will know. Heck – what's
oing on around here? Once upon a time style reflected
fe. All the units were light and twinkling and hopeful
nd beautiful. Cip 6 was sleek, ugly, cold and bare.
nd 7, the Hub. Desolate and empty, ringed with that
ink light that meant laser sheilds. Restricted access.
Danger. Authority.

Paradise is getting tacky at the edges.

Better do something about it.

And somewhere along the line, real or unreal – he'd
it Mah Level. He wondered if Dralon realised that?

NTERJECT: – ARCHIVE – ENTRY – REF:

C 273 Brightest 'Radio Star' – 'Quasi Steller
    Source' – or 'QUASAR'
ate of recession from Earth: 28,000 miles per
    second.
istance from Earth: 3 billion light years
 The answer to the question 'What are QUASARS?' is
ot yet known with any certainty, but the current
xplanation is that they are radio sources
riginally appearing in photographs as star like,
ut in many respects actually far more like
alaxies. In comparison to their relatively small
ize, often less than one light year across, their
utput of energy at all wavelengths is phenomenal.
 It has been suggested that a QUASAR may be the
output' side of a Black Hole – literally pumping
nergy from one universe to another.
 QUASARS are held in religious veneration by
embers of the Mah Religion sect. In this belief
stem, QUASARS are held to be the physical bodies
 Bodhisattvas. (Perfected beings.)

DATE: 23.50 MARCH 30 2031 TCT
LOCATION: LIMOGES SHUTTLE
BASE SPACEK LIMOGES
FRANCE WESTWORLD CCR 80

*'We shall sing of the great crowds in the
excitement of labour, pleasure and
rebellion; of the multicoloured polyphonic
surf of revolutions in modern capital
cities; of the nocturnal vibration of
arsenals and workshops beneath their
violent electric moons.'*

F.T. MARINETTI, *The Futurist Manifest*

The monorail was clunking to a halt at the end of
long deceleration run. It would take at least anothe
mile to meander into the terminal. Funny, Turne
thought, how all these super modern things end up ol
and clunky in the end. Could feel it now swaying fron
side to side, under the long ribbon of electromagneti
track that, along with a lot of other tracks like i
stretched nearly all the way around the world. Ove
oceans, farms, mountains, forests, cities and desert
and hills. Over millions of lives the monorail rar
Transport of the Future. Yes. All around the edges c
the giant belt cities that stretched from Tashkent t
Madrid in the South – Irkutsk to London in the Nortl
and still building. They crossed the North sea and th
Mediterranean on rafts held in position by nuclea
motors. Shipping lanes held open by tall bridge:
Corridor cities, housing and factories, huge artificia
leisure parks. Just south of Reggio, a replica of Bodmi
Moor, between Alpaca One and Fiat Zone Three, floa
ing over the ocean. Natural preserves – Parc Dordogn

a miles wide park in the midst of the towers a few miles from Limoges. Old town centres sometimes preserved like nuggets of historical reference in the midst of a linear city. Each massive conurbation groaned and travailed and smoked with life. For scale and grandeur – the orbital locations – despite their sophisticated living quarters, landscaped interiors and realistic climates – could never compare with the cities of the Earth, thousands of miles long – hundreds of miles wide. Cipola, Jefferson, Dev – they were mere frontier posts. It was planned that one day linear city corridors would track right around the globe. But that was for the future. 'Beltburg' Americans called the giant structures.

The inflight video had gone cold. Musak murmured softly. A tired Algerian waiter pushed an empty refreshment trolley between the rows of aircraft style seats. Wine stains and grease flecked the sleeves of his white jacket, dark stubble shadowing his jaw.

Turner looked from the Panoscopic windows down at the countryside beneath the metal and fibreglass shell of the monorail car. Dusk falling. Pale difference of French headlights and flat artistic neon. Pale green-ish French concrete. Long buildings slowly crumbling. An old abandoned works of some kind seemed to stretch for miles under the rail beside the line of a super highway. Away to the right – the old city of Limoges, spires and ornate towers amid tall blocks of elegantly designed modern housing. Ahead the shuttle base, like the mouth of a vast hanger. Glimpsed it as the monorail hung around a slow curve. Beyond that, flat hulls of Shuttle wings and four tall snouts of Direct Lift Vehicles – DLVs. Limoges. Headquarters of SPACEK – centre of the European Space Industry.

Normally the trip to an Orbital Location was a lengthy business. You took a shuttle to a Transfer Station outside the pull of earth's gravity and caught a liner to travel the quarter of a million miles out to the mini worlds. The liners were designed to travel under their own momentum after an initial shunt from a nuclear tug. A very cheap but leisurely form of travel.

A DLV was lifted by shuttle above the Earth's atmosphere and then burnt rocket fuel all the way to L5 at many thousands of miles per hour. It was quick – but very expensive. No private individual could ever afford the fare. DLVs were reserved for emergencies and the transport of top-ranking government, scientific and military personnel. Ellene was classed as scientific. So was Turner now. As her 'experiment'. Jesus, how weird. And the appalling Roger as 'medical assistant'. Her clearances had worked like a charm. Got through everywhere so far.

The monorail nosed into the vast cavern of the shuttle base terminal. Fluorescent glare replaced dusk and pale headlights. They stepped from the airconditioned chill of the monorail car into a smell of heat, tarmac and electricity. Ellene looked efficient and official. Roger, grim faced and staring eyed. Turner in his medicated tranquillised fog, hardly caring. Space – shmace. I never meant to go there. They left the platform through a milling throng of passengers and tourists wearing T shirts reading 'Astronauts do it weightless!' and *'En espace –la vue c'est la vie'*.

Doors read *Poussez* – Turner pushed. *Tirez* – he pulled. Other doors read *Passage Interdit*. It stuck in his mind. *Poussex, Tirer, Passage Interdit*. Thesis, antithesis, synthesis.

After a while he saw it. Green cards. Tourists, visitors and monorail passengers (Rail Services/SNCF) went through doors marked *Poussez* or *Tirez* then – *Passage Interdict aux Cartes Vertes*. Shuttle Passengers – Transfer Station, Dedicated Flights Only – *Cartes Bleues ... poussez tirez*. Then – *Passage Interdit aux Cartes Bleues*. DLV Pre-flight Induction Zones – *Cartes Blanches*. Then (funny eh? he thought *Cartes Blanches*) 'You have just reached the limit of the validity of all cards issued by SNCF or Rail Services. Those in possession of GALCOM Travel Credits and A12 Clearances – *PASSEZ! Attention! Passage Interdit à Toutes Cartes Colorées!*'

Asymetrical *poussez/tirez*.

'If in doubt as to your clearances – *Tirez la Poignée* and *attendez les fonctionnaires*!' Fat men in kepis lurked in glass booths, Gitanes cupped in chubby palms.

*Passage Interdict*.

Beyond he saw a huge holo enhanced sign claiming in all the European languages – 'The New Frontier Starts Here! GALCOM Space Division. Travel Services.'

Ellene pushed the door open, clutching three white cards, and they entered a new world. Earthside travel, however sophisticated was gone. A long white tunnel, clean, antiseptic and smooth, silent except for a faint hiss. A moving walkway whisked them gently towards the DLV flight check in. As they moved, the tunnel changed appearance – its walls shifting from pure white tube into a web of organic fibres like some ancient chemical structure of life, then they appeared to expand into a labyrynth like a spiral of galactic arms. Classic 'effect' architecture. Laserlight and vid to create 'effect' of an experience – life, expanding into the universe.

Under a low arch – robot checkers scanned their credentials – and they were in the departure lounge. Tall mushroom-like structures held the ceiling high. Weightless couches by low tables. A long bar. A team of GALCOM receptionists, a man and woman in unisex styled overalls were coming to meet them. Behind him Turner sensed Roger freezing. Over by the far wall of the nearly empty room – five tall men in brown military uniforms. The uniforms cut in incredibly good taste, like designer fashion clothes with a military theme – fantastically smart and business like, utterly suggestive of a New Age of enlightened centralised quasi-socialist world government.

No insignia, but on four of their shoulders a tiny green flash, and on the fifth, the tallest, a white flash. Tiny elongated triangle. CENTERCOM Shadow Command. Four Green Echelon rankers and a White Echelon leader. A Phalanx Unit. Global trouble shooters. The baddest asses in the world. Powers in excess of

Security and FTPA. Power of unlimited access as far as the *poussez/tirez* of Diaphantus locks and Mordell's Conjecture Probes allowed. A13 clearance for even the lowest ranks. Power of life and death over anyone, anywhere.

Turner heard Roger exhale softly. He too felt the rattlesnake and squirrel vibrations – only he wasn't the rattlesnake. First time he'd ever seen Shadow Command close to. Strange those Green Echelon men. Blank waxy faces. Even the one who was black. Odd. Nasty rumours about them. Room full of artificial wombs. Experimental embryos.

The reception team was processing their papers – happy effusive, welcoming – suitably concerned about Turner – 'the Patient'. He couldn't adjust to it. Laughing inside himself. Organ Implosion.

No doubt about –. From the far wall they were being scanned. Roger stood, frozen. His stoned eyes staring straight ahead.

'C'mon doc – camp it up,' Turner whispered – not knowing why. He couldn't have cared less if the phalanx had come over and seized Roger immediately. Except he somehow found the Shadow Command unit even more redolent of doom and danger than the Pranksters – actually there in the room with him. F.B. Turner – CANCELLED. As for Roger he had no doubt. When the right time came he was going to screw young Roger right up. No problem. Just wait till the Drive starts wearing thin ...

'Yes of course.' Gentle earnest voices of the reception team. 'He must take extra Stellachlorazine – for the g forces ...'

Roger broke out of his mould of fear.

'We have an increased dose prepared,' he barked efficiently.

'Yes of course. He'll feel so much better when he gets there. Lighter gravity.'

Ellene's voice was blurring softly into their stream of reassuring drivel. Why don't they ask me? Turner thought. His eye wandered. Caught sight of a stooped ashen-faced figure swaying weakly between two firm young upright people – a boy and a girl. A mirrored wall ran behind the bar. Christ! Turner thought. That's me.

'Perhaps you'd like to come through to the pre-flight preparation zone then –'

'Yes certainly.' Ellene moved with them towards two softly lit gangways opening from the far end of the lounge. Signs above read

Pre Flight Induction
ZONE A                    ZONE B

Gray minds. He felt the horror of them. Gray minds capable of triggering. Gray minds designed to preserve at all costs the interests of the system. Gray minds triggerable to perform psychotic acts. Gray pig minds.

Roger was close to panic. The massive shots of Drive were pushing him into paranoia. His mind was a red mind of anger. A black mind of nihilistic hate. If he wielded a gun – it was because he wanted to fight. To rebel against the crushing weight of oppression. The vast all-embracing mass control might of the New System. The huge enslaving global institution of which everyone was an inmate. The last resort he felt of the artist of life – to abandon creativity in a stultified world, to dive into the Black Hole and emerge Nihilissimus – Shiva – Lucifer – to bring light through the holy act of destruction. The gray pig minds would never understand that. He felt their terrible blankness – the ordered, efficient, command-obeying blankness. He felt it raping him. Raping his soul. They terrified him. He wanted to cut loose now – with a submachine gun and kill them before their psychic presence destroyed him. What had Herlechyn said? The rictus is the truest smile of comedy. He'd laugh too to see the Shadow Command Phalanx pirouetting, tumbling and clowning in the last bullet hail dance of death.

But of course he had no machine gun. No kind of clearance – not even the astonishing array of mojo

tickets Ellene seemed to be endlessly producing –
would clear a handgun to an Orbital Location. Rumour
had it there were some UAPWs up there just in case
one day Paradise started to get on somebody's nerves.
But no one knew for sure. A human society without
weapons? Impossible. His heart laughed callously at his
intellect. All he had were the transmitter implants in
his body, which even at this distance could still order
the detonation of a nuclear device in a tightly packed
luxury residential district a few hundred miles north in
another country and another zone. Soon they too
would be useless. Maybe as little as eight hours after
the shuttle donkey took off. Then his only insurance
would be – possession of the precious MCP. And to
back that up. A secret. Non magnetic – untraceable. A
plastic cylinder with a pistol grip. A flechette gun.
Compressed air fired a tiny plastic flechette at 500 lbs
per sq in. Used right, at close range – totally deadly.
Ellene wanted that probe desperately. He knew that.
No way she'd get it. Or Turner. Bastard was sick.
Smart too. Waste him if I get the chance. Once out
there he'll be badly in the way. Sentimental liberal
conservative pig.

Turner was thinking – MCP. Funny that. Mordell's
Conjecture Probe. Male Chauvinist Pig. MCP probes
masculinely into the vast womby female web of information. Tyranny of penetration. Diaphantus lock is a
chastity belt. Good thing he doesn't realise he's got the
wrong one or the neighbours would be getting a lot of
free central heating.

Ellene thought.

'*Links order rechts – in das Helldunkel des Umgangs –
Heir triffst, du "sie" sicher.*

Duck, *Dich in Spannung!*
*Aber keine Angst auch!*'

The Phalanx eyes bored into her.

'*Rechts.* Zone A. Couldn't someone have come clean
somewhere along the line and gotten hold of this probe
legally? *Wirkliches Leben ist echt, einfach und wahr – dhiss?*
Phantasie! I cannot sus them. I sense they are sensitive.

No. Weave a web. Protect all levels. Mah, Path, Oth, Kath – protected in a shell of light. Yet now surely – *Heir triffst du "sie" sicher!'*

At the tunnel mouth – the voice spoke to her.

'*Ascendez vous?* Going up?'

A joke – a light joke. The voice was only slightly French.

She looked up into the eyes of the White Echelon commander. About forty-five years old. Flat, handsome face. Eyes twinkled with strange merriment. Behind that, the huge weight of absolute authority. She wrapped the web tighter around her.

'Fear eats the soul,' she told herself. 'Let it pass by you on the wheel.'

She was fluently bi-lingual in German and American Basic, but now she spoke slowly and deliberately, thinking in German and roughly translating.

'Yes, going up. My friend is very sick. Here they cannot cure him, but at Orbital Location –' She smiled and gestured with a shrug, 'always let us hope so!'

'Please,' the sauve, not very French voice murmured. 'The A12 clearance for you and your party.'

'But already –'

'Please` – the clearance documents. It will only take a moment.'

She produced the documents. Her mind was empty. Now she felt nothing. An adept should have total control. She was very talented but still very young. She had won the first battle.

The commander looked at the clearances carefully. He pointed with his finger and head on one side, smiled.

'Hm. I see. Personally recommended – Raoul Vaux. Mandated CENTERCOM. A12 clearance.'

He folded the documents back into their plastic case carefully with the respect due to anything that was actually printed on paper rather than coded into the circuits of an electronic machine. He handed the case out to her elegantly, between index and second fingers. He bowed, smiling.

'There is no irregularity. And now – *bon voyage.*'

The reception team, looking baffled and embarrassed, ushered them through into the softly lit tunnel.

Nudging Turner with her elbow, Ellene dropped a few paces behind.

Turner was grinning. A sardonic world weary grin.

'We made it,' Ellene said softly.

'Yep,' Turner was still grinning. 'The worst is yet to come.'

## CHAPTER 17

DATE: LOCM 727 – 1240 H
(MARCH 31 2031 TCT)
LOCATION: THE SEVEN CITIES
OF CIPOLA L5

*'Doubt. Absence of definite belief, usually
with alternation between belief and
disbelief; sometimes obsessional.'*
JAMES DREVER,
*A Dictionary of Psychology*

Night. Engineered night. Starlight through a transparent cylinder. Starlight on a Terra style landscape.
Starlight soft on a Cipolan domicile dome.

Inside the dome a man dreamed. In the world of the
dreamer a surface began to flatten out. The uniform
green colours began to disperse into more colours,
filmy synthetic colours, until the environment began to
look like a huge 3D television screen. In the world of
the dream some kind of dusk was falling.

Morgan got up slowly from where he had been sitting at the end of the trench. He looked back. Behind
him the cloudscape of trenches swept up towards the
darkling sky like a construction from a Mayan nightmare.

Ahead, an automobile was parked across what
looked like a stretch of oil-stained concrete. Morgan
stretched and walked over to it. He got in, started it
and began driving down the wide belt of concrete into
the twilight. The buildings slowly rose up around him,
and the lights.

He was at the wheel of a strange car in a strange city
at night, driving on a strange expressway, watching
unfamiliar names roll by on alien sign boards, names of

streets, neighbourhoods, avenues and boulevards he knew he would never see again. Oodastadis, next ten exits. Vout Parkway, next right.

The lights above the expressway cast an eerie glow across the silent lines of automobiles which cruised endlessly six lanes deep ahead, behind and either side of him. Their soft tail lights were like a million unblinking eyes. Big, heavy luxury cars, light elegant mid-sized cars, small cheap economy cars. Cars for every purse and every purpose. They were never going to stop. It was the last rush hour of another world. A warm wind zipped through the smog laden air, through the windows of the car. The acrid fumes rasped his throat like powdered glass. Morgan checked the mirror. He could see cars coming from a thousand miles away. The expressway was endless and the span of the city skyscrapers stretched to the limits of his mind. The rush hour was going to go on for ever.

Morgan looked at the gas gauge. Empty. He knew then that all the other cars were running on empty too.

Billboards advertised products which had never, could never and would never exist and the names on the sign boards grew stranger and stranger still.

Morgan drove for hours and hours. The exhaust-stained concrete just kept rolling on and on, neighbourhood after neighbourhood, deeper and deeper into the inner city, getting dirtier and older, sootier and uglier, more desolate and dreary with every ceaseless mile. Merge after merge he followed the Thru Traffic.

A fly crawled across the windshield and fell dry and lifeless on the floor carpet. The air was like a warm, noxious gas. Morgan reached into the glove compartment. His hand closed around a half empty pack of cigarettes. As he groped for the lighter, filter tip drooping from his lips he saw on the side of the pack 'Cancer 100's – Your Favourite Brand'. Morgan spit the cigarette into the moist heavy air, shuddering.

The tenements were crumbling either side of the expressway and stretched as far as the eye could see in a grid as infinite and complex and unknown as the human imagination. Grim high-rises, streaked and smeared and stained like a giant's broken teeth reared into the murky sky from their roots in torn down lots.

Morgan began to sweat and the sweat was cold. Shooooooooom! The ceaseless cars cruised on.

'Concentration City is ten miles high,' Morgan thought, but he knew he hadn't remembered the quotation right. His heart raced. His stomach burned. Traffic this heavy was an ulcerated heart attack. 'God help me if it starts to back up!' He was trapped in the middle of a million tons of steady rolling steel.

Stress blared at him like the blast of giant motor horns. In the cars on either side of him gray, faceless men locked to the wheel stared straight ahead.

He looked down the immense length of the shiny dark hood and saw that the emblem mounted above the grill shell was a chrome death's head. He checked the mirror and on the hoods above the universe of pale headlights behind he saw chrome death's heads too. Silently he began to scream.

The sign board emerged out of the smog and grew and grew until it loomed over his car twenty three stories high. It filled the skies. The shadow it cast across the traffic crawled with menace. The reflector studded letters seemed to vibrate off the green painted metal surface of the sign straight into the neural activity of his brain.

'Ghetto,' it said. 'Right Lanes.'

And Morgan knew he was in the Right Lanes and the Right Lanes must exit.

'Oh no Dralon,' he said. 'I ain't NEVER goin' back to the Ghetto!'

He swung the wheel hard and savagely to the left. The long death's head hood began to plow through the gray men in their shiny cars. The tidal traffic broke in a screaming, whirling, skidding flood, smashing, tearing everywhere across the concrete, wrecking steel and burning rubber, gray men punctured and deflated flat, ripped and shredded, fly out window! BLAM BLAM SMASH! KEEEEEEERUNCH! CRASH!

The grooved pavement split apart beneath his wheels into a myriad slabs of light arcing out from a great deep abyss and Morgan was free falling ... over the rainbow's edge ... through the crack of dawn ...

Morgan woke to the sound of his own scream. The nightmare had been incredibly, eerily vivid. Shantelle, his Dyadic partner stirred beside him, groaned and carried on sleeping. No other sounds disturbed the night.

Morgan rolled from the low bioformed sleeping platform. He raised himself up from his knees and stood weakly in the darkness feeling groggy and sick.

So – there *were* after-affects. The kimono he used for lounging lay draped across a chair. He put it on, shivering slightly. Shantelle showed no signs of waking. She lay curled in the soft curves of the sleeping platform breathing gently. The honeycombed walls of their dome arched over her still form like a shell.

He moved quickly to the dining area, and got coffee from the autokitchen. He sat down and watched the steam rising from the cup towards the clear roof panel that provided daytime illumination for the area. Above him the soft Terra style landscape of Ultima – lakes, low hills, and woodland trees appeared as a dark mass on the far side of the vast cylinder that was now his home world. Shields masked the giant daylight mirrors suspended at each pole of Ultima's axis and engineered night filled the huge enclosure. Beyond that the real, eternal night of the Deep, pierced with distant stars – visible through transparencies in the cylinder walls. The Deep. Unimaginably vast. Unmeasurably cold. 3C 273 was silent now. Light years away. A voice of pure radio. Now he was alone.

After effects. There had to be. He suspected machinery. He suspected drugs. Three days elapsed – ex cloud time – in a kind of blurred limbo. Shantelle's lovely face – bemused and anxious as she looked at him. And now this dream. Based in some authentically dream-like way on his experience on the cloud (or in the Hub, depending how you looked at it) yet preying on his worst, long-buried subconscious fears. It was as though his strategy had been in vain. He had walked away from it, yet his block had come to him out of some unfriendly pattern of inevitability. He felt a shudder of terror. 'Nothing is inevitable – everything is possible,' he told himself, repeating Al Sharbasi's teaching. The mantra calmed him. He began to reflect calmly – on the events.

No word from Dralon. No news of the others. Only a message on vid.

'Participant ... thank you – for taking part – in this important experiment.

'Have faith. Everything will be ... explained.

'Until that time OCTAVE Committee appreciate your maturity in not divulging anything you may have seen or experienced to anyone. The Common Good ... may ... depend ... upon ... your ... silence.'

They had him over a barrel with that phrase 'The Common Good'. It was programmed deep in the psyche of every Cipolan. It was making things hard with Shantelle. As Dyads they shared everything. It hurt keeping her blocked out. He knew she longed to question him. Find out where he'd been. Why he was acting so strange. Now she wished she'd tried to go with him – as Dyads, ideal. Except that she had no eyes for deep space missions. Morgan had. Their relationship could handle it. Till now.

He felt like getting on CommVid and blowing the whole thing to everyone on the Seven Cities.

Anger replaced fear. What the hell was going on? Where were the others? Had they escaped too – or were they still in there, wrestling with the Blocks?

He tried to add it up. The 'Object' allegedly approaching the Seven Cities' orbital track. The volunteers for a space mission to investigate. The VPMBM. CENTERCOM. FINK. The Hub. Dralon. What else was going on in there? It floated before him almost like a visual hallucination projected on the Deep. The strands of a web. A web of secrets, half truths and conspiracy. Morgan had forgotten how to distrust. Life had been so good here. A real solution. Utopia at the edge of the stars.

The rapid five minute dawn began breaking at the eastern apex of the cylinder. No use trying to sleep now. He dressed without waking Shantelle (her mind would trace him) and caught a jumper over to OCTAVE Headquarters on Cipola 5. Dralon woud have to see him. He was going to demand right of Citizen's Access.

On Cipola 5 it was still night. Because its main purpose was to house SCICOM astronomical telescopes the cylinder's day/night cycle had been adjusted to effect a sixteen hour night and a four hour day. OCTAVE was located in an abstract-looking low rise amid cafes and theatres near the cylinder's residential section. The area was a favourite haunt of artists, bohemians and other 'night' people.

Outside Dralon's office it was the usual colourful scene. Tourists from Terra were emerging from an airlock subway on the opposite side of the foyer and, to greet them, a group of musicians playing trance music on synthesisers, saxophones and flutes led by a young girl singing 'The highest form of government is no government at all' in an eerie repetitious pattern that played on Morgan's nerves. But he didn't have to wait long. No one could get around Citizen's Access once it had been demanded. Not even Dralon.

'So, the masquerade is over,' Morgan said, as he was ushered into Dralon's cluttered office, crammed with books, tapes, VDUs, religious and scientific objects of all kinds. 'Was it all simulation?'

'Yes,' Dralon said. He had emerged from the living quarters in back, looking remarkably unruffled, clad in a long white arab style robe. Several mattresses were ranged on the floor in front of Dralon's desk – for periods of meditation, Morgan presumed. Dralon reclined on one of these and invited Morgan to do the same. It was hard to stay mad lying down so Morgan remained standing.

'Even the voyage out?'

'Yep.'

'I knew all along the cloud was a fake.'

Dralon raised his eyebrows, but said nothing. Morgan raced on.

'You see – it appeared flat like a plateau, but it had a gravity field. A heavy gravity field. There's only one way you can get that. Rotation.'

Dralon smiled, inclining his head knowingly.

'The laws of physics told me,' Morgan said. 'I knew that plateau had to be inside a cylinder or sphere. And then I figured – well probably here somewhere on Cipola.'

'Smart fellow,' Dralon said at last.

'Yeah. I need to be.'

Morgan stood over his tormentor hands on hips, breathing heavily. Dralon gestured languidly towards a futon a few feet from his own.

'Morgan – why don't you sit down. You'll tire yourself out standing there.'

It was one long act with Dralon – morning, noon and night. But no one could see it, Morgan reflected – except maybe for him. He sat reluctantly on the edge of the futon.

He realised suddenly that Dralon's face was motionless. Like he had walled up entirely. Was there a way? There had to be. Dralon was a con man – a trickster, Morgan had never seen it so clearly, but he had power and that was real enough. Morgan felt weak. No way he could take him on. The cloud had drained him.

Relax, he told himself. Contact the force within. Concentrate. Path – mental level. Blue light. Suddenly it was there, his mind filled with powerful blue light. Faraway, a voice of pure radio. 3C 273 had not deserted him. He felt his psychic energy returning like a great crackling hiss of mental static. Dralon reeled visibly as Morgan said,

'Dralon – let's go way back and work around the basics. Okay – animal, vegetable or mineral?'

'All three.'

'So – okay. The Terran takeover scam – it's a hype, right?'

'Yes.'

'And FINK?'

'They do exist. They are an extension of the Terran cult INK. But I am not a member.'

'So – the true purpose lies elsewhere? Wait a moment. Is purpose the right word?'

'Yes. Well no. Not really.'

'Yes. Or no.

'Yes. And no.'

'Dralon – give me the *whole thing*. Now.'

Dralon looked unhappy. He ran his hands through his long hair. At last he said,

'Very well Morgan. This is it. VPMBM. V is wrong. It's not what I told you. It's S. Self Programmed Mind Blowing Maze.'

Morgan watched him. 'Self?' he said.

But Dralon held up his hand, interrupting him.

'Morgan – do you know how OCTAVE is financed?'

'Yes. By CENTERCOM, and through various Trusts, based on Earth. Wealthy "Feet People" who are interested in consciousness research.'

'Correct. Those are the main avenues. And more recently there has been another. SIS.'

'Space Industrial? What for? Commercial considerations shouldn't have any influence over your activities!'

'I'm aware of that Morgan, believe me. But you know how it is with funding, you can never get enough. PMH alone is costing a fortune. And you know how mystics can be – naive! What harm will it do they said! I was convinced that SIS were merely trying to clean up their image at our expense. Anyway we had a few of their scientists over – Roland Vaux was very keen on the idea – and it developed. They have some incredible equipment. Including the SPMBM. There is no direct military application. I added that word "victim" to give the whole thing the worst possible slant.'

'For God's sake – why?'

'I'll explain – please –'

Morgan picked up vibrations. Shifty, raddled vibrations. Like an Archbishop leaving a chambermaid's bedroom.

'Anyhow – this is how we did it. The voyage out that you experienced was in fact the usual crew training stuff – centrifuges – thrust simulators – holoenhanced movies – and er, Real.'

'Real? Oh my God, Dralon! Real is a heavy drug! One of the few that have never been deregulated . . .'

'Morgan! Calm yourself! The dosage was minimal. Anyhow, your expectations coupled with your stored spaceflight memories plus the added boost of Real to add a little depth, were enough to convince you that the voyage out was genuine.

'Now – the Cloud. To put it simply – SIS boffins have been working intensively on developing some kind of modifiable IIRS vector. You know what that is? Identifiable Instabilities in the Structure of Reality. For years they were believed to exist. Out here in space, away from the pull of Earth's gravity they've not only been proved to exist – they've been located. So far SIS have been able to synthesise this gas. Now, with a computer to control the molecular structure it will take on different forms – gas, solid, liquid – and the forms can change at will. The will of a computer program.'

Morgan was watching Dralon carefully, letting his anger dissipate into fascination. No matter that his mind, and the minds of the crew had been violated – the important thing now was to stop this ever happening again. He stabilised his body in a half lotus position, feeling the fiery vibrations absorbing in a great coolness within him. He centred his consciousness in Path – mental level.

'Dralon . . . Who controls the computer?'

Dralon smiled.

'Isn't it obvious by now?'

'I think so. It's the only way to explain something

like that incident with the shard.'

'Yes. Of course nothing like that exists in nature.'

'The Towers?'

'I designed them. I trust you approved. How about the one that sounded like Cal Calhoun?'

'Beautiful Dralon. You son of a –'

'No Morgan – wait!'

Dralon sat up on the couch. Summoning his energies, he managed to look powerful and wizardly. He pointed dramatically at Morgan.

'That's all I did. You – all of you set up your own Blocks! *Self* programmed – remember? You said you thought you knew who programmed the computer. Do I have to spell it out? The computer responds to the human subconscious – and conditions on the cloud alter accordingly.'

Morgan said nothing. Lightning flashed in the space between their heads. He knew that was what Dralon had meant. But still his mind was reeling.

'I made the towers – just to get you all started. You were the ones who saw them as an obstacle. You Morgan, were the one who insisted they had to be destroyed!'

'They hurt us! We were nearly deafened!'

'Fire burns, if you get too close.'

'We had to reach the ship!'

'Why? Because I said you had to? There were a million million possibilities once you were in the magic world of the Cloud! You know I'm glad I ran this experiment. The kind of social system we run up here needs people with free imagination. Now I see what's happening to your spirit!'

'Okay. So say we'd stayed and listened. Just stayed and listened?'

Morgan was baffled. Suddenly tormented by doubt.

'Morgan – as Lester Young used to say, "It takes pretty people to make pretty music." Look, once you stopped fighting – really stopped fighting – what happened?'

'I found the ship.'

'Exactly.'

'Dralon you're ...'

'Morgan – control your anger. SIS wanted to market this thing! Something beyond any video, any holo-drama, any computer game ever invented! We had to test it. And CENTERCOM are involved. Their spies have been out here for months in various disguises – trying to figure it out. And I think they've succeeded tho' they've never been inside. Heaven knows what ...'

'You kidnapped us.'

'You volunteered. Look Morgan – you four were selected out of a thousand. Four of the most emotion-ally stable and intellectually sophisticated people anywhere in the Seven Cities. And what happened? One by one you all flipped out!'

'Why so many lies? Why invent an invasion from Earth?'

'I had to establish the worst possible set for it Morgan. Paranoia, fear, future shock – I couldn't take chances with something as powerful as this. Imagine – if it gets a licence. Not just Cipolans but "daytrippers" up from the Stack!'

'Lay off the Stack, Dralon,' Morgan said, his dream still fresh in his mind. 'That is an ugly and disrespectful way to talk about the more overcrowded areas of our Mother Planet.'

'Okay – but imagine. Somebody comes up here from Beltburg. Gets loaded on high grade Real. Hits the Cloud in its marketable form as leisure activity – My God! Monsters from the Id, Morgan.'

Dralon looked at Morgan in an attitude of impas-sioned entreaty.

Morgan didn't let up.

'You got a depressing view of the human subcon-scious Dralon. I would say that in spite of your occult studies and spiritual training you are still influenced by 400 years of Anglo Saxon Puritanism on a cosmic scale. The men in tall hats have grabbed your soul.'

'It's your opinion. Why didn't you make love to Angela?'

'Because of the crew harmonisation profile, because I am a Dyad, because I had to keep myself together, because maybe it wasn't really what she wanted to do, because I figured you might be watching!'

The two men sat in silence for a few moments, a tense web of anger and suspicion floating around them like an electrically charged depression before a thunderstorm. Finally Morgan broke the silence.

'Back there you said "One by one you all flipped out". I didn't flip out. Where are the others?'

'Look Morgan – you have to know. They weren't as strong as you are. We had to take them out of there. They're in the psychiatric unit at OCTAVE, under sedation, watching fish tanks, movies of the sea. That type of thing. They're responding to treatment. They'll be okay. Believe me.'

In the Cloud, he had touched Mah level. Had Al Sharbasi taught him how to forgive? Morgan didn't know. One thing was certain. Right now rage was pointless. He put his emotions into stasis.

'I'll have to see them.'

'Of course.' Dralon smiled blandly. 'We'll go at once.' He began to get up from the mattress.

'No. Not just yet.'

Morgan's voice was freezing. Dralon sat back down. His eyes were cloudy and troubled behind the smile.

'Dralon – there's something else about this cloud. Something more than a leisure device or something with scientific implications, however far reaching. Okay – I believe SIS scientists developed it from IIRS research. I believe, despite your unforgivably high-handed methods, your aim was to test it for the good of human kind. But there's something you're leaving out. I'm a citizen Dralon. Paragraph 4 do state' – "Unlimited access to information". I challenge you – on an Arnold's Oath – to divulge this information.'

'That's not fair!' Dralon's impassive face was blushing. His sonorous voice had become a high pitched squeak.

'You know that means I've got to tell you!'

212

Morgan laughed.

'Too bad. Now it's been said, baby.'

Dralon groaned and put his head in his hands. He looked up.

'It's a drag Morgan,' he said. 'It really is. But this is how stupid people are especially ...'

He pointed down through the floor. Naturally, he meant on Earth. Everyone knew Earth wasn't 'down' anywhere – it was 'out' there, just as the Orbital Locations or the Sun or Moon for that matter were 'out' there when you stood on Earth, and not 'up' anywhere. But very occasionally when the 'Feet People' really got on their nerves the Spacers resorted to a somewhat simian insult.

'Uh huh.'

Morgan nodded knowingly and waited.

'The CENTERCOM Elections,' Dralon said. 'The three main candidates have spies out here in heavy disguises. By now, they know what's in there.'

Morgan said nothing. His mind was working fast, but he couldn't get it.

'Think of the Info Sphere,' Dralon said. 'At first a theory, now known to exist. Like Teilhard de Chardin's "Nuosphere" – a worldaround psychic web produced by the human mind – but in the case of the Info Sphere, actually electrically produced by informational equipment used in high volume by modern technological civilisation. The entire web of produced and transmitted information that encapsulates the globe like a second atmosphere. Some of it is beamed – some is in wires. All of it leaks, eventually spreading everywhere. Gray flashing sheets of information. The medium through which rumours of a mystery in the Hub reached Earth in the first place!'

Morgan breathed deeply, watching Dralon like a hawk.

'Fascinating professor. But so what?'

'So this, Morgan – so this!'

Dralon leaned forward. His voice became a whisper as though he were afraid that what he was saying

213

might leak out the same way.

'Imagine,' he said, 'you could feed the characteristics of the Cloud into the Info Sphere. But first you had programmed the experience the way I did with an initial set – promoting your policies as a CENTERCOM candidate straight into the subconscious. Only this time it isn't interactive. It's only one way. Your glittering vision of the future – as experienced reality! Don't forget Morgan, you don't *need* a cloud of gas in a cylinder – it can all be reduced to information and transmitted, like the old Soviet Fission Ray.

'Imagine several billion people with computers and wristwatch radios. All waiting to vote. Whoever controls the Cloud – controls the vote.'

'Whew.' Morgan lay back on the futon. At last.

His mind felt clear. Brilliantly clear.

'Dralon,' he said, 'let me see if I have gotten this straight.'

Dralon smiled, an aquiescing smile.

Morgan launched into it, and Dralon continued to smile as Morgan spoke.

The Cloud, Morgan summarised, was a kind of gas. It could be contained in a cylinder, or for that matter any other convenient container. It could be solidified or liquified, and take on many forms. Its molecular structure was contolled by a computer.

This computer could be programmed by someone outside the cloud, to make the cloud assume different forms. Or it could be programmed by whoever was inside the cloud. Only those people wouldn't know it, because inside the cloud the computer responded to the subconscious.

Weirder yet, the characteristics of the cloud in any shape could be reduced to electronic information in the form of a ray and transmitted – one way only. Then it could have a gigantic subliminal brainwashing effect on whole populations. The Info Sphere, the worldaround web of electronically produced information, would be imprinted with whatever images the programmer desired.

214

Morgan fell silent. He stared at Dralon.

'That's the great game,' Dralon said. 'You see that's why we needed you and your companions to test it out. Four of the most together people we could find.'

'Flattery will get you nowhere.'

'But it's true. Do you see the implications? The human mind – even four human minds in concert – just can't handle it. You see, whether it's interactive or one way, whether it's the ultimate leisure activity or a means of political gerrymandering – the Cloud is too dangerous to leave lying around. In some ways it's a shame. As a psychological research tool alone, the Cloud could be invaluable. But put yourself in my shoes as a member of OCTAVE. We watch over the minds of millions, Morgan!'

Dralon lapsed into silence. Then as if thinking aloud he said, 'What we need is something that will over ride the Cloud's computer – permanently.'

Morgan watched Dralon carefully. Surely not even he could weasel out of an Arnold's Oath?

'There's one way to do it,' Dralon said at last. 'A Mordell's Conjecture Probe.'

Morgan didn't interrupt. This was it. The mother lode.

'See, a Mordell's Conjecture Probe is linked to the structure of an Arnold Device – right? It structures and restructures information. Infinite and variable. The most powerful informational tool in the world. It can alter any electronic reality in an instant. You follow me?'

'No.' Morgan shook his head. 'You better tell me.'

Dralon leaned back, searching for the right words.

'Look – think! The Cloud is controlled by a computer. As the computer responds to the human subconscious – e.g. you and your chums, or – the will of an outside programmer – e.g. me and my creation of the four towers – so the molecular structure of the gas alters to create a new situation. A situation which is as real as anything else that can be called real. Forget the physics, forget the philosophy, remember the experience!

'What we need to do is to put the Cloud into stasis. Permanent, benign stasis, before CENTERCOM election candidates, SIS fun salesmen, or anyone else can get to it.'

A linear probe entering and ordering an organic web of information. Yin–Yang, mish–mash, Morgan thought – but he didn't know where the thought came from.

'In theory,' Dralon was saying, 'according to OCTAVE's scientific wing, a Mordell's Conjecture Probe which can break any code up to infinity could do this. How? By penetrating the mysterious cybernetic "mind" of the Cloud, measuring and understanding every variable the Cloud is capable of, and then – the master stroke! Programming the Cloud into a final, permanent state. Because the programme – though simple in result – will be so complex in form that the Cloud's computer will never be able to think of a way around it.'

'Actually,' he said smugly, 'our peopled have worked out the program the Probe will feed in.'

'So, the Cloud becomes a harmless Disneyland,' Morgan said.

'Something like that. Actually I thought it might have been nice to create the world of a great painting – say something from Monet – "The Beach at Trouville".'

'Nice,' Morgan said 'but for you rather uncharacteristic. I would have thought you would have picked something with a spiritual or even religious theme.'

He studied Dralon's face carefully, but Dralon only smiled mysteriously. Morgan let it ride and said, 'There's just one problem. As far as I know there is no MCP anywhere in Space. That's where the "Feets" have got us cold. We are the new industrial zone. We make the wonder products and cook them with cheap energy. They are ahead of us in informational technology.'

'Right.' Dralon looked sly. Tricky people – wizards. 'But there's one on its way.'

'Oh. Uh HUH!' Morgan looked conspiratorial and trustworthy. Even an Arnold's Oath you could only push so far.

'An agent – an OCTAVE agent – a girl agent ...'

'A glamorous girl agent?'

'No. A tough no-nonsense but not-altogether-unattractive girl agent is on her way out here – in possession of – yes – you've guessed it. An MCP.'

'Uh huh.' Morgan laid his index finger along the side of his nose.

'She's got cover, and she's got clearance,' Dralon said. 'Officially, she's bringing back an implosion case who's been rescued from the dubious practitioners of Earthside medicine and technology to take part in our Psychometric Healing Programme.'

'Lucky guy,' Morgan said thoughtfully. 'This must be how you people always get to win Boy Scout of the Month. How did she come by the Probe? I suppose she just shimmied into Shadow Command's White Echelon recreation room and asked for one.'

'Morgan,' said Dralon, suddenly stern. 'I detect a subtly sexist tone to that remark. Male Chauvinism plays no part in our society.'

'So sorry,' Morgan said.

'Nevertheless,' Dralon's voice was thoughtful, 'it wasn't easy, I'll say that. And, of course, men will respond to feminine charms so long as there is a need for reproduction. Which may not be all that much longer ...'

His voice trailed off and he stared at the ceiling as though lost in a sudden reverie.

'Forget the Future! Let's deal with right now!'

'Yes, yes.' Dralon appeared to snap out of it, and leaned forward.

'Shall I say we heard a rumour?' Dralon smiled a sardonic and gentlemanly smile.

'Oh yeah?' Morgan wondered if he push the Arnold's Oath a tad further. 'A rumour ain't no merchandise.'

'Quite. You see inefficiency increases in inverse

proportion to the size of the command structure in any organisation. Shadow Command, by the very nature implied in its title, is no exception – despite their much vaunted "phalanx" system. Paramilitary organisation with a human face – and I might add there are grave doubts about that statement at many levels. Not the least of which is philosophical and biological – not to mention politico-social. ...'

'Quit jeffing, Dralon. Get to the point!'

'At once. My point is that even in an outfit like Shadow Command mistakes occur. And recently a very serious one. They lost a Probe.'

'Whew!'

'Yes. January 3rd 2031 TCT on Earth, Pranksters seized control of an SSET station in Arizona, USA. One of them, apparently smarter than the average Prankster, convinced the er, "investigating authorities",' Dralon's mouth wrinkled with distaste, 'that he knew how to operate the attitude and pitch control equipment installed in the receptors. As you know, the obliquity of the ecliptic dictates that the receptors alter their pitch to remain on full stream as the rotation of the Earth ...'

'Yeah yeah yeah – c'mon –'

'Okay.' Dralon grinned infuriatingly. Morgan's guess was right. He wouldn't break an Arnold's Oath. But he'd try to weasel out by sidetracking Morgan any way he could. The question was – who's mind would tire first?

'Anyway, he convinced them that he could direct the beam of microwaves across Arizona into Colorado – thus adversely affecting the rain shadow of the San Juan Mountains and thus causing rain at a mean temperature of 98 C to fall on the new American city of Empyrean Park. A hitherto unheard of ecological catastrophe.'

'Boiled futurists – right?'

'Right. Actually stir fried – as cooked in a wok. Don't forget that downtown Empyrean Park is sealed beneath a geodesic dome in a style devised by the

American inventor Bucky Buckminster whose advanced ideas are at last in vogue.'

Morgan made a face of entreaty.

'Ah yes, well – Shadow Command were called in. They used a Mordell's Conjecture Probe as an override, i.e. to shut down the plant and to open the security systems.'

'And . . .'

Dralon's voice had gone cold. By now Morgan was getting a creepy feeling.

'No one inside was left alive. The team had been Coco Beans. A suicide squad.'

Morgan shuddered. Such awful things did not jibe with the happy fulfilled way of life in the Orbital Locations. It put a hurt on his mind.

'So – how come . . .'

'I said no one was left alive *inside*. Pranksters have their cell systems, a mirror image of Shadow Command's Phalanx – the one based on the concentric circles of the circus ring. The other upon the layers of a pyramid. One Prankster, the head of the cell, was missing. To this day no one knows how he did it. But he got out as the troopers charged in. Two White Echelon commanders waited at the perimeter of the site directing the operation. He shot them both and drove off in their truck, which contained the Probe.

'Of course having no base or secret world headquarters, the Pranksters had nowhere to hide it, so they passed it from hand to hand through their cell system. That way it was constantly in motion, around WestWorld, one cell member handling it at a time. Obviously it became very hard to find.

'As you may know like everything else at CENTERCOM Shadow Command, when all the talk of echelons and hierarchies is done, is managed by a committee – largely composed of civil servants. At this time a member of this committee fell severely ill. Organ Implosion. He was a Promethean – 98 years old – an old time CIA and FTPA man. Marshall Peredur. CENTERCOM wanted him kept alive at all costs. A key man and a big investment. One of the first of the "lab built oldsters" as I believe the slang is. They did a deal with Roland Vaux and had him shipped out here by DLV to be put on the PMH Programme. Can you imagine the opportunity? To study the mind and soul of a man like that?'

'Keep it coming.' Morgan would keep Dralon pinned down at all costs.

'Well – like so many people who arrive here for the first time – his personality and psychology underwent many changes. Or developments, one should say. His quarters were on Ultima in a green dome filled with plants, overlooking a beautiful lake. From there he could stare out into the Deep and see Earth in the distance. A small blue planet.

'This, and the therapy released the censor bands and repressions that had for years subconsciously tortured his mind. The fantastic culturally conditioned urge to control himself, that had lead him to devote his life to the control of others. Faced with his own death – a quarter of a million miles out in space, he opened up to life. At one point he said – (we have taped transcripts) – "I feel the neurosomatic rapture – one foot above the ground".'

'Yes Dralon – marvellous. PMH is really the tops. A control freak flips out. The facts. Please let's have the facts!'

'Ah yes. Well after these – dare I say it – "mystical" experiences, he opened right up. The game of ruling the earth seemed as a "childe's toye" compared to the wonderful vistas of inner and outer space suddenly revealed to him. Roland and I now know more state secrets than Madame Feng – CENTERCOM's Mistress of Mystery. Did you know for example that Goodrich cries at the sight of a sculpture by Henry Moore? Apparently the reason is – his mother was ...'

'Dralon – get the lead out!'

'Obviously, he told us about the Probe. He laughed! By the way he's still here. Quite cured. Never going back. He's taken religious orders in the DCCH.

CENTERCOM are a bit miffed!'

'I'm not surprised! He must have told you more than that.'

'Yes. He said that it was believed that the Probe was currently circulating around that part of the Beltburg Stack known as London.'

'Ego, Dralon. Ain't that where you started from?'

'Guildford, actually . . .'

'Yeah – okay. Foot on the gas . . .'

'We assigned agents. We succeeded where Shadow Command had failed. We found that the current holder of the Probe – a cell leader – code name Pagliachi – very young, very talented, very dangerous, was currently busting his brains out as an INK Seraph. His cover, you see?'

'Our agent by a subterfuge . . .'

Morgan looked old fashioned.

'Okay, by seduction – gained possession of the Probe, substituting a worthless mockup based on a securilock programmer in its place.'

'Risky. I would have thought that if this dude is as smart as you say . . .'

'Don't forget Morgan – that Probe has passed from hand to hand through the Prankster's underground grapevine right across the world. In fact we were in some doubt as to whether our merchandise would by this time be genuine.'

'And?'

'It is genuine.'

'Yes . . .?'

'Our agent is speeding spaceward by DLV at this very instant.'

'. . . and?'

'There are complications.'

'There always are. Like what?'

'As well as her patient, the Prankster is with her. He suspected she was up to something. When she suddenly vanished into the arms of a Reclaim Inc deprogrammer – he became convinced.'

'Oh my God! Who has the Probe?'

'She does, at the moment. You see she did a double double switch when he tried to get the Probe back. She was holed up with her "patient" waiting to ship out.'

'That's enough! Spare me the details! What do we do now?'

'Dralon's voice became chilly.

'Well you – Morgan. *You* don't *do* anything. We have this under control. We have the arrival zone surrounded with a telepathic thought barrier.'

'Like hell you do! Besides Dralon I think you owe me . . .'

'All right.' Dralon capitulated suddenly and completely. Morgan had won. 'You can get involved if you want to, but as spiritual adviser to this city I must warn you that psychic exhaustion may be rapid, and moreover . . .'

'Dralon – I hit Mah level.'

'When?'

'In the Cloud.'

'Good Lord! My dear boy, I had no idea. The brain waves, the trance! Why didn't I realise?'

'Dralon, it's okay. First off, I want to see Angela and the rest of the team. Just to know they're all right.'

'You have my wor . . .'

'From here on out – seeing is believing.'

'Very well. A naive assumption after all you've been through but . . .'

'You know what I mean.'

'Of course.'

Dralon stood up, walked over to his desk and pushed a switch. A bank of screens lit up on the far side of the office wall. Each screen showed a room filled with soft orange light.

Angela, Datsun, Platinov.

Morgan watched intently.

Their backs were to him. Angela lay on a low couch. Datsun sat cross-legged on the floor. Platinov appeared to be assembling some kind of puzzle made from wood.

The picture on the first screen moved into close-up. Angela turned towards the camera. Her face was pale and calm. She seemed lost in thought.

'Are there two-way mikes?' Morgan found he was gripping the edge of the desk very hard.

'No,' Dralon replied quickly. 'You can't speak to them yet.'

He pushed another switch. The screens went into diagram form. Complex webs and lines. A coloured dot slowly traversed each diagram.

'There,' Dralon said. 'See what's happening? They're slowly working it out. When the dot reaches the far side of the diagram – they'll be straight again.'

'Prognosis?'

'It's good. They're strong people. That's why we chose them. You found the answer. Ultimately it's up to them.'

A loud bleep sounded from Dralon's desk. A red light began flashing in a panel on the ceiling.

'My God!' Dralon yelled, springing frantically towards the door.

'The Probe! It's here!'

ARCHIVE – INTERJECT – ENTRY – REF:

Dyads: Dyad = the number two. Dyads are a life style option arising out of OCTAVE initiatives designed to restabilise society after late C20th disintegration made the early years of the C21st, a sociosexual maelstrom. Dyads are men and women who have decided to share their lives physically, spiritually and intellectually for eternity. Lo Credit Dyad training courses are available from OCTAVE at several Orbital Locations and thruout the CENTERCOM region.

Mystical overtones: Dyads believe that together as binated male and female they make up one complete human psychic unit. Dyad theorists cite Yin/Yang – DNA/RNA dialog and many other examples from science, psychology and philosophy to assert correctness of '2' as basic universal integer.

Applications: After the establishment of the Orbital Locations long distance space flights to the outer planets became an increasingly

viable possibility. CENTERCOM recommends that
where ever possible Dyadic units should be
selected as space crews – shortcircuiting the
need for sex suppression through Enketholin or
the inclusion of 'ancillary staff'
(Male/female sex therapists). [Note: SIS
flights still use porn, sex holos and
'therapists'].

Gays demand to be included in the Dyad system,
esp. gay women. So far women crews have
successfully operated the two month round trip
reaction freighter trips between L5 and Geo
Synchronous Orbit.

OCTAVE as consciousness advisers to CENTERCOM
refuse to acknowledge gay couples as Dyads –
believing that the 'Dyad state' must reflect
an actual union of male and female. This
uncompromising position is becoming
increasingly hard to maintain in the face of
organized peaceful protest. (Controversial).

General Usage: Many customs, styles and
expressions originating in Space have a
special 'frisson' for Earth dwellers. The term
'Dyad' is no exception and Earthside, is
loosely applied to describe any couple whether
they have undertaken formal Dyadic training or
not.

DATE: MARCH 31 2031 TCT =
LOCM 727 – 40

*'But the new order of things, rational
enough as compared with earlier
conditions, turned out to be by no
means absolutely rational.'*

FRIEDRICH ENGELS,
*Socialism; Utopian and Scientific*

The DLV soared through space – thousands of MPH –
thousands of miles above the Earth. The interior was
like the inside of a huge airliner, with weightless
couches instead of aircraft seats, and more spacious.
There was no in-flight video. Travel had temporarily
transcended the abstractions of the late twentieth
century, and become an experience again.

The passengers – largely composed of scientists on a
visit to the SCICOM installation on Cipola 5 and
CENTERCOM diplomats charged with the mission of
reassuring the space communities that whoever won
the forthcoming election everything would still be really
jake – lay back on their couches viewing the Deep
through transparencies in the DLV hull, or floated
dreamily and uncertainly between the food automats
and their seats. 'Far out' and 'out of this world' weren't
just expressions any more as they blissed out one
by one above the atmosphere. 'Weightless' some of
them said laughing with new found knowingness, finding out for themselves the reasons for space people's
favourite expression of approval.

The flight had been fabulous. Turner had to admit it.
Too fabulous, considering the circumstances. One foot
above the ground. Even the Stella could not dull it. Yes

– and it still seemed to excite the crew who you'd think would be blasé by now. Even sight seeing to do. They'd pointed out the old defence laser stations that had once helped to terrorise and cow the mass populations of Earth. Everyone on board booed. Yes it did seem silly, zooming above the planet. Seeing it as a beautiful blue ball. Easy to forget how those tiny minded territorial concerns had once seemed so important. A glimpse of human folly.

Ellene had been joyful and exhilarated. Now she seemed to be fighting for control. Work to do.

As for Roger, you could never forget he was dangerous. Very dangerous. His stoned eyes, raw and red splintered from lack of sleep, his skin, pale and oily from the effects of the stimulants, his head had seemed to burn a halo. Strange vibrant ecstasy. At one point he had looked at Turner floating back to his weightless couch with a soft drink and said,

'Gravity is a myth – Earth sucks! You sus that?'

He laughed. A high crazy laugh. Somehow it seemed blasphemous, face to face with wonder. Laws of nature no longer in a book, but real.

Turner strapped himself back in carefully between Roger and Ellene. Was there nothing he could do? By now Roger's implanted transmitters must be out of range. They were thousands of miles up and moving. Dodman's Ley was temporarily safe. Maybe it was time to put some pressure on.

'How do you expect to get away with this?' Turner said, staring into Roger's bloodshot eyes. 'You can't kid me those transmitters will reach all the way from L5. I bet they're even out of range now.'

Roger's face split into a leer. His jacket lay across his lap. He lifted the edge of it. Turner was staring into the plastic snout of the flechette gun. So – the implants had done their work. Roger had gambled correctly. Neither Turner nor Ellene had dared sic Shadow Command onto him at the Shuttle Base or alert the security forces in any other way, for fear of blowing up Dodman's Ley. The deal had held good so far.

Now in order to overpower him they'd have to risk the lives of the passengers on the DLV. Because he'd use the gun. There was no doubt of that.

'I see,' Turner said slowly. 'I might have known there'd be something up your sleeve.'

He lay back on the weightless couch quietly. There was no point in doing anything while the ship was in motion. Just have to sweat it out till they reached Cipola. Then Roger would make a move. But what? Turner guessed that he would almost certainly try to take Ellene or himself hostage and demand admission to the mysterious Hub. That was the standard terrorist procedure. Most worrying of all – how would OCTAVE handle it. It was doubtful if any weapons existed anywhere on any of the Orbital Locations. And Roger was armed – and extremely dangerous. Mercifully he was still duped as to the true whereabouts of the Probe – ie Ellene's flight bag. Either way, there was going to be some kind of showdown.

Now the DLV had begun to decelerate. The pilot's voice had announced, '*Voilà! Le Centre Industrielle Pendu L'Orbite Lagrange d'Autour!*' And sure enough there in the distance could be seen, rotating in the dark vastness of the Deep, a really garish, schmaltzy, super-technological anarcho-paradise. Six white plastic-like cylinders of enormous size, rotating around a central hub.

A great cheer went up from all the passengers and Turner felt a sharp momentary pressure against his ribs and heard Roger's voice, sinisterly quoting a sacred Prankster text, murmur, 'George, don't make no bull moves.'

The DLV had docked, dwarfed to a tiny needle against the side of one of the gigantic Cipolan cylinders. Smiling, untroubled-looking Cipolan hosts of both sexes looking surprisingly (to Turner) much like people anywhere, had welcomed them. And now – this part they were in – you could be anywhere. Some sort of elevator had brought them up from the DLV docking point – Roger always slightly behind them – out through a metal door and this part, it could just be an airport lounge.

Turner glanced round moodily. There were lakes and parks – countryside he'd heard – as well as industry. Weightless gymnasiums. But here concrete and glass. Above – infinite darkness pierced with bright stars. He'd been looking forward to his first sight of the moon looking really big. Still, patience. Earth normal gravity – a little lighter perhaps. Made him feel easier. Hard to remember though – that was space out there.

Doorway. Reception desk. Sign over doorway read 'OCTAVE – The Mystery of Consciousness is Within Our Grasp'. In a corner of the foyer some musicians were playing. Turner recognised it as trance music. Nice touch that. Shame about the music. Two men sat on a long bench by the far wall. They were hand in hand. Turner had forgotten. Space was very popular with the gay community. Chance to begin anew, without the old prejudices. Suited CENTERCOM. They didn't want the orbital population to grow too fast. What the heck was going to happen next? He suddenly didn't care anymore a quarter of a million miles from Earth. Roger was no longer his job.

Turner froze on the spot. He realised that Roger and Ellene were motionless too. He felt a sudden pressure, paralysing him, as though a giant hand had seized his mind. The little group was suddenly surrounded by people. He realised with a shock it was the people in the foyer – the musicians, the two gays and various loafers he had hardly noticed. In all about twenty people in a wide circle.

The pressure increased. Their eyes were staring straight at him. Huge, saucerlike and luminous. He couldn't move. Christ! All along these freaky sods had seemed too normal! He saw Roger from the corner of his eye crouched in slow motion – like an athlete trapped in a swamp. The eyes were focusing in on him. Roger's hand was moving, trying to reach the flechette gun. Time stood still.

Turner heard voices. From the doorway under the

OCTAVE sign two figures emerged. A tall black man and a long-haired bearded figure in a white robe. At that moment he felt the pressure drop, as though the diversion had weakened the powerful circle of concentration – and Roger was off and running. Running at full speed towards a hatch-like door marked 'Jumper Entry – 4, 6, and Hub'. Without any warning Turner felt his knees buckling. Everything went black. He was unconscious before he hit the deck.

Roger knew a lot more than either Ellene or Turner thought. Ellene was telepathic at Mah level, but only to the point of picking up general moods and vibrations. She didn't receive specific thoughts or scenes, nor did she usually transmit them. Also Roger – though he generally despised psi as a mental luxury of the bourgeoisie, was himself sufficiently physically attuned to know how to keep his mind shields in place, which he did whenever possible, imagining his mind surrounded by a high dark wall. Thus Ellene could not detect any hint of knowledge. She constantly came up against a sensation of dim, blank, determined stupidity. It had saved him now – from the full force of OCTAVE's thought barrier which had felled the unfortunate Turner. It had kept Ellene literally in the dark as to his plans.

Because in the short period of time between Turner snatching Ellene so he thought, from the clutches of INK, and Roger's appearance at Dodman's Ley, Roger had been briefed. The Prankster cells had vibrated with activity – a great amorphous body without a head – the Pranksters. No leader – only a common desire to destroy a system they hated and feared. 'No ring master – only Clowns,' Herlechyn had said. The five nearest cells had coagulated, voted – and Roger was chosen and elected. To get to the Hub, with the Probe, and sus the scam out.

Roger was briefed rapidly by a dissafected SIS worker who'd lost the use of his arm assembling a solar panel and returned to Earth, where he existed as a 'Poodle'. Poodles were ancillary backup to the Pranksters. People too feeble or depressed to attack society themselves, but who admired the Pranksters for doing it. 'Poodles can't be clowns – because they only perform,' Herlechyn said. The failed emigré told Roger everything he knew about the topography of the Seven Cities – which was plenty – told him about the inter unit transport by motorless jumper – told him as much as it was possible to know about the Hub. When he was through, he sat up and begged, like a performing dog should. Roger shot him with the flechette gun and put him outside in the garbage for the sanitation man. The Clowns laughed till they cried. They hated the stupid poodles. Almost as bad as the Zombies. Night of the Living Dead. Nerds, Mothas and Shits. Everywhere.

Roger knew how to get *something* out of a Mordell's Conjecture Probe. Not as much as Ellene. He couldn't have discerned the colour of President Goodrich's underpants at the flick of a digit – but he knew enough to do something when he got inside the Hub.

He was, therefore, very distressed when he discovered that what he had hugged to his bosom for the last forty-eight hours was in fact not a Mordell's Conjecture Probe – but some kind of devilishly similar looking, but altogether inferior high access multi-channel controller. The bitch had tricked him again. This was in the jumper – drifting at a stately 500 mph towards the Hub.

The full weight of it all suddenly exploded. Even nihilist terrorists with a devil spirit in them are human. He sat down and cried. Long shuddering sobs of agony. Then he froze up – because somehow there still had to be a way. Something he could do. The jumper docked softly against the side of the Hub. He pulled on his Prankster's harlequin mask. He wrenched open the exit hatch and hurled himself through. He came up rolling onto his knees clutching the flechette gun. But there were no guards. No security. Fate was working hard to keep human ugliness out of the Orbital Locations. So he didn't shoot anyone. Nor did he get burnt up by the famous and offensive laser shields.

They had been arranged to avoid the jumper entry. Like so much else to do with security – they were mostly a symbol.

Ahead of him stretched a long echoing metal tunnel, ridged and grooved as if to take the installation of complex machinery. Overhead, a translucent roof through which stars twinkled in the everlasting night of the Deep.

He walked down the tunnel easily, sure in the knowledge that it was happening – he was into it – this was it. The right place at the right time. The right person. Fear left him.

He knew that the controller was sufficiently sophisticated to function any standard security code. He flipped it through its scramble program when he reached the tall steel door at the end of the tunnel. After a few moments the door swung open.

The masked man stepped through, into another world.

As soon as Dralon had grabbed the real Probe from Ellene, he too was running – Morgan hot on his heels. They climbed aboard a jumper moored next to the one Roger had left on and turned it loose. The vehicle began speeding across space towards the Hub. Morgan stared into the void between the cylinders. Suddenly he grabbed Dralon's sleeve.

'Look!' he yelled.

Faraway on Cipola 6 a Scoot Ship had cast off from the docking hatch of an old space tug slung in close orbit around the SIS headquarters. It accelerated fast now into the jumper's wake.

Morgan knew that space tug. It had been named the 'Valhalla'. Now it was the home of the 'Immigrants' – barbarous and primitive – who had allegedly 'materialised' on Cipola 6 a few weeks before the first 'sighting' of the mysterious gas cloud had been reported by OCTAVE.

'It must be urgent – the speed they're going,' Morgan said. 'And they're headed for the Hub!'

'Yes. What a drag!' Dralon groaned, leaning forward in his seat as if to make the jumper go faster.

Morgan eyed his companion thoughtfully.

'Dralon, wouldn't it be easier if you told me EVERYTHING you know?'

Dralon looked at Morgan wearily.

'The Immigrants,' he said. 'They aren't from another dimension. Not the way people think. More literally they're from another planet – Earth.'

The Scoot Ship was gaining rapidly. Morgan's eyebrows raised incredulously.

'Shadow Command,' Dralon said. 'The spies I told you about. Madame Feng got in first with the "Mongols". Then they were infiltrated by Amalrik – the "Tartars". And last but not least the latest arrivals – working for Goodrich. The "Vikings".'

'Cal Gold as well?'

'Oh, he's playing by the book. He's going to wait till the other three have finished fighting it out, and then expose them. He's decided there's more capital to be made that way, politically.'

'Why the weird disguises?'

'Remember the Declaration of Bogota? They aren't supposed to be here. It seems that by some bizarre coincidence all three conspirators hit on a similar idea? It will be interesting to see which faction has got there first.'

'What do they do then?' Morgan asked. His jaw had dropped so far he could hardly speak.

'Secure the Hub,' Dralon said, 'and contact their side's scientists who are probably hidden among that motley crew of diplomats and what have you that just arrived by DLV. Funny to think of, isn't it? Each one sitting there with a brilliant plan for feeding the factors of the SPMBM into the Infosphere, unaware that a rival is probably in the next seat!'

The jumper was docking. The Scooter had overshot the Hub and was backing up. Morgan and Dralon pounded down the passageway towards the chamber where the SPMBM was housed. The airlock was open.

Behind them, the rattling of feet and hoarse cries. Morgan dragged Dralon behind the airlock door.

The Immigrants, waving their shields and weapons went charging through, but they were so dishevelled it was impossible to see which tribe they were supposed to be.

Morgan sneaked out from behind the door and peered in, Dralon following him.

Of the green plain Morgan remembered, nothing remained.

Only a whirling shifting gaseous expanse, in which images blurred and flickered at the edge of identification – a low rumbling sound – images of pure unknowable abstraction.

'My God! What's happening?'

'It's breaking up,' Dralon said. 'It's swallowing everything!'

He punched buttons on the Mordell's Conjecture Probe.

Patterns zigzagged through the whirling miasma.

'I can't control it!' he said.

But he didn't have to any longer. The MCP was glowing – hot like a white diamond. Dralon dropped it to the floor.

A series of incredibly rapid calculations of enormous length appeared in the fabric of the gas – then it began drifting out past them – down the corridor and out of the still fastened outer airlock, as though it wasn't there.

Gray flashing sheets of information

Gray flashing sheets of information

Gray flashing sheets of infor

Gray flas

Soon they were looking into the floor of an empty cylinder. Meteorite metal and concrete blocks. A void, empty, flat, drear vacuum.

'It's gone,' Dralon said. 'Vanished into thin air – taking the last thoughts of Roger and the Immigrants with it.'

Gray flashing sheets of informat

'Well, that's that then.' Dralon shrugged, looking helpless.

Morgan grinned. He couldn't help himself.

Gray flashing sheets ...

A jumper docked at the far end of the tunnel. Members of the Council and the OCTAVE Committee were approaching down the corridor.

'Better get ready to put in a preliminary verbal report, I suppose,' Dralon said.

'Yes.'

'It's gone now. Into the Infosphere.'

'I'd love to know what you put into it before it left,' Morgan said reflectively, 'while the Probe was still working.'

'Oh no!' Dralon was almost laughing. 'No more oaths!'

But then they were surrounded by a chattering throng of scientists, adepts, and councillors.

... of information.

DATE: LOCM 827 – 441 J = 7.30
APRIL 1 2031 TCT
LOCATION: THE SPACE TIME
CONTINUUM

*'One fact of outstanding importance for
our purpose is that the motifs of flight and
of ascension to Heaven are attested at
every level of the archaic cultures.'*
MIRCEA ELIADE, *Myths, Dreams and
Mysteries*

The worlds were waking to a new dawn – in different
times, and at different places.

FOR INSTANCE –

In the Museum of the Twentieth Century on de
Kooning Street, Empyrean Park, Colorado – in a softly
lit room away from the main galleries, the glittering
informational presences of James Joyce, Albert Einstein,
Charlie Parker and Pablo Picasso (physically recon-
structed from the information left behind them in their
work – pulsating clouds of information – stored in a
vacuum, positioned over electro magnetic display
plinths – shimmering in tall columns – almost visible)
were waking up.

Picasso broke up into a pattern of interlocking planes
of flat opaque colour which rapidly transformed into
long organic tendrils intertwined with eerie shapes.
Joyce rose slowly into the pale cool waves of light, an
emanation of thought, impressions, languages, sigla
and symbols. Near the ceiling he began undulating
between male and female forms. Charlie Parker soared
upward in a gorgeous plume of whitehot sparks which
rapidly beautifully and logically arranged themselves
into series of aural vibrations. Einstein sat calmly puff-

ing his pipe – watching them.

In the Stack, Leisure People took breakfast snacks from their food vendor units and switched on the Wall to Wall T.V.

On the highways and freeways of Earth, commuters hurried to work. Everyone everywhere was making sure their wrist watch radios were working – because at 17.30 TCT '*les populations radiophoniques*' would be voting – in the final stage of the CENTERCOM elections.

On Cipola 3, Ultima, prime residential zone for scientists/workers and visitors to Cipola, Frank Turner sat in a green dome filled with plants – overlooking a beautiful terraformed lake. From there he stared out into the Deep, seeing Earth in the distance. Mysterious planet. A small blue ball he had once called home.

PSYCHOMETRIC HEALING PROGRAMME PHASE I: A restful, yet stimulating environment. (Somewhere to unwind.)

Yes because whod have thought it would ever be like this new worlds for old seeing the earth is that the main thing this feeling no ads can capture that a blue ball all these miles away from you never felt so free like they say its fabulous here grass trees buildings all around you space the vastness theyve got and later you could take an explorership to the outer planets anything you want to feel the future forget the past Trace yes I forgive her hope shes happy my fault a lot of it hope she forgives me insisted insisted I remember I insisted our child should be a natural if we had one and she didnt want to go through that why not Frank incubate it in an artificial womb its so much easier for me Frank Id like it but Im afraid of the pain Frank and these days you dont have to go through it but I wouldnt agree to it not my child a plastic they call them wrong of me yes I hope shes happy somewhere Paris maybe

as for this I love it are these my sex feelings this fire thats flowing through me is it the bliss of life returning?

INTERJECT - ARCHIVE - ENTRY - REF:

SUBJECT: Turner, F.B. Origin: Terra. U.K.
    Westworld.
CONDITION: Organ Implosion
TREATMENT: Psychometric Healing Programme. Cipola
    3 Ultima. OCTAVE Auspice.
RESULT: Spontaneous Remit - LOCM 827 - 441J
FUTURE: Subject requests Citizenship Status -
    Cipola.
APPLICATION INCEPT: LOCM 828 - 442 J
RESULT: Request Granted LOCM 829 - 443 J

THE CENTERCOM ELECTIONS 2031

COMPUTERISED GLOBAL GOVERNMENT ELECTIONS
ON A SYNDCALIST MODEL #
AFTER LA COMTESSE SIMONE DE LAUTREC

le chef/La chefette

traditional system     □     le système Nouvel

```
                 ∧
               □ □
              ∧ ∧
            □ □ □
           ∧ ∧ ∧
         □ □ □ □
        ∧ ∧ ∧ ∧
      □ □ □ □ □
     ∧ ∧ ∧ ∧ ∧
   □ □ □ □ □ □
  ∧ ∧ ∧ ∧ ∧ ∧
□ □ □ □ □ □ □
∧ ∧ ∧ ∧ ∧ ∧ ∧
□ □ □ □ □ □ □ □
```

Centercom
committee    les administrateu▪

POLITICAL    A POLITICAL

local national    les etats
politician    industriels

une population    une population
radiophoniques    radiophoniques
(toutes les mondes)    (syndicats)

238

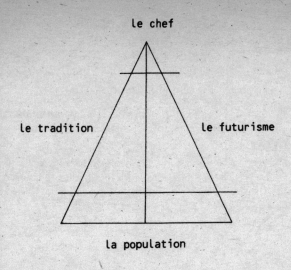

le chef

le tradition

le futurisme

la population

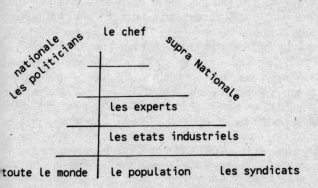

nationale
Les politicians

le chef

supra Nationale

les experts

les etats industriels

toute le monde | le population | les syndicats

le système Nouvel
comme un oeuf

*'Personne n'achetera celui-ci pendant dix cent mille années'*

*(They'll never buy this in a million years)*

Conclusion to the preface of
*La System Nouvelle* by Simone de Lautrec

**two**

## Biographical Note

'Simone de Lautrec was foremost among the brilliant political theorists of the late twentieth century. Her central thesis was a daring synthesis of syndicalism and centrist democratic ideas admirably suited to the state of the world and of course ruthlessly rejected and derided by the demagogues of right and left when they bothered to mention it at all. Something of a prodigy Simone had completed her "magnum opus" – *The System New* – by the age of twenty-four. Ten years later finds her close to death from poverty and Enketholin addiction having renounced her title and mortgaged her estates to the cause of world peace. Held in high repute by many friends world-wide she is persuaded to emigrate to the Russian space city Mir i Druzhba in the year 2011 when she is now over forty-one years old. Here she begins a new epoch – in the field of space architecture.'

(Translated from the French by Anatol Snark)

N.B. Simone de Lautrec's ideas – despite their almost universal rejection by most political influences were, however, held in awe by Edwin O. Goodrich styled by many 'The Father of CENTERCOM'. As luck would have it also they were popular with Andrei Tsarchovsky of the Soviet Union who as history relates was elected first President Chair Person (PCP) of that body in 2001. However the vast amounts of double dealing cooked up between them to get these ideas cunningly incorporated into the structure of CENTERCOM would be sufficient on their own to fill another book.

# APPENDIX

# three

**Glossary of Terms and Abbreviations**

Arnold's Oath: In an age of information – secrecy was the greatest sin. And of course, the greatest prize. Arnold's Oath, named for the man who made 'total access' possible, was usually sworn by computer operations people and others in the information industry.

However the Arnold's Oath could also be used as a direct challenge *or* bond face to face in normal human (non-cybernetic) relations by citizens of the world of information.

Depending on the context, the oath taker swore either to divulge everything he/she knew – or conversely keep everything she/he knew a secret.

Arnold Device: Computer capable of breaking any code up to infinity. Potentially it can decode any information of any sort anywhere in the universe – given enough time. Both the 'E.Z. Analyzer' and the 'Mordell's Conjecture Probe' are types of Arnold Device.

CENTERCOM The Central Communities 2001. Political and

economic federation of USA, USSR, E/W Europe, China, Japan.
(See Appendix No 4)

Citizen's Access: Moralis based on an informational world view.

Any citizen could demand to see any politician, govt official, or religious leader at any time of the day or night, anywhere – by invoking 'The Right of Citizen's Access'. It was assumed that Citizen's Access would only be invoked in a case of emergency.

This traditional right or custom derives from New System Constitution Preamble Para 4.
'We also hold this truth to be self evident that it is the inalienable right of every Wo/Man and child on Earth or any planetary colony or orbital location to demand and be granted free and unrestricted access to all human, cybernetic or printed sources and repositories of information, all artificial or natural resources and means of nourishment, all commonly owned or public property, existing anywhere on Earth or in Space.'

Legal Note: Corporation Lawyers argued that Space Industrial Services were legally justified in restricting access to the Hub as their status as Lessees rendered the area no longer 'Commonly owned or public' property as defined by the Preamble – the lease giving them statutory rights 'analogous to' private ownership.
Human protestors argued that CENTERCOM had betrayed its trust as 'collective common owner' of the Hub by leasing it to SIS in the first place.

DCCH: Drongo Church of Christ Hallucinogen.

Australian religious sect popular among dwellers at the Orbital Locations.

**DLV:**   Direct Lift Vehicle. Rocket that takes off directly from the surface of the Earth to inter-orbital or inter-planetary destinations. For reasons of cost alone, most long distance space travel begins outside the pull of Earth's gravity at a Way Station in 'Geosynchronous' orbit.

**E.Z. Analyzer:**   Space craft maintenance tool. See 'Arnold Device'.

**Faboid:**   Neologism coined by 'OCTAVE' theorists to replace late twentieth century misuses of the word 'Myth'. By late century the word 'myth' had lost its original meaning viz;
'a true history of what came to pass at the beginning of time'
and had come to mean a fable, a childish misconception, a downright lie.

On OCTAVE's recommendation, CENTERCOM Mandate MEFPTZ 155 disallows the perjorative use of the word 'myth' except for literary purposes. (Controversial)
For all their faults, OCTAVE were far too wise to ban something without providing a viable alternative. Hence – substitution of the FABOID; Factual Assumption Based On Insufficient Data.

**GALCOM:**   Galactic Commerce.
**(see SCICOM):**   One of CENTERCOM's Big Three. Early in its development CENTERCOM anticipated colonisation of the outer planets and possible (commercial) contacts with ex terrestrial civilisations.

**Geosynchronous Orbit (GSO):**   (Geostationary Orbit). An orbit 22,300 miles above the Earth where objects (eg satellites etc) remain in position relative to locations on the surface of the Earth. Hence GSO is ideal

for communications satellites, SSET
transmitters, 'waystations' etc.

Infosphere:
Gray flashing sheets of information.
Like Teilhard de Chardin's 'Nuosphere' – a
worldaround psychic web produced by the
human mind – the Infosphere is actually
electrically produced by informational
equipment used in high volume by modern
technological civilisation. The entire web of
produced and transmitted information. Some
is beamed – some is in wires – all of it leaks,
eventually spreading everywhere. This is
how rumours of a mystery in the Hub
reached Planet Earth in the first place.

IITS:
Instantaneous Information Transfer Services.
A subsidiary of GALCOM.

L5:
Lagrange Point Five. There is no general
solution for the '3-body problem' of a body's
movement under the gravitational pulls of
two others. Five special solutions were
determined by the French mathematician
Lagrange, for points where the third body
could hold a stable relationship with the
other two. The whereabouts of Ls 1, 2 3 and 4
need not concern the general reader. L5 is
ahead of and behind the moon in its orbit,
equidistant from the Moon and Earth. Lest
the use of the term 'point' should cause any
imaginative misconceptions it would be well
to note that the region L5 is an area of space
encompassing many thousands of square
miles.

LOCM: (see
TCT)
Libration Orbit Chronological Metering.
Taking full advantage of their status as
artificial environments – the Orbital
Locations have abandoned Earth style time
measurement, dictated by sidereal
conditions. For example CIP 5 has a 16 hour

day and a 4 hour night in a 40 week month.
The climate alternates between mild spring
and warm summer on a five monthly cycle.
CIP 4 on the other hand offers a full range of
seasons, including a perpetual 'Winter
Playground' at the centre of the 'Space Park'
freedom area.

How to read LOCM
    827 — 441 J
Month year time day segment
    (TCT adjusted)
H = Daytime
J = Evening
N = Night

E.g.: Interpret the above date as:
8th month – 27th year – 44th hour – 1st
day – Evening. (N.B. 27th year (TCT
adjusted) means 27th Earth year since
habitation. Obviously the Cipolan year by
LOCM reckoning would soon be out of
synch with Terran Calendar Time].

Mordell's
Conjecture: Mathematical puzzles based on the
arithmetic of the Ancient Greek Diaphantus.
Gerd Falting's (1983) solution to Mordell's
Conjecture, raises a number of questions
which are semantic rather than
mathematical. For example – the practical
definition of infinity and the question of
where all answers to Fermat's Last Theorem
must lie – between 0 and 1 or between 1 and
10?

NMS Faction: Normal Members of Society (Media creation)
A1 Security and Credit rated.
It has also been claimed to stand for;
Nerds, Mothas and Shits – or –
Nembies, Marijuana and Snow – or –
New Moderate Sensibility – or –
Nasty Media Scam.

| Psycho Dramas: | Television shows featuring heavy emotional and psychological situations. Interactive communications techniques permit viewer participation – adding a 'computer game' element. Many watch under the influence of the drug Real (a powerful psychotropic halucinogen) and come to believe the PDs are actually happening, while their own lives are merely a television programme. |
| --- | --- |
| SCICOM: (see GALCOM) | Scientific Community. One of CENTERCOM's Big Three. |
| SPACEK: | Space Exploration Executive. Headquarters of European space industry. |
| Syndicalism: | A movement among industrial workers having as its object the transfer of the means of production and distribution from their present owners to unions of workers. |
| TCT: (see LOCM) | Terran Calendar Time. Meantime measurement on Planet Earth, based on sidereal year – as opposed to LOCM – artificial time measurement constructed to suit the various needs and fancies of the inhabitants of the Orbital Locations. Note: All year numbers in LOCM readings appearing in this volume have been TCT adjusted. |
| UAPW: | Urban Anti Personnel Weapon. Riot control weapons designed primarily to subdue and deter rather than to kill. But as in the case of the rubber bullets and CS gas of the late twentieth century, nevertheless lethal when used incautiously. |
| | Particularly popular with the FTPA were: 'Poseidon's Net' – a one person handleable, ground-to-air launchable, explosive cannister containing a net of thin nylon fibre capable of ensnaring up to 100 people |

and

'The Electric Bolas' – three strands of weighted nylon cord reinforced with electrically charged copper strands fired from a bazooka style tube. The Electric Bolas – named for the Argentinian gaucho's lassoo, tripped people up and gave them an electric shock at the same time.

UNIMED: (see SCICOM)

Unified World Medical Services. One of CENTERCOM's Big Three.

Publicly owned medico – industrial combine acting as medical supply manufacturer and hospital administration agency for all CENTERCOM regions.

Way Stations:

Large space stations positioned at GSO relative to launch pad sites on Earth, functioning as intermediate transit bases for travel to the L5 Orbital Locations and points beyond.

Outside the pull of Earth's gravity well, huge 'reaction liners' powered by nuclear motors make space travel a relatively cheap if leisurely business.

Zombies:

Prankster term for the 'NMS Faction'.

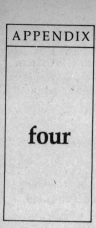

APPENDIX

four

**Economic Structure of CENTERCOM**

CANCELLED!
CENTERCOM MANDATE 1/27 April 4 2031 TCT

# interzone

## SCIENCE FICTION AND FANTASY

Quarterly                                                    £1.50

- *Interzone* is the only British magazine specializing in SF and new fantastic writing. We have published:

| | |
|---|---|
| BRIAN ALDISS | M. JOHN HARRISON |
| J.G. BALLARD | GARRY KILWORTH |
| BARRINGTON BAYLEY | MICHAEL MOORCOCK |
| MICHAEL BISHOP | KEITH ROBERTS |
| ANGELA CARTER | GEOFF RYMAN |
| RICHARD COWPER | JOSEPHINE SAXTON |
| JOHN CROWLEY | JOHN SLADEK |
| PHILIP K. DICK | BRUCE STERLING |
| THOMAS M. DISCH | IAN WATSON |
| MARY GENTLE | CHERRY WILDER |
| WILLIAM GIBSON | GENE WOLFE |

- *Interzone* has also published many excellent new writers; graphics by **JIM BURNS, ROGER DEAN, IAN MILLER** and others; book reviews, news, etc.

- *Interzone* is available from specialist SF shops, or by subscription. For four issues, send £6 (outside UK, £7) to: **124 Osborne Road, Brighton BN1 6LU, UK.** Single copies: £1.75 inc p&p.

- American subscribers may send $10 ($13 if you want delivery by air mail) to our British address, above. All cheques should be made payable to *Interzone*.

- "No other magazine in Britain is publishing science fiction at all, let alone fiction of this quality." *Times Literary Supplement*

- - - - - - - - - - - - - - - - - - - - - - - - - - - - - - - - - - -

To: **interzone** 124 Osborne Road, Brighton, BN1 6LU, UK.

Please send me four issues of *Interzone,* beginning with the current issue. I enclose a cheque/p.o. for £6 (outside UK, £7; US subscribers, $10 or $13 air), made payable to *Interzone*.

Name _____

Address _____

_____